ENFORCER

Book Eighteen of the Hayle Coven Novels

PATTI LARSEN

ALSO BY
PATTI LARSEN

The Hayle Coven Universe

The Hunted Series
Fiona Fleming Cozy Mysteries
The Nightshade Cases
The Clone Chronicles
The Diamond City Trilogy
Didi and the Gunslinger

and much, much more.
Find your new favorite author at
pattilarsen.com
Sign up for new releases
bit.ly/pattilarsenemail

chapter one

I lifted the tea cup to my lips in an effort to hide my fake smile was morphing into a grimace of anguish.

Huan Wong, the Santos Council member, sat across from me, her round cheeks flushed as she fixed her narrow eyes on my empty left hand. Considering the fact it was August and my twenty-first birthday had come and gone months ago, I knew the absence of a wedding band was the main reason for this little visit from the High Council.

That's right. The entire High Council of North American Witches sat in my living room, sipping tea from Mom's china while I ground my teeth together in an effort to keep from kicking the lot of them out of my house.

It's not like I didn't expect this visit. Mom warned me long before now I'd have a price to pay for ducking my head and barreling through my birthday at Beltane, June, July and now part of August in clear rebellion of Council law. I was supposed to be married by now.

Grumble, mumble.

Freakout.

"Not to put it indelicately, Sydlynn," Willa Rhodes said, clearing her throat as her cup tinkled on her saucer, a drip of tea washing over the edge to stain the flat of the white plate. "But you have put your coven in a terrible position." The old witch's face scrunched in an apologetic, apple smile.

The Council members all nodded while Mom held her peace, calmly nibbling one of the little sandwich Shenka hastily prepared for our unexpected guests.

Thank goodness for my second and her fast-on-her-feet abilities. I'd have stared stupidly at them in the kitchen doorway when they arrived in a flurry of blue fire, probably slammed the door in their faces.

If it hadn't been for Shenka. She took the entire thing in hand, guiding the Council into the living room while I struggled with the need to run as far and as fast as I possibly could in another direction—any direction. She seated me graciously, her smooth and together manner calming me enough I didn't bolt for the hills.

All while wrangling the nitty gritty details as my temper simmered under the gathered Council members' stares.

The offer of tea and snacks seemed to have diffused some of their agitation, but it was clear I wasn't getting out of this with a little hot double double and a handful of crustless munchables. And yet, Mom's relaxed state gave me more confidence than perhaps I should have felt. I learned a long time ago to follow her lead. And since I had my real mother back, free of the influence of the Brotherhood, I could trust that lead more now than ever.

"I've studied the law," I said, grateful Shenka suggested it about the time true panic set in. Two weeks before the big birthday. So powerful and all-consuming I almost ran to Demonicon to hide from the inevitability of wedding bells.

Funny how running came up so frequently when I thought about committing to this particular responsibility. I wasn't typically the type to flee from problems.

But this particular problem was all kinds of different.

How was I supposed to choose? Liam and I were still a little distant, all my fault. I had, as of yet, to commit to the love he professed, freaked out to no end by the thought of making the wrong choice. And though the handsome and charming Piers Southway pressed his case on a regular basis, I didn't love the Steam Union sorcerer. And wasn't sure he'd be a good fit for the coven anyway.

Excuses. Enough I talked myself into a frenzy of flight, only to be pinned down by my faithful second who shoved a copy of coven law under my quivering nose and offered a solution.

Temporary, yes. But a solution nonetheless.

Erica Plower's eyes widened as she set her cup aside, glancing sideways at Mom. The former second of my coven, now my representative on Council, wasn't exactly on my side. "The law is clear, Syd," she said, blonde hair, once a cute bob, now grown out to rival my mother's long, black locks. "And you've broken it. We've pushed our willingness to accept a little leeway, but with the approach of conclave..." She sat back as the others—minus Mom—murmured their agreement.

So that's what this was about. *They're worried about saving face?* I sent the tight mental question to Mom.

Witches are always worried about appearances, she sent with a heavy dose of laughter in her voice.

Nice to see someone found my imminent doom amusing.

Just tell them what you discovered, Mom sent. *I'll do my best to back you up. But don't hold your breath.*

Shenka refilled my cup with steady hands, her pleasant smile far more natural than it should have been. Her dark eyes met mine, her calm as comforting as Mom's.

Breathe, Syd. Just breathe. "According to law," I said, "I have until my twenty-first birthday to marry if I want to remain coven leader. Correct?"

The assembled ladies nodded, murmuring their agreement.

"Actually," I said, stomach quivering with butterflies as I delivered the punchline, "that's not quite accurate." Shenka lifted the scroll of law from the end table and handed it to me like a illusionist's perky showgirl, all prepped and smiling.

My lovely assistant.

I unrolled the scroll to the place she'd marked for me, speaking out loud while I read, the words rising to etch in blue fire in the air.

"'And it shall be that all Coven Leaders wed well and true, in the year of their twenty first.'"

The words burned over my left shoulder, solid, unwavering.

"Yes," Huan said. "Precisely."

"No," I said. "I think you missed it." I pushed my power against the hovering script. "In the year of" popped out, bigger and brighter. "According to this, I still have nine months to find a suitable partner and wed."

Phew. I already felt lighter now I'd said it out loud.

Willa frowned, head tilted as she stared at the floating words, but Huan spluttered out some tea.

"You are purposely misconstruing the letter of the law," she said.

"No," I said, tossing the scroll into her lap. "I'm following it. To the word." Clearly no one ever contested it. I guess I was the only person who actually thought it was nuts to make me marry at such a young age.

Witches were crazypants.

Mom's mind hugged mine. *You made your point*, she sent. *Let me handle this.*

Go for it.

"An interesting interpretation," Mom said.

"You would think so," Huan bit at her, bitterness heavy in her voice.

Mom's blue eyes pierced the Santos Council member, her faint smile gone in a flash, face now cold and blank. "Are you accusing me of something, Council Member Santos?"

Huan backed down immediately, head bowing. "Not at all, Council Leader," she said, though her hands twitched around the scroll like she wanted to whack me with it.

"I'm afraid I have to side with Sydlynn on this one," Willa said. I felt my stomach loosen, the knot releasing. Willa and her sister, Coven Leader Violet Rhodes, were both sticklers for the law. "I have to confess, I've never read this particular passage myself. But it appears, as Sydlynn states, we've been misinterpreting it for centuries."

Holy. Did I just win?

From the angry looks on the Council member's faces, Willa's opinion wasn't appreciated.

"Coven Leader Hayle has done more for this Council and all witches than any other in her few short years," Mom said. "For that reason, we have allowed her leeway in her marriage choice and timing."

Whoa. Choice? Were they planning on saddling me with someone they picked or something?

My demon snarled, Shaylee's power rumbling far beneath the house even as my vampire hissed in outrage. The family magic swirled in protest, though I did my best to hide my unhappiness from the Council.

We'd see how long their little Prince Charming lasted.

Mom went on, her mind chuckling in mine. Because she clearly knew where my thoughts were.

"For now, I agree with her assessment of the law as well, bending to the input of Council Member Rhodes." Instant protest, though Willa nodded to Mom. My mother held up one hand as I scowled at Erica for being a traitor. So much for old family ties. "However, I understand the importance of Coven Leader Hayle's marriage." *I'm sorry, sweetheart,* Mom sent. *But it really is important.* "While I know many of you would prefer she married before conclave, it is obvious, the very event now only a day away, she won't be wed by then."

They scowled at me as a group. What, were they going to drop off some guy, zippity do da me down the aisle and present me, officially hitched, to the rest of the World Councils?

So not going to happen in my lifetime.

"The very fact one of our most powerful coven leaders"—one of? Seriously—"blatantly flaunts the fact she thinks herself outside the law makes our position on the international stage all the more precarious." Huan's lips pinched into a straight line, her straight, black hair swinging as she shook her head. "And while I'm as grateful to her as anyone"—sure she was—"this kind of defiance is unconscionable."

"I seem to recall," I shot back, "I was granted carte blanche by this very Council."

That shut them up.

But Mom sighed, shattering my little advantage.

"While we have granted you the freedom to act in our best interest," she said, "your marriage isn't included in that agreement, Coven Leader Hayle."

She just had to hack the floor out from under me, didn't she?

Huan lurched to her feet, face set in a mask of anger. "I, for one, am embarrassed at this state of affairs," she said. Turned on Mom. "And I insist the Council act on the problem before it becomes a larger issue." She returned her gaze to me. "I would hate to see you forced to step down as coven leader of the Hayle family."

Such. A. Liar. She was in bed far enough with the Dumonts I was sure she'd be happy to see me fall. Her old allegiance with Odette, the now deceased leader of that hated family, couldn't have ended with the matriarch's fall. In fact, I had no doubt the Santos coven was still heavily invested with the Dumonts, especially now Odette's son, Andre, served as coven leader.

"I'm certain Sydlynn will make the proper choice," Mom said, rising to her feet with a gracious nod to Shenka and me. "And in time to fulfill the letter of our law."

The others rose, nodded to me, Shenka leading them out. I stayed where I was, swiping in irritation at the still floating letters hanging beside me, popping each word like a bubble while blue sparks fell to the floor.

Damn it.

Just damn it.

Mom sat next to me as the sounds of Shenka saying goodbye echoed from the kitchen. Her hands reached for mine, her power hugging me.

"I'm sorry, Mom," I said. "I hate to put you in this position."

"You too, sweetheart," Mom said. "This excuse of yours will only last so long. I doubt they will allow you to go the full year. It's been a battle to make it this far."

"Thanks for backing me up." I sagged against the puffy armrest of the sofa, feeling defeated. "I just have no idea what I'm going to do."

A fat, silver body landed in my lap as Sassafras, my demon Persian, settled himself against me, amber eyes on fire.

"Interesting conversation," he said. Eavesdropper. "Do you have to be so stubborn or are you enjoying yourself?"

Smartass cat. "Okay then," I said to him. "Who would you pick if you were me?"

He sniffed, swiping one paw over his nose. "I'm not you," he said.

Argh.

"See," I turned to Mom as Shenka sat across from us, "this is the help I get."

"No one can make this decision for you," Mom said. Paused. Bit her lower lip. "Have you spoken to Quaid?"

Oh. My. Swearword. She did so not bring him up just now.

"No," I snarled through my aching jaw.

We were meant for each other. If he hadn't chosen a life with the Enforcers, cutting off any chance we had to be together, he would be my first and only choice.

But no. Quaid was out.

And I couldn't bear to pick someone else.

I hated how weak this made me feel.

"Stop being so picky." I spun at the sound of Gram's voice, staring as she scowled at me from the entry to the living room. But not my familiar Gram, not the powerful woman full of vigor and snark. This old lady with the withered skin and fluffy white hair looked petulant, reduced. Felt that way, too, magically at least. And had since Ameline Benoit stole her power a year ago.

Power I promised Gram I'd retrieve for her. Except I couldn't, could I? Not while I needed Ameline and her dark maji self to defeat the Brotherhood.

Guilt.

"Gram," I said. "You were the one who told me how important this was—"

She swatted the air in front of her, frowned so deep her brows almost touched in the center of her forehead.

"Get on with it," she grumped. "Hurry the hell up and pick one already." She turned, shuffled a step. "They're all the same anyway."

I watched her go, heart aching, wishing I had my Gram back. When I returned my attention to the others, they all watched me, expectant.

And the pressure of their expectation was way too heavy for me to bear.

"I'll pick," I said, standing, dumping Sassafras on Mom. "But I won't be pushed into it."

I know it wasn't fair to be angry with my mother, my cat, my best friend.

Or myself.

But life wasn't fair sometimes.

chapter two

I retreated to my room, my favorite refuge since I was a girl. Different geography, maybe, but the idea was the same. Escape from the family, from responsibility, if only for a little while.

Sassafras wasn't interested in giving me space, it turned out. As I tried to close the door behind me, he slipped through the gap, sauntering his fat cat body to the bed before leaping onto the quilt. I sighed inwardly, expecting a lecture as I crossed the room and glared at him where he perched, watching me with those judging amber eyes.

"You're being ridiculous," he said. "The law is the law. And it's not like you don't have choices."

"So, you're telling me I should just get married and oh well if I make the wrong selection. Is that it?" I prodded him with magic, stomach churning.

Sass's tail thrashed once, but when he spoke again his tone was lighter. "I know you're worried," he said. "There was a time you put yourself first. But these days, like the great leader I always knew you would be, you put the coven ahead of your own heart." I sagged a little as he went on. "Syd, we only want you to be happy. And if that means choosing someone you love, but who might not be the best choice for the family, then do it." He reached out with one paw, swiping the air before letting it fall. "I've watched so many Hayle witches struggle with just this issue over the years, wished I could help them more than I did when it came to these things." His ears drooped sideways, whiskers quivering. "But you are the only one I really don't worry about. Whoever you decide to marry, he will be right for you." Another twitch of his silver tail. "And the coven can suck it up."

I sank to the edge of the bed and kissed the top of his furry head, loving how soft it was. He leaned in, purring so loudly I felt myself vibrating from it.

"Thanks, Sass," I said. Swallowed the lump in my throat threatening to choke me. "I guess I've just been worried about everything, it's making me crazy."

He head-butted me. "Our fault," he said. "We put too much pressure on you."

I leaned back to stroke his fur as he continued his rumble. "It took me a long time to understand how important the family is," I said. "And while I know my choice isn't life or death, I just can't bring myself to..."

"Let go of Quaid." Sassafras's voice dropped to a whisper as he licked my fingers in sympathy.

A small sob escaped me, both hands rising to cover my mouth, to keep in the sadness pushing on my chest, making it hard to breathe. I managed a nod, finally admitting the truth to him.

To myself.

How could I possibly marry anyone but Quaid? The power inside me swelled, yearned for him. The connection to him remained, thanks to the family magic, a constant reminder of who I needed, loved, had to have.

Couldn't.

I fell on my side, tears leaking onto the quilt as Sassafras curled up against me, whiskers tickling my cheek as his pink nose came within an inch of mine.

"I love you," he said. "And I'm sorry this is so hard for you. But it might be time to finally let him go."

I shivered, nodded. "You're right," I choked out. "I just don't know how."

Sassafras sighed deeply, entire body rising and falling with it. "When Thaddea first rescued me, I loved her so much, Syd." A hit of shock broke through my own melancholy as Sass spoke. He never talked about his past. "It was the first time I really knew what love meant, the first time I thought of someone else before myself."

I hardly breathed as he went on, flickers of images

passing between us as he showed me a gorgeous young woman in Victorian dress, her long, red hair in an elaborate updo, lifting him from a dirty puddle, his Persian body broken and filthy.

"She saved my life," he said, his own voice now thick with emotion. "But more than that, she saved my soul." He paused, eyelids closing slowly over his burning yellow gaze before he went on. "I thought we would be together forever." Another image, this time of him happy, clean, Thaddea laughing. It was so odd to see my ancestor as a young woman, no older than me, to think of her, not as my history, but as a real, breathing person who Sassafras knew and loved. "But we weren't meant for such a fate," he said.

A new image appeared, this one of a tall, broad shouldered man, a kind smile on his handsome face.

"I hated Orin," Sass said. "Because I knew, the moment they met, their magic connected. They were born for each other."

I shivered. "I feel that way about Quaid."

Sassafras nodded slowly. "I know," he said. "There are times when certain witches meet and their power combines in a way which cannot be denied." He nudged my nose with his. "I watched it happen to Thad. To Auburdeen with Gabriel. And with you and Quaid."

"So we have to be together." Was that relief, Syd, coursing through your veins suddenly?

Sass didn't respond right away, but when he did, I felt my newborn hope die.

"You should be," he said. Snorted softly. "And I'm afraid you will both be miserable if you don't. But he is as stubborn as you are," his amber eyes flashed fire, "and I have no doubt has the determination to do what he wants regardless of how he feels for you."

"So I'm doomed," I said, trying to keep my voice light though fresh tears found paths to the damp quilt. "Thanks, Sass."

He shuddered, fur fluffing out. "I'm sorry," he said. "I didn't tell you this story to make you unhappy." He shifted position until his full body was pressed to me, head tucked under my chin. "But I want you to understand why you're resisting making a choice. And that you will be forced to fight how you feel for Quaid for the rest of your life."

Considering how long my life was supposed to last, thanks to my immortality...

Just. Freaking. Lovely.

But it did put things into perspective. "Is there a way to break the connection?" I thought of my werefriend, Charlotte, now princess of the werewolf nation. She and I had been bonded, a connection which shattered when she'd almost died. Then again, by choice, last winter when I freed her and her people from the sorcerers.

Sassafras shrugged. "I don't know," he said. "But I

doubt it. All the research I've done indicates it only ends with the death of one or the other, and even then a gaping hole remains."

Wow, he was really making me feel better.

"I think about Gram," I said, breathing in Sass's fur, "about Grandfather Ivan. Mom and Dad. And I wonder if love is really worth it." My arms tightened around my demon cat. "And there's my immortality." Should the law even apply to someone like me? "Whoever I marry will grow old and die, Sass. And I'll be alone."

My egos stirred, comforting and soothing, but I had to talk about it.

"That's true," Sass said. "There are very few races you could choose from who could even hope to match you."

Demon. Sidhe. Vampire.

"Have you talked to Liam about this?" Sassafras lifted his chin, one paw on my cheek.

Sigh. "He just wanders around all heartbroken one minute, determined to win me over the next." I rolled my eyes. "It's driving me nuts. Besides," I poked his tummy, "I thought he was the wrong one for me. You and Gram both said so."

Sassafras's ears twitched. "I know," he said. "And yet, perhaps I was wrong. Liam O'Dane is a lovely young man, Syd. Not strong enough for you, no. And he never will be. But he loves you and will treat you and our coven with respect. That may be enough."

Was it?

"As for young Piers Southway," Sass said. "I know you don't feel about him the way you do Liam, but he is a power to be reckoned with. And marrying a sorcerer of the Steam Union can have political advantages."

My brows came together in a frown before I could stop them.

"I don't want to marry for politics," I said. Paused and thought about it as I forced my temper to back off. "Then again," I said, "since I can't have the love I want, maybe politics is the best choice."

Sass's warm body wriggled closer as he closed his eyes and let his purr rise in volume.

"You must choose," he said. "No more thinking."

Thinking was all I'd been doing.

"If you were to toss a coin," he said, "with Liam being heads and Piers tails, who would you wish for as the coin rose?"

Smartass cat.

"You're forgetting Sebastian." I still felt terrible my vampire friend, the former leader of the Blood Clan DeWinter, remained trapped and suffering at the hand of Celeste Oberman. The desire to rush to the vampire mansion and murder the traitor and spy was so powerful I knew it was a delay tactic. My brain didn't want to make a decision and happily created a scenario to save me from thinking further.

Sassafras's paws kneaded against my chest. "Unless you can find a way for the undead to father children," he said, "I'm thinking he's not an option."

Sigh.

"I'll decide," I said, feeling my eyes pulling closed, the strain of so much emotion driving me toward sleep. "I promise."

Sass's purr lulled me into quiet as he softly chuckled. "Of course you will," he said.

Liam pulls against my left arm, his dear face twisted in need. "I love you," he wails. "Why don't you love me back!"

Someone grasps my right arm, jerking me away from Liam. "Marry me," Piers leers, long, blonde hair hanging over his shoulder as his gray eyes burn holes through me. "We're the perfect combination of power. You'll never miss love."

I lurch from both of them, stumbling from a castle hallway and into a garden, surrounded by flowers and the scent of lilacs.

"You have to choose." Mom's desperation gives me goosebumps.

"You have to choose." Shenka's hands try to pull me to her, but I spin and run.

"You have to choose." Sassafras's claws catch me, pull me back. I stagger to my knees, look up as the High Council surrounds me, ranks of witches, faces I know, those I don't, crowding close, pushing against me. I huddle in fear and heartbreak as they loom over me.

"Choose," they chant. "Choose. Choose. Choose—"

I jerked awake, shuddering from the afterimage of the dream, disoriented and crying all over again.

A groan escaped me as I pushed myself up from the bed, still fully dressed, the dark of the room and the rumbling of my stomach telling me it was long past dinner. Sassafras had left me to sleep, though I desperately wished he was here with me now. The dream was a clear response to the stress I felt. Sadly, this wasn't the first time I'd had this dream or one like it.

I shivered and hugged myself as I stood there in the black and tried to pull myself together. Clearly, Sassafras was right. I had to find a way to move past the need I had to hold onto Quaid. I didn't want to believe he was the real reason I struggled so hard. But it became crystal clear to me now where my panic came from, what spring the palpitations of my heart drank deeply of.

Quaid.

Through pain and hurt and heartache. In love and excitement and more joy than I'd ever felt in my life. Past trouble, disaster, risk of death.

Always Quaid.

So how exactly was I going to shed this impossible need I had for him? Maybe I could do some research. Dive into the Sidhe archive in the Gate cavern. Every book that ever existed resided there and I was sure, if it meant breaking this hold Quaid and I had over each other, Liam would be more than happy to help.

But even as I imagined opening a large, dusty tome, reading the words providing the relief I needed, I shunted the thought aside. And that, I knew, was my downfall.

I didn't want to let him go.

A deep breath of frustration and longing turned into a meep of fear as something rattled against my window, shattering my private misery. Since the family wards didn't respond, fear left in a rush of anger.

My temper came willingly, happy to smother heartache, my favorite answer to everything. Instinct took over, forcing me across the room to the curtain. I whipped it back, jerking on the sash as my temper lit inside me. Probably some local kids throwing rocks at the house.

I'd thrash their little behinds.

The moment the window was open, though, I realized my mistake. And fell back with a cry of fear as power surged at the gap before rushing through the wards and into my room.

chapter three

I stumbled back, gathering my maji power even as the egos inside me paused.

And recognition dawned.

The swirling mass of magic separated into ribbons of color, amber and blue twining with red and green and white. A final zigzag of black crossed the lot as the glow from their energy lit the room in a rainbow of power.

I knew these scraps of elemental magic, had freed them myself from the crystals the Brotherhood used to trap the Dumont family magic. Each of these wild fragments escaped the clutches of Belaisle and his evil group.

Demetrius Strong had been happy they were free. The crazy, former Steam Union sorcerer and one time leader of the Chosen of the Light believed as I did--the Brotherhood lost a power source when I shattered the crystals holding the slivers of wild magicks in thrall.

But I hadn't seen them or thought to ever again once they fled captivity that night. I stood there, mouth hanging open and unable to react as they swirled around me like giddy children, their energy light and full of joy at seeing me again. At least, that was the impression they gave me as they stroked my skin on the way by in their happy, acrobatic dance of enthusiasm.

Amazing and beautiful as they explored first me, then my room, burrowing under my quilt, poking into my closet before alighting in various places like contented butterflies.

But what did they want?

The moment the thought crossed my mind, they leaped into action again, increasing their speed, now agitated. Love poured over me, loyalty and adoration. But a dark warning lay within them, trying to reach me.

So I reached back. Felt my individual egos connect with them. And shuddered as darkness enveloped me. The feeling of travel through emptiness. Then light, a laboratory of some kind. The remnants of the machine in which they'd been trapped.

Were they showing me their old fear or a new one?

Belaisle's face appeared, his arrogance, the nasty little goatee on his chin. So this was a reminder?

"Yes," I said to them as they came together again into a ball of swirling light. "I remember."

Another push of power and the vision changed. I fell into a mirror, surface rippling like a pond.

A flash of light.

Nothing.

I gasped a breath as they released me, sinking back to sit on the bed, their fear now mine.

"But what does it mean?" I reached for them again.

I felt someone cross the family wards at that moment, the familiar touch of the Hensley coven's power an instant distraction.

The cloud of wild magic sighed in frustration, spun in a vortex and zipped away even as I tried to pull them back, heading for the window.

I almost fell out as I lunged after them, watching as they flared in the night and vanished.

At a loss, still muddling over the message—if there was a message—I moved before I realized I opened the door, my feet padding softly down the stairs to the kitchen to find out why Tallah was here.

Found her whispering with Shenka in my kitchen. The pair looked up, Tallah a little angry, Shenka with guilt, my second jerking free of the hold her older sister and former leader had on her arm.

"Syd," Tallah said. She'd been cold with me ever since Shenka chose to leave her and join me. Not my problem. Though I hoped the young coven leader would get over her snit eventually. I really did like her and wished things could be different.

Still, seeing Shenka rub the place where Tallah held her, the confused flicker passing over the younger Hensley face, my temper returned before I could stop it.

"Can I help you with something?" It was after midnight, only 8pm in California, the home of Tallah's coven. So it was a natural mistake to come here and forget time zone issues were in play. I did it all the time. Still, from the frown on Tallah's face, her uncertainty, I figured she knew exactly when she'd be arriving.

And hoped to talk to her sister without me finding out about it.

Now, fair enough. If Tallah had a private conversation with Shenka, her family by blood, who was I to interfere? Except when my second met my eyes, it was pretty obvious whatever Tallah was here to discuss had nothing to do with personal matters and everything to do with the coven.

My coven.

Hell no.

Tallah shrugged and stepped away from Shenka, her dark hair in a tight, shiny ponytail, deep-toned skin flushing red at the peaks of her cheekbones. "I'm here for Sashenka," she said. Paused. "That came out wrong."

Did it ever. "I assumed you didn't intend to kidnap my second," I said, keeping my voice light, even as Tallah's brows came together in a quick frown. Time for her to get it through her stubborn skull Shenka was mine.

Until she decided she didn't want to be. But it would be Shenka's choice, not her sister's.

"I should be going." Tallah's mysterious visit ended there. She tried to hug Shenka who did a quick back pat before pulling free.

I wanted to ask. I so wanted to. Needed to know.

But instead, I just waited as the door closed behind Tallah, the surge of her magic fading as she left.

Waited for Shenka to tell me what she needed to tell me.

She hesitated, arms around herself, head down. Swayed like a young tree in a storm.

"Okay, well," she said. "Good night, then."

And rushed past me, up the stairs to her room.

Closed the door firmly behind her.

Restraint has never been one of my strong suits. Keeping my temper, allowing others secrets when I worried they might affect me and my family. But this was Shenka.

I had to trust her. Didn't I?

I half spun, ready to go after her, heart clenched against the need to believe she had my best interest—and that of the coven—in mind. Of course she did. She worked so hard to protect the family, was the one who managed the day-to-day so deftly I was hardly necessary most of the time.

26

But Tallah was her sister, had a blood connection I couldn't counteract.

Stopped myself at the bottom of the stairs, feeling like a total bitch for allowing my anxiety to make me doubt her.

Forgot all about Shenka and Tallah and my need to uncover the mystery about the wild magicks and what they wanted of me, when a second power crossed the wards, this time in the back yard.

I turned like an automaton, feet carrying me without my permission, heart nudging me out the door and into the grass.

The bond between us left me no choice but to go to Quaid.

CHAPTER FOUR

I tried to count the months since I'd seen him as I stepped outside into the cool grass and deep of evening. Unable to process how long it had been, all the while not really caring the moment my eyes settled on him.

His hands bulged in the pockets of his jeans, fisted inside the denim, dark head down, wavy hair longer than I'd ever seen it hanging over his face. His broad shoulders rounded inward, black t-shirt wrinkled over his wide chest, the scuffed toes of his leather boots damp from dew.

I had no control over myself, the way my breath caught as our power linked. How his magic, reluctant in the instant I saw him, surged in answer to mine and wrapped me up in the heat of his power. It was so hard not to run to him, to throw my arms around him. Now that I understood the connection we shared, it was all the more painful. I knew I'd carry this aching longing the rest of my days.

My demon moaned her unhappiness as I forced myself to a halt a few feet from him, arms tight to myself to keep from grabbing him even as his familiar scent drifted toward me on a soft breeze.

Traitor air, carrying temptation my way.

When Quaid finally looked up, I almost lost myself. So. Close. But the flicker of agitation in his eyes, the tension in his tall body, was enough to hold me back.

To make me wonder.

"Nice to see you." I wanted it to come out with sarcasm. Intended it to sting, to bite, my longing driving me to hurt him for the choices he'd made, the pain he'd caused. Instead, I whispered it, heart on fire for him.

Only him.

"I thought it was best if I stayed away." His voice growled low, gravel over a thick throat. No snark from him either, nor the smirk I expected.

"You've been avoiding me." I release the tension in my arms, hopelessness making me want to cry all over again. Why did he have to show up, tonight of all nights? When I was already weak from tears and unable to commit to letting him go?

Quaid's shoulders twitched as he half-turned from me, the chocolate deliciousness of him pulling back.

"Have you made your decision yet?"

Oh. Boy.

I could have sank into despair, but felt a twinge of temper spark and seized on it, my old friend, my faithful companion and protector of my heart. Better anger than grief.

Always.

"I wasn't aware it was any of your business." Crackle. Pop. Damn it.

He looked up, no anger, just the same agitation, deep and swirling, feeding his magic, his sorrow.

"I'm sorry," he whispered.

Choke. "So am I," I said, anger falling away. Not like I could stay mad at him, considering how I felt.

How neither of us thought we had a choice.

Our gazes locked, held. For a long moment we stood there, just staring at each other, so many words unsaid, so much love held, trapped, excruciating between us. My yearning grew, but my feet remained anchored by the knowledge he wasn't here to tell me he'd changed his mind.

He was here to say goodbye.

Quaid groaned softly, power surging around me again and closed the gap between us in a rush. His mouth felt hot, his breath in my lungs and I clung to him, to the burning kiss and the hardness of his body.

His hands curled into my hair, pulling me closer,

deeper, as I lifted myself from the ground, wrapping my legs around his waist, hugging him with my entire body, the pressure of his need tight against my own.

I felt him moving, didn't care where this led us, as long as my bed was our destination.

As he climbed the stairs, panting over my lips, hands pulling at my clothing, I unwound my heart and power and welcomed him home, the door to my room closing softly behind us.

Dark eyes studied me, shining waves of hair hanging over my hand. I tried a smile as the morning sun lit his beautiful eyes even as my lower lip trembled.

Quaid kissed me, first my lips, then my forehead, pulling me closer until it seemed his body was mine. I trembled against him for a moment until my sadness passed. When he finally released me, we both smiled this time.

Soft. Sweet. Delicious.

"I love you," he said.

"I love you, too." I kissed him, tried to believe this wouldn't be over soon. Let myself believe Quaid and I were together. Forever. "Breakfast?"

He stretched out his long body, the muscles in his chest rippling, pentagram tattoo dancing on his tanned skin. When his chocolate eyes met mine, dark with passion, I felt my pulse increase.

"I'm starving," he said.

And devoured me.

I loved how he didn't flinch from the heat of the shower, though I didn't have the ability to really feel it anymore. When we finally descended to the kitchen, his fingers wound through mine, I actually started to believe it. Not just imagining, but believing Quaid made his own choice.

And now mine was simple.

The shocked look on Shenka's face flashed quickly away as she smiled and welcomed Quaid, but I could tell from the tilt of her head and the questioning look she gave me behind his back she was as surprised by this turn of events as I was.

Sassafras's tail thrashed against the table-top as he glared at our visitor with flashing amber eyes.

"Quaid," he growled.

"Sassafras." Quaid didn't try to touch the demon cat, just nodded gravely to him as though understanding exactly what my furry protector was thinking.

What I started thinking when reality hit.

Was he here to stay, or to break my heart again?

Demetrius sat at the end of the table, scooping in a fork full of scrambled eggs. His big, blue eyes smiled at Quaid as he waved. But it was Gram's reaction that caught everyone's attention.

She lurched to her feet, face twisted in fury, frail body shaking. My grandmother jabbed one sharp-nailed finger at the Enforcer trainee and snarled like a caged animal.

"How dare you!" She lunged at him, pushing against his broad chest, so weak now she didn't budge him even a little as he gently grasped her hands to stop her from pounding on his broad chest. "Betrayer of your heart, betrayer of your order!" She pulled free, staggering, almost falling as Shenka flew to save her.

Gram pushed my second away, wavering as she glared at Quaid, wiping her mouth with the back of one wrinkled hand.

"Get out," she hissed. "And never come back."

"Gram." I didn't mean to be so harsh. I really didn't. I loved my grandmother, knew how much pain she had to be feeling.

She turned on me, then, pounding her thighs with her fists as she shrieked a curse. "What were you thinking?" Gram shook her head with so much violence she almost fell over again, swatting at Shenka who continued to try to help. "What were you thinking, you stupid, stupid girl?" Gram's face fell, collapsed, tears rising in her faded blue eyes, coursing down the deep creases in her skin as she began to sob.

Demetrius rose slowly, calmly, and took Gram's hand. She didn't seem to notice as he patted her shoulder gently before turning to me. I could tell from the lucidity in his gaze he'd come back to us as he sometimes did, and wondered why he'd managed at this moment. Yes, I'd forgiven him the things he'd done to me, knowing now he was brainwashed and tortured by the Brotherhood. But I'd never really considered him compassionate.

Until now.

"Forgive her," Demetrius said with a small, apologetic smile for Quaid. "Ethie just needs to rest."

I stood frozen, wanting to reach out to her, knowing I'd be rejected as Demetrius slowly led my sobbing grandmother from the room, leaving us all in heavy silence.

My happy hope shattered into dust.

"I shouldn't have come." Quaid turned, headed for the back door. I went after him immediately to the sound of Sassafras sighing. I caught the love of my life as he strode in long, thudding strides out the back door and to the yard.

The thrum of the Wild Hunt, its sleeping magic stirred by the disturbance in our power, fell still as Shaylee soothed the ride back to sleep.

I wished I was so easy to calm.

"Why did you come here last night?" I jerked Quaid around to face me, fingers digging into the bare skin of his arm.

I had to ask. And yet, I didn't want to know the answer.

Coward.

Quaid spun toward me, mouth twitching, jaw working, his power bubbling with frustration and anger and grief until he shook his head.

"I don't know," he said. "I wanted to stay away, Syd." Quaid's voice rumbled through me, his words hurting worse than any blow. "I tried so hard. But I heard the Council was here, that you're being forced to choose and I just couldn't..." He turned from me, a curse bursting from his lips. "I don't know!"

My magic flowed around him as I pulled him back to me. Quaid finally met my eyes, body tilting toward me as I did my best to force myself into quiet.

"It's not your fault," I said. "It's destiny."

He didn't answer, just stood there, lost. As lost as I felt.

"I will always love you," I said. "I have no choice. Just like I know you love me and will forever." That much was true. Absolutely true, the magic inside us confirming my words. "But love can't keep us happy, can it?" He flinched. "Not if one of us feels trapped." Another twitch from his broad shoulders. "Not if it means sacrificing what you really want."

Quaid's hands lifted, as though to grasp onto me. But he didn't try, just stood there, heart and soul in his eyes.

"Syd," he whispered. "I don't want to hurt you. I want to stay."

Hope bloomed anew, found a small, fluttering home inside.

"I'm here," I said. "And we have time." We didn't, I knew that, now. The Council would be on my back, pushing hard from here on in. "If you ask me to wait, I'll find a way."

I hated the bond for making me weak. Any other guy, he'd be kicked to the curb long ago. But Quaid, our fate, our power... I meant every word.

He finally shook his head, hair swinging as he relaxed, came to me, hugged me. I savored the heat of his skin, the scent and touch of his body, the deliciousness of his power even as I felt him pull away again.

He left without a word as I watched him go and wished there was something I could do to change his mind.

And mine.

chapter five

I almost ran into Shenka on my way back inside as she emerged from Gram's room, Demetrius behind her.

The sad looks on their faces told me my grandmother wasn't taking Quaid's departure any better than his arrival.

"She'll be fine," Shenka said.

"No," Demetrius's lucid moment had gone, his small body doing a spinning jig, reminding me of Gram at her worst. "She's not. Not, snot, lotta good you'll do in there." He danced away, humming to himself, listing off rhyming words as he went.

I paused, eyes locked on my second, only then remembering our late-night visitor. "Can we talk after?"

She sighed, nodded. "I don't have any secrets from you," she said.

I hugged her before gently moving Shenka aside. "I

know," I said. "Thank you for not giving me a hard time this morning."

Her lopsided grin tore down the last of my worry about last night. "And thanks for not chasing me down and accusing me of betraying the family to my own sister."

Eep. Did she guess I'd had those concerns?

I laid one hand on Gram's door. "I'll handle this first," I said. "Go make sure Demetrius doesn't freak out the neighbors. And then we'll talk."

She bobbed a nod before hugging me so hard it hurt. Didn't care. I hugged her back.

"Damn Quaid," she whispered in my ear before fleeing toward the kitchen.

Sigh.

I found Gram sitting on the floor next to her bed, knees drawn up to her chest. Her thin nightgown had risen to expose the mottled skin of her calves, her narrow ankles lined with veins, skinny feet topped with jagged nails. No fuzzy socks. She'd stopped wearing them, since Ameline.

So much had changed with her since Ameline.

I sat next to her, mimicking her position, resting my chin on my knees.

"I could use some help," I said.

Gram grunted, turned sideways away from me. "Figure it out yourself," she said. Sniped, really, a bitter old bat instead of the crusty woman I loved. "You're so smart, aren't you? Sleeping with one while another loves you and a third wants your power." She mumbled something I missed before ending with, "self-important brat."

Snarl. "That's so not fair," I said, doing my best to hold my temper. "And you know it."

"Fair doesn't live here," she snapped. "Hasn't ever." Her white hair trembled around her in a soft fluff. "Not ever."

"I'd think you'd understand how I feel." No whining, Syd. "That you'd want what was best for the coven." Better.

Gram twitched. "To hell with the coven," she said. "And to hell with you."

Gasp. Tears bloomed in my eyes, the edges of my soul crumbling as I fought to keep from hugging her and begging her to come back to me. Even when she was crazy, lost in the darkness of her insanity, she was always bright, sharp. Snarky, yes. But cruel and angry?

This wasn't my grandmother anymore.

I don't know what made her suddenly relent. Maybe she finally heard what she'd said to me, processed it through her own pain. Because she turned back toward me with a sigh, shoulders slumping.

"She told me, you know." Gram's voice came out harsh, rasping sandpaper anger and sorrow as deep as mine. "About Ivan."

It took me a moment to make the connection through my grief of wanting my grandmother back.

She? Told her what?

And then it hit me, a ton of bricks in the face. Guilt slammed into me right after.

"I'm sorry, Gram," I said, thinking of the maji chamber under the vampire mansion. Of Ameline and Iepa, of the dark maji guide, Trinol, and the story they told us.

Of Ameline's heritage.

"He was her grandfather." Gram breathed the last word, as though still struggling to believe it. "Ivan and Odette..." She choked, coughed softly. Stared at the floor. "They had a daughter."

I didn't say anything, could barely breathe, knew if I tried to speak I'd sob instead. I'd never been able to uncover what happened the day Gram was attacked, when Ameline stole her power. I was off chasing Alison, trying to stop her after she stole the tainted vampire essence from me. She was the reason I left Ameline with Shenka and Gram and Charlotte. My second and werefriend had both been knocked out early in the fight, before the Enforcers Ameline killed even showed up.

It was my fault Gram lost her magic. No blaming Alison.

My fault alone.

Gram looked up, met my eyes, hers dull and empty. "I tried to fight her," she said. "The moment you left to hunt Alison, Ameline tried to leave." Gram's voice wavered, thin and soft. "Shenka chased her, we all did. I thought that Benoit bitch killed Charlotte." She ran one hand over her face, wrinkles sagging as she seemed to collapse in on herself. "When Shenka fell, I called the Enforcers." She shuddered. "I held her, fought her. I stood against her." No pride, not even a glimmer of satisfaction. "I know they could have captured her, if I'd only held my ground."

Against Ameline? Gram was strong—had been—but she didn't stand a chance.

Did she? Maybe I underestimated my grandmother. After all, she'd been an Enforcer once.

"I think she knew she was about to lose." Gram snuffled, wiped her nose with the sleeve of her sweater. "So she told me."

I saw the last of Gram's light leave her just before she turned from me for the second time and pressed her cheek to her knees, only the back of her head visible, white hair thin and wavering.

"She told me about Ivan," Gram whispered, "and I fell."

Oh, Gram.

I heard her crying, saw her shoulders shake. But when I tried to comfort her, she shrugged off my hands, my magic.

"I always knew he betrayed the coven," she said with so much bitterness I worried for her state of mind. "But I believed him. I believed he never betrayed me."

I couldn't help the aching sob that escaped, but Gram just seemed to grow calm.

"She knew what to do," she said. "That nasty piece of work. She knew how to break me, and I let her." Gram sighed. "I gave up so much over the years. Everything I ever wanted. Fought so hard to be worthy, to make amends for my mother, my grandmother. To keep my family safe." Gram sagged over on her side, curling up in a sunbeam. "All for what? For nothing, in the end." Another sigh. "I just don't feel like fighting anymore."

"Gram." My hands fluttered at my sides.

"So do what you want," she said. "Make your damned choice already. But don't forget, whatever you do, it's always going to end badly."

No matter what I did, no matter how I pleaded, Gram fell silent and refused to speak to me after that.

I left her, still in a ball of emptiness, now tucked onto her bed under a quilt, unable to stand her blankness any longer.

chapter six

I wanted to go to my room and climb under the covers. To hide from the pain I felt, the slow and unrelenting crushing of my heart. To push aside the promise I'd made to sit down and talk to Shenka when I was done with Gram. But as I paused at the bottom of the stairs, I felt someone cross the wards before hearing the sound of knocking on the kitchen door.

Retreat still sounded like the best plan. Shenka was there to pick up the slack and even if it was Tallah all over again, I knew my second had it handled despite my fears the night before. But I needed the distraction, longed for something to break the heavy weight of grief I carried. And so, despite myself and my desire to escape into solitude, I found my feet carrying me down the hall and into the sunlit kitchen.

Shenka turned to meet my eyes, hers hooded in

dislike just as I shifted my gaze from her to the open door. And the young woman standing on the other side.

Mia Dumont's wavering smile almost did me in. That, paired with her tears and the soft cry of desperation she uttered was surely aimed to crush my already fragile hold on my empathy.

I went to her, embraced her as she shook in my arms, guided her inside and to a chair at the table. Avoiding Shenka's glares of irritation, I held Mia's hands as she pulled herself under control. She smiled again through lashes thick with mascara, eyeliner forming twin rivers of dark pigment down her pale cheeks.

"Oh, Syd," she said. "I'm sorry. So silly of me. It's just so nice to see you."

I turned to Shenka who tossed a box of tissues at me. It thudded into my chest, a dash of energy behind it. Okay, I knew my second didn't like Mia, but she never told me why.

And now really wasn't the time.

Considering Mia once hated my guts and blamed me for the loss of her family magic to Andre, tried to have me burned at the stake for my involvement, it was amazing she and I were even remotely considered friends. After all, she'd lost her crap over the theft of the Dumont family power. Not that she'd really had her life together in the first place. But she'd shattered completely, reduced to the weak and fragile witch who now sat before me.

But I'd known Mia for a long time now, since she called herself Pain. My abnormal, unpowered Goth friend, a long way from the witch whose magic had been sealed away by her own mother to protect her from Odette. Leaving her brother Quaid to suffer at the hands of the Moromonds.

I would not think about Quaid.

Would. Not.

"I hate to dump all of this on you," Mia said, squeezing my fingers while Shenka made a strangled noise behind me. "But I don't know who else to turn to." She pulled me a little closer, cold lips pressing to my cheek. "I can always count on you, Syd."

She could. She was my friend, no matter what happened. Even if Shenka didn't agree.

Mia continued to ignore my second, like she always did, focused completely on me. In fact, Mia rarely acknowledged anyone outside herself. Made me wonder if the cracks in her personality somehow damaged her focus. Though her selfish absorption could have been one of the reasons Shenka disapproved of her.

Though it wasn't like Shenka to care.

I pushed away my worries about my second and listened as Mia went on.

"I'm worried about my family." I almost winced, afraid she referred to the Dumonts, only to understand a moment later. "They are lovely, don't get me wrong." She released one of my hands to dab at her face with a tissue. "But I'm not as strong as I was, and they are so weak."

Ah. She meant the small "coven" she built from the ruin of her old life. A handful of witches booted from the Dumont family after Andre took over, beneath his notice and without enough magic to protest their expulsion.

"What if I'm leading them astray?" Mia's ice blue eyes, Ameline's eyes, widened in worry, her face reminding me of a porcelain doll or an anime character come to life. "I'm doing my best, but I want to make sure they are happy."

Guilt sizzled around my edges, the need to help my friend overwhelming me with its sting. I didn't blame Mia for her reaction. Understood she was doomed long before I met her, as a baby. Too young to understand, spending her whole life with part of herself missing. Being thrown into that horrible family as an impressionable young woman already damaged by years of loss. I was amazed she'd stood up at all, especially against Ameline, when Mia tried to claim the right to lead the Dumont family.

It wasn't her fault she failed.

I offered once before, told her I'd welcome her into the coven with open arms, accept her as a Hayle, give her purpose again. And meant it. Maybe this was the perfect time to renew my pledge to her.

If you welcome this creature, Shenka's mental voice cut

through my thoughts, *grant her a place with our coven*, anger crawled over me as she snarled her fury, *I'm leaving*.

What is your problem? I turned to glare at Shenka who scowled right back.

She didn't respond, simply turned her back and went to stand at the window, shoulders stiff.

Seriously?

Fine. Whatever.

"I'm sure you're doing a wonderful job." The words sounded hollow in my ears as I turned back, but Mia beamed at me.

"You think so?" She puffed up, as though she needed my approval.

She was doomed.

We talked a few more minutes, Mia rattling on through thought after thought, mind flitting from idea to impulse. I shrank from her emotionally, guilt more powerful than ever as I watched her spiral into insignificance right before my eyes.

Shenka finally spun and joined us, pulling out Mia's chair with a single, harsh jerk of energy.

"Forgive us," she said in a grating tone, "we have preparations to make for conclave. If you'd be so kind."

Mia acted as if Shenka hadn't spoken, rising to her feet like it was her decision to go.

"I really have to leave," she said, hugging me, kissing both of my cheeks. She felt cold, almost vampire-before-dinner cold. "So much to do before the Councils arrive."

I hesitated. "You're coming to conclave?" Only coven leaders were invited.

Oh, right. She thought she was one.

"I'll see you there," she said, eyes bright, still with tracks on her cheeks from her makeup. She waved with an airy smile, letting herself out and I watched from the open door as she drifted down the driveway, paused to look both ways. Talked to herself in a singsong voice a moment before turning and floating away to the right.

I had no idea where she was going, but she clearly wasn't here anymore.

As I turned to give Shenka hell for being so rude, she stomped into my space and shook a finger at me.

"You listen to me, Sydlynn Hayle," she said, the family magic crackling between us. "You made me responsible for the nurturing of this coven. As your second, it is my job to ensure the happiness of each and every family member."

"I'm still leader," I growled back. "And I say who joins and who doesn't."

Our first fight. Okay then. At least she was standing up to me finally instead of going all quiet and weird.

Though as her power trembled on the edge of our connection, I almost wished she shut it.

"I've worked too damned hard to bring balance to this family for you to barge in with your crazy-ass refugee plan and tear our coven apart." Shenka's eyes snapped with blue magic, a testament to her anger. "You want a healthy, strong family to come home to after you've saved the world? Then you stop being such an idiot about Mia Dumont." She shivered. "Syd, seriously. Even if we weren't facing bigger issues, even if there wasn't a giant battle to the death coming, I still wouldn't want her or her ragtag band of nutjobs in this family. And neither should you."

It was hard to hear Shenka, so hard. I wanted to save Mia—

"You can't rescue everyone," Shenka said, finally calming, resting her hands on my shoulders. "It's not your fault and I want you to stop beating yourself up over people and events that had nothing to do with you." She let out a long, gusty sigh. "We need you to be focused, to keep your attention on what's happening out there." She jabbed a finger toward the door. "While we maintain the stability and quiet you need when you're here." Another jab, this time at the floor. "Inviting Mia and her brood into this coven is inviting trouble and strife." Shenka shook her head, glossing black hair waving around her. "I know you're buying her 'all's forgiven and let's be friends' routine because you want to believe you can save her, that she's salvageable. But Syd. I'm here to tell you I can see right through her little act." Shenka dropped her hands. "She will destroy you if she can. And there's nothing of the girl you knew left to save."

Um, what? "How do you know that?" Mia wasn't lying to me. She forgave me.

Didn't she?

"You walk around with your head in the clouds most of the time," Shenka said, now with a wry twist to her lips. "And I can hardly blame you, with all the mess you have on your plate. But I'm down here with the rest of the witching world, and I pay attention to details." She crossed her arms over her chest. "I have sources who've chatted up her little coven. And they were more than happy to badmouth you and this family."

More sadness. More anger.

"And so," Shenka said, driving in the last word, "was Mia."

I bobbed a nod. I had to trust Shenka.

"I just..." I raised my hands, dropped them as my heart, already beaten black and blue today, cracked a little further.

"I know," Shenka said. "You care so much. Too much." She turned and left the kitchen, pausing at the door to the basement for a parting shot. "But it's time to toughen up and move the hell on."

Not even the sunlight could warm the chill passing through me.

Would have been nice of her to tell me just how to move on.

chapter seven

I had just sat down, my legs no longer willing to hold me up, when Sassafras leaped onto the table and fixed me with his amber eyes.

"I agree with Shenka," he said.

"Of course you do." I sat back, refusing to look at him. "Just beat it, cat. I'm busy."

"Feeling sorry for yourself." He snorted. "Typical. When will you tire of your little pity parties, Syd, and grow up?"

I wanted to snap at him, almost did. But as I turned to deliver a scathing line, I saw the twitch of his whiskers, the way his big eyes looked so sad, his drooping ears telling me loud and clear how much he was suffering.

Aw, hell.

Sassafras purred against me as I scooped him into my arms and propped my feet up on the next chair, leaning back for a cuddle.

"Funny," I said. "I never seem to see you anymore and yet here I am, for the second time in less than twenty four hours, leaning on you."

Sassafras's body settled. "I'm sorry," he said. "I've been spending as much time with Ethpeal as I can."

Ah. Choke. "Thank you," I whispered.

He batted at me before going on. "Shenka's assessment is accurate. You spend too much time feeling guilty over things you can't control, worrying about those who have their own lives to live. You give up so much time and energy to caring for others, you forget you are the most important person in your life."

This time I did try to protest, but he barreled on.

"If Mia had been strong enough in the first place, if her mother hadn't walled off her power in an effort to save her, if Ivan hadn't been such a lying, conniving, cheating bastard..." Sassafras's claws dug into my skin as he snarled softly. "None of it has a scrap of connection to you."

I hated it when he was right.

"If anyone is to blame," he said, "it's your grandmother and I. We spent so much time when you were still developing inside Miriam, giving you power, teaching you to love, honor and protect those you care about, I fear we pushed you too far."

I shivered at the thought those two had a say in my

creation. And yet, I couldn't have been more grateful.

"Your loyalty is one of your most commendable attributes," he said. "And your greatest weakness. Though I know it goes against your heart, you must learn to release those who don't deserve the kind of love you have to offer."

Was he just talking about Mia, or was Quaid in this mix?

Sass left me, padding off to Gram's room as I mulled it over.

Remembered I wasn't done with my second, just yet. Rose with a sigh and descended to the basement in search of Shenka.

I heard her before I spotted her, the sound of flesh on leather, the grunts of anger. I rounded the stack of boxes blocking off the view of my heavy boxing bag from the staircase and stood there while Shenka ineffectually whacked away at the hanging target.

I watched her for a few minutes before stepping into the space and putting my body behind the bag as she staggered and almost fell trying to kick it.

"You suck at this," I said.

"So what?" She tossed her long hair back, dark cheeks pink. "You suck at a lot of stuff. I'm allowed."

I laughed. Couldn't help it. Saw her anger crack open. Her lips turn into a grin.

"Why don't you let me teach you how to hit," I said,

thankful to my trainer, Sage, for being so thorough in his instruction I was comfortable sharing my knowledge. "And you can teach me how stop being an idiot."

Shenka tilted her head, eyes narrowed, but still smiling.

"I'm not sure that's a fair exchange," she said. "My job is so much harder."

"Har har, smartass," I said. Sobered. "Shenka, I'm sorry."

She dropped her hands, still held in boxing stance. "No, I am." She came to my side, hugged me. "It's not your fault you care about people. And I'd hate to think you lost that part of yourself." She leaned back. "But you have to trust me when I argue with you, okay? Because I'll only do it when I know I'm right."

"Promise," I said. "But you have to do the same. Trust me."

She tensed a moment before tossing her hands. "Tallah," she said.

"If it's personal..." I gave her an out, but Shenka's face hardened as she squared herself.

"Not personal," she said. "You need to know she's been at me to come home ever since I joined this family."

I wasn't really surprised. Tallah didn't strike me as the kind of person who quit easily. We had that in common.

"But it's more than that." She thudded one fist against the bag. "She's been hinting at a power shift. She's in talks with someone she says can help her, supposedly help all magic users, come out to normals."

She what?

"Has she lost her freaking mind?" It was only sheer will keeping me planted in one spot.

"It's always been Tallah's greatest wish," Shenka said with a hint of misery in her voice. "That we with power could walk freely among normals, heads high. Accepted and pursued as much desired assets by those in control of our plane."

Cracked. Tallah was utterly cracked.

"I suppose she's forgotten about the whole 'there's a witch, let's kill her' history we have with normals?" Aggravation and anxiety made me bounce on my toes. "Jumped up jackrabbit on a joystick, Shenka—tell me you don't agree with her?"

"I used to," she said. Softly. Sadly. "There's a part of me that wishes it was possible."

That settled me down. "Me too," I said. "It would be fabulous if we didn't have to hide, run from place to place out of fear we'll be revealed." A huge reason I was grateful for the Gate and Wilding Springs. Thanks to the Sidhe portal's presence, we could probably have let off a magic bomb in town square and the residents would smile and point at the pretty fireworks.

But there was zero hope we could get along with normals. Witch history was written in enough blood it was no wonder the use of creation magic was banned during the Inquisition. There was no way normals would accept who we were without mass hysteria, fear and, ultimately, jealous hatred rearing their collective ugly heads.

"Who has she been talking to?" My chest tightened as I processed the next bit of Shenka's announcement.

"The Steam Union," Shenka said. Paused. "So she says."

Crap. And more crap. "You're worried it's the Brotherhood in disguise?"

Shenka's misery punched me with a hit of panic.

"I need to talk to Mom." But I waited. For permission. While Shenka's face crumpled before she nodded.

Suddenly shrieked.

I spun, power pulling tight, only to find the wild magicks swirling in a liquid dance behind me. Shenka covered her mouth with one hand, eyes wide as they came to touch her, sliding around her. Her fear quickly turned to wonder as she smiled at me.

"Are these what I think they are?" She stroked the blue fragment as it nuzzled her cheek.

How had I forgotten their visit?

Quaid. Oh yeah. Right.

He'd make me forget my own name.

"The wild magicks I freed," I said, confirming her

suspicion. "They showed up out of the blue last night." Neither of us mentioned tall, dark and yummilicious. "I think they are trying to communicate, but I don't know what they want."

She frowned a little, cupping her hands so the white spirit ribbon could pool there a moment.

"Any idea where they came from? Where the Brotherhood found them?"

"I don't know." I smiled as the magicks did their dance of joy around us. "But I think Demetrius might."

She rolled her eyes, but smiled. "I'll work on him," she said. "He might be able to remember something if I'm careful."

Shenka gasped out loud as the image of the machine flashed in my head.

"You too?" I reached out and took her hand as she nodded, breathless.

The next image built on the first, the crystals being broken. This was a new show, not the same as last night. I saw myself from their point of view, as they were freed, one by one.

"Amazing," Shenka said. "Maybe they don't want anything. Maybe they are just telling you they are grateful?"

The darkness came again, the empty place reminding me of traveling with sorcery. I shuddered from the image, the memory of Demetrius taking us to Austria along the channels of black and silence as Shenka's hand tightened on mine.

The air beside me tore open, amber fire pouring through as the veil opened. The element fragments squealed in musical protest before fleeing in ripples of panic, out through the concrete foundation and gone in a flash.

I turned, still slightly dazed, to feel my demon grandmother's spirit touch me. I sent love to Ahbi Sanghamitra as my sister's tall, muscular form crossed from Demonicon to my plane. She towered over me in her platform boots, floor-length black jacket topped with spikes. Her polished horns curved back into her glossy curls, large wristbands studded with more dagger-like metal flashing as she waved at Shenka.

The veil sealed shut behind her, leaving us in the semi-dark of the single, dirty basement window.

"You two look like you've seen a ghost." Meira's voice, deeper and smoother than any human's broke through my bemusement.

"We had visitors," I said.

"You'll have to tell me all about it," she said. "And Mom, too."

"Mom?" Right, Mom would probably want to know. Along with my worrisome news about Tallah.

Meira grinned at me, her body shrinking, clothes altering to a pair of jeans and a blue sweater, her skin now pale pink, eyes the same blue as mine. She now looked like a cross between Mom and Dad, my height and absolutely ordinary.

If stunningly gorgeous could ever be ordinary.

"Silly," she said. "We have lunch. Did you forget?"

Oops. Right. It was family lunch day.

I really needed to start keeping a day planner.

Shenka grinned and stepped aside after hugging Meira hello. "Ask Syd who else came to visit."

Traitor.

I didn't give Meira a chance, her evil grin enough to tell me she already guessed.

Just what I needed. Mom would have a cow.

Glaring at my second, I grabbed Meira's hand and tore the veil again, leaping inside with my sister in tow, willing to blurt Shenka's news out at lunch if only to deflect the obvious questions.

chapter eight

I hadn't noticed how frazzled Mom looked when she sat with the rest of the Council while they lectured me on my unweddedness. But now I focused on her and not my own troubles, I saw the slight darkness under her eyes. How she looked more tired than usual.

Mom returned my hug before latching onto Meira. I caught a flicker of motion to my right, glanced over and spotted Maurice watching with a pinched and bitter expression. Looked like our little family lunch was on his list of unnecessary events.

"Council Leader," he said in his whiny voice, round belly rising and falling as he spoke with his nose in the air. "You realize we have much to do between now and this evening?"

I have no idea where Mom found her patience. Instead of dropkicking his rotund little body out the nearest window like I would have, she smiled and nodded to him, waving him aside. She led Meira and me through the doorway he attempted to block as he spluttered at her for forcing him to move.

"I need to eat," she said over her shoulder, tone light. "We all need to eat, Maurice."

My demon acted before I could stop her, snapping my teeth together in his face.

"Yum," she said through me in her graveled voice.

Maurice flinched and backed away before spinning and trotting off.

Snicker.

A huge stack of paperwork greeted us as Mom magicked it to a nearby chair with a smile of apology.

"I'm sorry, girls," she said. "This conclave has taken on a life of its own." Her hands clasped tightly in front of her. "It's been a balancing act to not only bring everyone together, but keep our search for Brotherhood taint under wraps. You know witches and ruffled feathers. If any of them found out we were planning to search their power without their knowledge…" Her fingers wound together, the only sign of her growing nerves. "And I'm certain, as you are, Syd, Liander Belaisle is quite aware of the main goal of our little get-together."

Little. Yeah, because the logistics behind gathering all the Councils together was the definition of "little".

"Can we help?" She'd insisted I stay out of it from the

beginning. I rushed to pour Mom a glass of wine, trying not to allow myself to worry too much about the Brotherhood. Belaisle was always ahead of me anyway, so I was sure she was right. But what else could we do but be as proactive as possible at this point?

Mom accepted the offered glass with a soft kiss on my cheek.

"Not at all," she said, sinking with a happy sigh into the chair at the head of the table, Meira and I on either side. Both of us leaned forward and focused on Mom, our energy meeting in the middle, offering her support as we offered it up.

Mom laughed and batted us away with a flicker of magic. "Silly girls," she said with a fond smile for us both. "I'm fine."

She really shouldn't have been surprised we worried, not after what she'd been through. The fact she'd almost lost herself to the Brotherhood thanks to the theft of her family necklace still bothered me. Yes, more guilt. And while I knew she was a grown witch and more than capable of taking care of herself, I also knew if it hadn't been for the pentagram pendant she'd given me, embedded with her magic, now around her neck, I wouldn't be sitting here having lunch with her.

I'd probably still be in a cell.

"The first of the families will arrive tonight," Mom said, shaking out her napkin as flares of magic delivered lunch. I sniffed in appreciation as my bowl filled with soup. Curry sweet potato, my favorite. I dug in as Mom went on. "I just hope the site is ready in time."

Meira slurped her own appetizer. "I'm sure it will be," she said. "Are the coven leaders still giving you a hard time over the location?"

Mom shrugged, eyes twinkling as she winked at me. "I haven't given them an opportunity lately," she said. "The biggest naysayers have been loaded down with the most work."

Nice way to shut up someone. I resolved to remember to use her trick when the opportunity arose.

Still, I almost agreed with some of the protesters. I was about to have the world's most powerful witches in my back yard. The reminder rose to smother the hurt and worry of the last few hours.

"And the old coven site is secure?" I picked at a hang nail even as I admitted to myself my mother was a genius. Still, as brilliant as her idea was, it made me queasy. "I'm happy to add magic to the wards."

Mom shook her head over another sip of wine. "The Council's power is more than enough," she said. "Along with the Enforcers. Pender has seen to it himself." Mom's Enforcer Leader was nothing if not thorough, still blaming himself for Mom's trouble with the Brotherhood. "And since the site used to house the Hayle family power, the elements there are still more than easy to manipulate to our purposes."

Considering the Sidhe Gate also kept normals in Wilding Springs from even noticing magic, it really was an excellent choice of venue for the once a century meeting of witches.

Still.

Yikes.

"I'll give you a tour after lunch," Mom said.

And she did, much to my surprise. Usually something catastrophic—at least according to Maurice—would arise before we even finished eating and he'd hustle Mom away to put out what amounted to a tiny fire. Sometimes I thought he believed he owned my mother.

Pissed me off.

This time, he kept his distance, not even protesting when Mom rose and took our hands. I pondered the best time to dump Tallah's little meetings with sorcerers and the arrival of the wild magicks back into my life on my mother. She had so much to handle right now, just spending the majority of a nice meal with her was much more appealing.

Deciding I'd talk to her once we reached the conclave site, I opened the veil and slipped us through. Ahbi greeted Mom with a spark of power before we stepped out into the late afternoon sunlight.

Mom waved at her face, tiny beads of moisture rising on her upper lip, Meira grinning. I didn't notice the heat or humidity, thanks to my changing physiology and missed the warmth of the August day like a knife stab.

All that, and the rising urgency I felt to share what I'd learned, faded as I looked around with my mouth hanging open. Giant white pavilions dotted the landscape, filling not only the clearing where we'd once held our family rites, but stretching out through the tree line, expanding the site to five times its old size. Enforcers whizzed by carrying various bundles while witches hurried between the impressive tents, heads down, chattering details to each other.

The sizzle of magic greeted us as we passed over the line of wards and into the main site. Mom's distress at the heat faded and even I felt the cool wave of air as we passed. How civilized of Mom to offer the gathering temperature controlled comfort. I counted pavilions as we went, all circling a large main one towering over head.

"Africa," Mom said, gesturing to her right. "Asia." Another just beyond it. "South America." On the other side of the center pavilion. "Australia and New Zealand." Beside South America. "Europe." My chest compressed as I thought of Council Leader Margaret Applegate and her thrall to the Brotherhood. "India. And North America." I looked up at the big tent that was to be my home for a few nights and sighed.

"Mom," Meira said. "What are those for?"

I noticed smaller tents dispersed between larger ones

just before Meira pointed them out. The still impressive pavilion sat between Asia and South America, reduced size intended for a smaller number of occupants.

Storage? Dining tents?

"Come see." Mom led us there, stopping next to the first one. "I thought it only fair." She gestured to the flag hanging from a pair of poles stuck in the ground and felt my eyes widen.

"Demonicon." Meira laughed and clapped before hugging Mom. It was the first time in a long time I remembered, despite what she looked like on the outside, my sister was still a fourteen year old girl. Yes, she'd matured beyond her years in many ways, but the sweet young woman she hid behind her power and presence showed up occasionally.

Made me smile.

"I'm sorry to split up you two," she said. "I originally wanted to put your tents together. But this way I have the two of you in strategic placement around the site."

Was okay with me.

"And this one." Mom showed us the Sidhe banner, tent crouched between South America and Australia. She turned to me with a smile. "Liam has already extended our invitation to Queen Aoilainn and King Odhran."

Had he, now?

The next, tucked in the shadows of Australia and Europe, bore the banner of the Wilhelm family. "Frank and Sunny have agreed to come," Mom said. "Though I'm afraid there's no word from Queen Pannera." The Sthol flag sagged in the dropping breeze as if in answer to Mom's words."

The second to last tent had the head of a wolf howling at a full moon. "You invited the werewolves?" Why was I so surprised?

"They are a nation themselves, now," Mom said, arm slipping around my shoulders. "And they, of all magickind, have the most experience with sorcery."

Did they. I'd only just freed them this past January of centuries of servitude to the Black Souls and their corrupt leader, Yure Danko. I was happy the Czar was dead, but still thought about his second in command, Vasyl Krajnik, and wondered how Liander Belaisle greeted the sorcerer after he'd failed in his task to recruit the werewolves.

At least, I assumed that was Belaisle's aim.

Who knew what the Brotherhood leader was really thinking?

As much as I figured it would give me an advantage, the thought of understanding his twisted mind made me want to throw up.

"You do realize this is going to raise a stink the likes the witching community has never seen?" Meira grinned at Mom.

"Epic," I said, finding her amusement contagious.

Mom's smile turned wicked. "Should be a show," she

said.

And Sassafras wondered where I got it.

"And the Steam Union?" Just bringing them up raised the image of yummynom Piers Southway's face in my mind. I fought the blush warming my cheeks as Mom spoke.

"Yes," she said. "I've just spoken with Eva. I believe they are sending a small contingent and hope she herself can attend." Gestured at the tent between Africa and Asia.

I understood her motivations. "We need to make sure everyone is here."

She nodded. "To foster good relations between the supernatural races," Mom said, tone light and practiced. Until her eyes narrowed, voice dropping. "And so we know everyone is clean."

Of the Brotherhood.

Good luck with that.

I didn't get a chance to talk to her about Tallah. The wild magicks. Demetrius. Because the inevitable finally happened, a witch rushing up to Mom and dragging her off. Promising myself—after a firm ass kicking—I'd fill Mom in as soon as she was free, I drifted through the tents while Meira wandered into her pavilion with a saucy grin.

As I rounded a corner, still a little in awe of the set up, I caught a flash of movement and peeked between two tents.

Caught Quaid standing with his back to me. But he wasn't alone.

The buxom blonde Enforcer trainee who stood next to him had no idea how close she came to death that day. Payten hovered beside him, her face in the light, her generous rack pushed against his arm.

Her fingers twined in his hand as she laughed.

Oh.

My.

Swearword.

I turned and stumbled away, unable to draw a breath, choking on my anguish even as something inside me snapped and fire poured over the chill of my hurt.

Bastard.

Just try that again.

The next time he showed up in my back yard, I was burying his arrogant ass next to the Wild Hunt and leaving him there to suffer for all eternity.

chapter nine

Meira caught up with me, her face falling at the sight of my expression. She linked arms, not asking questions, just offering her energy for support. My demon took it, used it to soothe me while my alter egos soaked me in love and understanding. Walking was good. Moving on was better.

Mom appeared a few moments later to join us.

"Excellent," she said with a smile. "We now have confirmation from everyone but Europe." None of us were surprised we heard no word from Applegate. Though I fully expected the thralled Leader to show up at some point and cause trouble.

Prepared for disaster? I was born for it. And speaking of disaster... "Mom," I said. "I have some things you need to know."

She drew me along with her as we strolled again, as

though unconcerned by the conversation we were about to have while my sister's false smile echoed our attempt at subtlety.

I shared what I knew of the wild magicks, what they'd shown me, shared with Shenka and I in the basement. Mom's frown flashed only for a moment before she nodded pleasantly to a passing cluster of witches.

"You think this goes beyond gratitude?" Mom kept her voice low. "Maybe they have some kind of message they are trying to deliver?"

"That's my guess," I said. "But Mom, these are wild creatures we're talking about. Just getting them to settle down and tell me what they want me to hear is a bit of a struggle."

"Sounds like Shenka's idea to talk to Demetrius is a good one," Meira said. Hey, that had been my idea first. "Crazy or not, he seems to know a lot about things we've never dealt with before."

Made me miss Gram's quirky presence all the more. She would probably be able to figure it out in a flash.

"From the expression on your face," Mom said, "and the fact you said you had 'things' to talk to me about, I take it there's more?"

Bless her for not sighing or rolling her eyes. I would have. Wanted to, and I was the one passing on the trouble.

She pulled to a stop when I told her about Tallah's

dream for witch equality and the fact she'd been in contact with the Steam Union.

"Syd." Mom's cheeks went pale, eyes wide, not even trying to hide her distress.

"I know," I said as Meira huddled close to us, a tight frown on her face.

"She's nuts," Meira said, skin taking on a reddish hue as her control over her real form slipped just a little. "We're already trying to circumvent a magic war. Now she wants to start one with normals?"

"Do you believe it may be the Steam Union she's speaking to?" Mom's blue eyes drilled holes through me.

I fought over my conscience with that one. "It's possible," I said. "Piers told me there were other branches of the Union in the world that had nothing to do with his people."

"Who are we kidding here?" Meira's eyes flared amber as her demon made it through. "She's been duped by the Brotherhood and we all know it."

I hated to say it was the most likely scenario.

"Only one way to find out," Mom said. "I'll speak to her. But you'll have to be there, Syd. I'll need her tested for the taint."

Shenka would understand. Agree with me 100%, I was sure. Still, I felt guilty thinking about her sister this way.

"I could just take a little trip to California," I said. In

and out of the veil. Presto magicko.

"No," Mom said. "If she is under Brotherhood influence, I want to keep this official.

I don't want to warn Belaisle we know what he's up to." Mom's hand twitched over the front of her skirt, smoothing it in a reflexive gesture I associated with stress. We'll wait to talk to her when she arrives tonight."

Great. I had lots of time to torture myself over this.

Fair enough.

"Let me know when you're settled into your pavilion," Mom said. "We'll take care of it right away."

Ack.

"I don't know why it's necessary for me to stay here." Mom and I already had this talk but the whiner in me couldn't let it go.

"As a show of faith," Mom said.

"You know how risky it is." Every time I thought about leaving the family for a few days, I felt nauseated. Yes, I was still inside our family boundaries. But we were effectively stripping each of the major territories of their most powerful and influential witches. If the Brotherhood wanted to strike, the timing couldn't have been more perfect.

"Enforcers will be posted with each of the families," Mom said, her tone soothing, hand on my arm. "We've talked about this."

We did. Okay. "But what about the conclave itself?" I

shuddered, sudden panic rising. She didn't know Belaisle the way I did, how he always seemed to be ten steps ahead of me. "We're sitting ducks here. Might as well paint giant bull's eyes on the tops of the pavilions."

"Had that done this morning," Mom said. "Biggest targets on the most important tents. So the Brotherhood knows exactly where to strike."

I gaped at her as she laughed and hugged me.

"Syd," she said. "I'm kidding."

Okay, I knew that. "It's not funny."

"No," she said. "It isn't. But we're doing everything possible to assure the safety of our covens and our visitors. You know this is necessary. We have to stand as one against the Brotherhood."

Grumble, mumble.

"This place will be swarming with foreign Enforcers, werewolves, vampires, Steam Union, Sidhe." Mom turned to Meira who nodded. "Demons."

"I've already gathered a contingent," my sister said, "demons with effigies available here on this plane." She nudged me. "Quite an impressive list."

We were safe. I had to believe it. So why didn't I?

When Mom was called away again, Meira and I took our leave, sliding through the veil to the basement of my house while I struggled with worry and the understanding no matter what happened, the next few days were going to be very interesting.

chapter ten

"So," Meira said as we stepped out into the dim light of the underground. "Since Shenka obviously wasn't talking about her sister's arrival, mind telling me who came to visit you last night?"

No way. Not now I'd seen Quaid with...

Her.

He met Payten during his first summer Enforcer camp. He claimed they weren't a couple, had shared only a fling. And yet, she seemed to think otherwise and, surprise surprise, any time I saw them together she was all over him.

Okay, so holding his hand wasn't technically "all over him". But when her impressive chest was in his space, it qualified.

"It doesn't matter," I said. Hating how much it really did matter.

Meira didn't push me. Just hugged me as her body shifted back to demon form. I really had to get her to teach me how she altered her clothes in the process because by the time she released me, she towered over me in those damned boots she loved.

My sister winked before turning and tearing open the veil. Ahbi answered instantly, embracing both of us with magic before Meira blew me a kiss.

"Love you," she said before stepping through.

Love you, Ahbi's mind whispered.

And then, they were gone.

"Love you, too," I said into the quiet air.

Sighed.

A snorting snore caught my attention, the sound leading me past my heavy bag and to the small, partitioned corner of the basement Demetrius claimed as his own. I'd tried a few times to convince him move to upstairs into the main part of the house. With Charlotte back and forth between here and her family's home in Ukraine, my old room was available most of the time.

But he refused, preferring to hide down in the cool and quiet. Lurking like a cockroach. Okay, not really fair. Still gave me the creeps.

I found him lying on his side on his cot, hands tucked under his cheek, blue eyes closed. He looked so peaceful, almost young, only the scar he'd acquired marring the peaches-and-cream of his complexion. A surge of empathy drove me to cover him with a quilt, smoothing it out over him as he muttered in his sleep.

Aside from breakfast, I hadn't seen much of him lately. He'd been chasing down my old bestie-turned-insane ghost echo, Alison, not to mention trying to track the Brotherhood. He was barely home, mostly just to sleep as far as I knew. I wanted to wake him and ask him about the wild magicks. After talking to Mom about it, I felt now more than ever their appearance had to be important. But I couldn't bring myself to disturb his rest.

Time enough later. Besides, the fact he was here meant he probably had something of his own to tell me, and would come find me when he woke up. I could bring it up to him then.

I left him, sleeping peacefully, and returned to the kitchen, trying not to feel bad about leaving him alone in the basement.

I didn't even think to check the house for other magic, my head in the old coven site, tied up in the coming conclave. So when I emerged into the early evening sunlight and spotted Liam sitting at the kitchen table, I actually froze in place.

Galleytrot grumbled beside my Sidhe friend, the giant black hound of the Wild Hunt staring at me with his black eyes, red flames flickering in their depths. Instant resentment fired in my gut. He'd warned me in the past not to hurt Liam and I'd done my best.

Clearly my best wasn't cutting it.

Nice of the stupid mutt to remind me.

I didn't get a chance to comment on the dog's attitude, not when I turned at a flicker of motion on my right just before being pulled into a strong embrace. I hugged Charlotte back, happy to see her, at least. She smiled when we parted, white teeth flashing before her face settled into her more stoic expression.

Yes, she was much more open now with her emotions, happier, even chatty, much to my surprise. But the more time passed, the more she settled into her familiar quiet expression, years of training in hiding what she felt a hard habit to break.

"Grandfather says hello," Charlotte said. "He's hoping you can spare time for a visit."

I bobbed a nod. "Sure thing," I said, feeling the extra enthusiasm behind my words bubbling like a desperate wall between me and Liam.

Charlotte's blue eyes softened around the edges as she turned to the Sidhe Gatekeeper. "Perhaps you could join us, Liam." He looked up, perking a little from the sad, silent stare he'd fixed on me the moment I emerged from the basement. "I'm certain you will find the library at the palace of great interest."

His easy smile flashed a moment, handsome face happy.

I missed his happy.

"Thank you, Charlotte," he said. "Sounds fantastic." Enthusiasm replaced his angst. "I've been wanting to talk to one of the werewolves who lived there about Chernobyl and the effect the meltdown had on your race's physiology."

Charlotte flinched, just a little, enough I knew it had to be a touchy subject.

"I'm sure one of our people would be willing to discuss the dark time," she said even as Liam's face fell.

She turned back to me, cocking her head to one side. "You smell like outside," she said.

No question, just the statement. Cracked me up.

"Mom gave Meira and me the tour of the conclave site," I said, taking a seat at the end of the kitchen table as Shenka appeared with a smile.

"How does it look?" Her magic flared, glasses floating to each place setting, a bowl appearing for Galleytrot, another as Sassafras leaped onto the table to listen. I sipped the cold juice in my glass with a grin of thanks before answering.

"Big," I said. "Busy." I clinked glasses with Charlotte. "Your family is coming?"

She nodded, taking a drink. "Grandfather has agreed to come, most eagerly." A soft frown pulled her perfectly arched brows together. "Though there are those who worry about exposing ourselves to witches at this juncture. Before we've fully established our freedom."

"No one will oppose you," I said. "While not everyone may know what happened last winter, they'll find out soon enough."

Charlotte nodded, her glass thudding on the table as she set it down. "I have no doubt Miriam and her Council have things well in hand. Nor do I worry about my people's standing. And Grandfather feels the same, or he would have declined the invitation."

So odd to talk to Charlotte this way. While it had been over six months since I freed her people from the Black Souls sect, it still amazed me she was so talkative. I think she'd said more to me over that time than she had the entire duration of the rest of our association.

I liked it, don't get me wrong. It just took some getting used to.

"Both courts have agreed to attend," Liam said, deep voice soft as though afraid he interrupted by speaking up. I shifted my focus to him and smiled, a real smile, though I still felt uncomfortable.

I looked into the hazel eyes of the man I could be marrying in the next little while and felt my insides shudder.

"How nice they are getting along well enough they're willing to share a pavilion." I didn't want to be part of that logistical nightmare.

Liam chuckled, green sparks in his gaze. "Well, I wouldn't go that far," he said. "But they are coming. So it's a start."

We smiled at each other for an awkward moment before Galleytrot cleared his throat like a rumble of distant thunder.

"I know you're concerned about the safety of the family," he said. "You have to stay at the site?"

I nodded, feeling glum all of a sudden, staring down at the thin trail of orange pulp on the side of my glass. "Am I the only one who thinks this might be a perfect opportunity for the Brotherhood to act?"

No one argued, Sassafras's tail twitching so violently a small cloud of silver fur rose.

"I'm happy to play guard dog," Galleytrot said. "Miriam's Enforcers can keep an eye out for witch magic, and I'll keep track of Sidhe. I can't promise you I'll sense sorcery if it comes up, but I've been around enough of it now, I think I'll know if the Brotherhood disrupts earth magic."

Sudden relief lifted my shoulders. I leaned sideways in my chair and scratched the big hound behind one ear.

"That makes me feel much better," I said. "Thank you, Galleytrot."

"While I understand your concern," Sassafras said, "I think you're focusing on the wrong threat."

"What do you mean?" I settled back into my chair again. "The conclave?"

I'd thought of that. But with all those witches and

Enforcers, Belaisle would be insane to attack now we knew how to counter his power by dropping our wards and shielding. Without access to the extra magic, it would be easy for me to mop up the mess.

At least, that's what I told myself.

My demon cat's eyes sparked as his tail continued to thrash. "Liander Belaisle has remained several steps ahead of us," he said. "At every turn, we find he has three more planned."

I hated that part.

"You're saying you think he has an entirely different goal in mind?" Shenka's fingernails danced over the side of her glass, the musical sound almost hypnotic. I couldn't help but think of Tallah and her mysterious Steam Union friends, wondering, even as I did, if my second's thoughts were also with her sister.

"I'm saying," Sassafras swiped at his whiskers with one paw, "we need to be open-minded and release our pre-conceived fears about what may happen over the next several days." He turned to me again. "While your temper has gotten us into trouble in the past, it is that same temper, and your reflexes under pressure, which are your most powerful weapon against the Brotherhood." He shrugged, took three laps of his milk. "Worrying about a specific event will only dull your attention to what he really has planned."

Fair enough. I stroked his fur.

"When did you get so smart?" He shivered under my touch, nose twitching.

"Oh, shut up," he said.

"I should be getting back," Charlotte said, standing abruptly. She still had trouble with social niceties, but no one held it against her.

"I'll run you home." Anything to escape the hang-dog look now returned to Liam's eyes, the irritation in Galleytrot's.

I followed Charlotte outside, ignoring Shenka's sigh and soft shake of her head.

Whatever. I'd deal with Liam later.

Honest.

I was such a liar.

Charlotte turned before I could take her hand. There was no need to leave the house to travel anymore. The family wards didn't give me a hard time, not now I had access to maji power. But it turned out she wasn't thinking about me.

"Syd." She bit her lower lip, shrugging her shoulders, looking guilty. "I have a confession."

Okay. I braced myself for impact, knowing if it was coming from Charlotte, it had to be a doozy.

She hung her head as she spoke in a whisper. "I went on a date," she said. "With Sage."

She did what now?

"I'm sorry." She hugged herself, fitted leather jacket

creaking. "I went to the gym to see if you were there, but you weren't." Pause. "He was, though. He teased me." She looked like she wanted to cry. "And I was free, don't you see? My pride, Syd. My foolish pride."

I gaped at her as she rushed on.

"He challenged me and I accepted." Oh boy. "I beat him, of course I did." Poor Sage wouldn't know what hit him. My normal marital arts instructor was an awesome guy, very attractive, but he wouldn't stand a chance against my werefriend. "When I was done, he laughed." She shook her head, blonde hair waving around her. "Laughed! And asked me out on a date."

Giggles bubbled in my chest as she grasped my hand, face wreathed in guilt.

"I should never have gone out with him," she said. "He was yours and I infringed on your territory."

Okay, I just couldn't hold it in any longer. I laughed, belly laughs, tears trickling, ribs aching until I had to gasp for air. All the while Charlotte watched me with an anxious expression, slowly easing as I finally pulled myself under control and hugged her as hard as I could.

When I leaned back, she smiled, impish and daring. "You're not mad," she said.

"I'm not even a little." A tiny flare of regret passed through me at the thought of Sage. He was delicious, kind, strong, brilliant. If only he had power, I might consider him. But there was no way the coven would accept a normal. My other choices already pushed the boundaries of acceptable.

I winked at her. "Was it fun?"

Charlotte giggled like a girl behind her hands before arching an eyebrow. "Most pleasant," she said.

We laughed together in the driveway for a long moment, our good humor silenced briefly as Liam and Galleytrot left the kitchen and almost ran into us.

Charlotte took a step away, the big dog joining her as Liam stopped beside me. He felt miserable, emanating anxiety. I wished I could comfort him, but there was nothing I could say I hadn't said before.

Liam bent and kissed my cheek. Left me there, good mood shattered as he strode off with his shoulders slumped, head down. Galleytrot heaved an irritated sigh in my direction then trotted after the Gatekeeper.

Charlotte watched them go, waiting until they'd left our view before taking my hand.

"Trust yourself," she said, her wolf rising in her eyes. "Laws and rules and witches be damned. You must do what is good for you, Sydlynn Hayle. Believe me, I have experience with these things."

She'd spent her entire life enslaved to others up until recently. So, yeah. I believed her.

I just wished I knew what the right decision was.

Falling back into my own melancholy, I tore open the veil and took Charlotte home.

chApTeR eLeVeN

Summer did wonders for the Ukrainian countryside. I liked it much better without all the snow and ice, thanks. Even though cold didn't affect me anymore, I still preferred the green and multi-hued beauty of this time of year.

I'd meant to drop us inside the palace foyer, but, instead, found myself stepping out of the veil on the giant front lawn, my sneakers crunching over gravel and old asphalt at the edge of the curving drive. The quiet of dusk washed everything in deep blues and shadow as the sun set here in Eastern Europe.

Puzzled and a little irritated I'd somehow missed the mark, it wasn't until I looked up and saw the tall, handsome blonde striding toward us, a smile on his angular face, I realized I'd been manipulated.

Ahbi chuckled in my mind as the veil sealed behind

me, just before Piers Southway came to a grinning halt before me. He didn't pause, speak, or ask as his hands dove into my hair, mouth descending over mine in a hungry kiss.

This wasn't the first time he kissed me without permission. Probably wouldn't be the last, either. I could blow a gasket and be a bitch, or...

Well. He really was a great kisser.

Charlotte's soft laugh drifted off and she was gone before Piers finally lifted his mouth from mine, the last of his exhale in my mouth.

Peppermint and coffee. Now I craved caffeine.

"Hello there, beautiful." His sorcery butted up against mine, as close as his body pressed my full length. One thing about Piers, he had zero issues with contact.

I really wanted to be irritated with the blasé way he treated his attraction to me, but I found him so refreshing, his open honesty a delightful change from sullen darkness and angst ridden sorrow I just couldn't help myself.

"Piers." I gave him a gentle push to put some distance between us even as he backed off as if it was his idea. "What are you doing here?"

He spun on his heel, gray longcoat swirling around his legs, his familiar uniform in attendance despite the warmth of the evening. One arm extended, offering some chivalry, and I simply couldn't resist taking it.

"I was hoping to see you, of course." He winked one sparkling gray eye before laughing as I glared back, deadpan. "Mum wanted me to check in with the werewolves to coordinate our joint arrival at the conclave."

Made sense. "Are you coming?" And why exactly did I care?

Oh, Syd. Just keep lying to yourself, girlfriend.

He didn't comment on the loaded question, keeping his sarcastic come-ons to himself. "I am," he said. "While my mother might not be your biggest fan, she understands your power and position with the North American High Council and hopes my presence can sway your opinions."

I had to laugh, as we stepped through the massive front door and into the Faberge egg interior of the palace foyer. "I'm sure she told you to put it exactly that way," I said.

Piers shrugged, eyes full of laughter and more than a little wickedness. "Considering I'm a candidate for your husband," he said, "I figure full disclosure will serve me better than diplomacy."

He had to remind me, didn't he? I slid my hand free of his arm and forced a little smile.

Piers didn't let me escape so easily. He bent over me, eyes tightening even as his own mouth curved into a small frown.

"You do realize," he said in his crisp British accent, "you're going to have to make a choice eventually? Running away from it won't solve anything." He pulled back, long, blonde hair falling over one shoulder. "Regardless of whom you choose, avoiding the topic is only making things worse."

"Thank you, Captain Obvious," I shot back, temper searing through me as my demon grumbled.

Piers laughed, kissed me swiftly. "I adore you," he said. "I can't tell you how much."

Grumble mumble.

"Any sign of the Brotherhood?" Topic changing was one of my most polished avoidance tactics.

Piers just sighed and shrugged, taking the massive hint at last. "Not from our end," he said, falling into serious, gray eyes brewing a storm behind them as he leaned into me. "Mum's been vigilant, but they're still in hiding."

Creepy crawlies traveled up my spine, paired with frustration. "What are they up to?"

Piers's gaze locked on mine, grim and dark. "You can be certain," he said, "whatever their plans, you will somehow end up in the thick of them." We'd talked enough over the last six months or so, him cheerfully appearing in my kitchen whenever the hell he felt like it. Our conversations about my dealings with the Brotherhood meant Piers was fully informed as to my trouble magnet nature.

Even knowing that didn't scare him off.

Brave boy.

"Lucky me," I said. Paused. "You said there were other Steam Union groups, one in my territory, correct?"

He nodded, squinting in curiosity. "Why do you ask? Looking to make some new allies?" Was that jealousy in his voice?

"I need to keep my husband options open," I said. Elbowed him with a smirk. "I'm kidding," I said as his little frown turned into a snort. "One of you in my life is more than enough."

He swept a bow before going on. "I take it there is a point to the question?"

Why did I hesitate to tell him? Right. Sharing Shenka's secrets with Mom was, well... she was my mother. I didn't have many secrets from her, especially any big ones. But telling Piers was crossing the friendship line.

Wasn't it?

Still. This was important. And any information I could give Mom would help when we finally talked to Tallah.

My Steam Union friend was scowling by the time I finished telling him what Shenka told me.

"I highly doubt anyone from our order would suggest exposing witches or any other magical race to normals," he said. Stopped. Whistled softly through his teeth. "But I can't be sure."

That was helpful. "Can you poke around for me?"

Piers didn't answer right away, and when he did, his voice was distant. "I have some people I can ask," he said, giving me the impression he was already doing so. The moment passed, his full attention returning. "We'll know soon enough."

Okay then.

That left me with my other curiosity. "Since you seem to be the go-to guy for answers, what do you know about wild magicks?"

I might as well have punched him in the stomach. Piers gasped, grasped my upper arms in his hands.

"Tell me they've returned," he said.

Um, wow. Chillax dudilicious. I pulled free of him, scowling.

"I told you I freed them," I said. "You didn't seem all that excited before."

He shook his head. "I've been doing some research," he said, backing off a little, though his excitement didn't retreat far. "What happened?"

I told him while he nodded and grinned at me before hugging me swiftly.

"This is brilliant," he said. "Can you summon them?"

"Maybe if you actually filled me in," I said, "I'd consider trying."

Snap.

Piers's deep chuckle made me all warm in places I wished it didn't.

"Here's what I've learned," he said. "According to Steam Union records, the wild magicks you freed were captured centuries ago by the Brotherhood and enslaved to their use."

What else was new? The Brotherhood was great at making slaves.

"Here's the best part," he said, eagerness rising. "If you truly did free the full fragments the Brotherhood stole, you now have access to all that power yourself. Power our enemies are now lacking." He bounced once on his toes, white teeth sparkling as he smiled. "You need to trap them, Syd. So the Brotherhood can't capture them again."

A horrible feeling settled in my stomach at the thought of trapping the wild magicks.

Piers must have seen the resistance in my expression because he calmed a bit, drew a breath. "Everything you've done," he said, "has reduced the power of the Brotherhood. From forcing them to abandon one of their bases of power," the mansion Belaisle burned, right, "to breaking their hold over the attack on the Sidhe," with Ameline's help. Still made me furious to remember. "But by setting free one of their major sources of power, you've crippled them beyond what they expected."

I wasn't so sure about that. My mind went to the woman in the rainbow shielding, the one we'd seen when Ameline and I worked together to save the Sidhe realm from Belaisle's attack, as I spoke. "If so," I said, "does that mean you think they've gone to ground for good?" I couldn't bring myself to hope I'd done that much damage.

Had I?

Piers shook his head. "There's more depth to their power than the wild magicks," he said. "But if you were to claim them, you would have a distinct advantage."

"I'm sure that's true," I said, skin crawling at the wrongness of the thought as my alter egos prodded me to reject the idea.

Piers seemed almost desperate for a moment before visibly calming and taking a step away.

"The Brotherhood can't be allowed to reclaim them," he said. "Just promise me you'll act if necessary."

What, did he think I was an idiot?

There were times I liked Piers a lot, times I wondered if he'd be a good choice to marry, my partner in crime.

This wasn't one of those times. In my heart, and in the souls of the powers living inside me, I knew the only place for the wild magicks was out there.

Free.

"Syd." Charlotte waved at me from the entry to the throne room. When I turned back to Piers from her distraction, his ready smile had returned.

This time when he kissed me, I cut it short, the buzz of anger still humming through my veins.

He didn't comment, as cocky as ever. "I'll see you tomorrow, gorgeous," he said. Gestured as a large, black hole formed. Saluted with a wink before disappearing through it.

I ground my teeth together in a mix of frustration and nerves as I joined Charlotte.

chapter twelve

After a quick hello to Oleksander and Raoul, I was off for home again. While I'd thought the king of the werewolves had an important message for me, considering Charlotte's mention he wanted to see me, it turned out to be nothing of the sort.

"Sydlynn." The huge were with the iron gray hair and beard engulfed me in his massive arms, crushing me to his broad chest a moment before setting me free. "It is wonderful to see you."

Oleksander had blossomed as much as his granddaughter. The pensive, serious werewolf I'd first met was gone, a benevolent monarch left behind. It was clear his people worshipped him by the way the gathered pack members watched him, bowed as he bent to kiss the back of my hand. Good to know the werewolves were in such dependable paws.

"You too," I said. "You're coming tomorrow?" Wow, was it really tomorrow? Conclave already. I thought I still had lots of time.

Not so much.

"I am." He reached out for Charlotte, one arm draping around her shoulders as she smiled up at him. "And my delightful granddaughter is joining me." He bowed his head. "Many thanks to your mother for the invitation. We werewolves understand it is a great risk she takes, bringing us to America for such an important meeting. But her goals to unite all magic races, to create dialogue and partnership where once we all toiled alone, bring me great hope for the future."

"We're honored to have you." Okay, so I was picking up on the diplomacy thing after all. Mom would be impressed.

"Most excellent." Oleksander kissed both of my cheeks before clasping his hands behind him. "We will see you then."

Um. Great.

Charlotte escorted me to the front door, giggling.

"He is so excited," she said. "And so very proud. You have given him something he's never had before, Syd. A sense of purpose, a reason for being. Our people are his reason, without fear of others trying to control our destiny." She shrugged. "I know this meeting might not have meant much to you, but he thinks fondly of you, as though you were his granddaughter, too. Forgive an old wolf for wasting your time."

I hugged her immediately. "Don't be an idiot," I said, tears burning my eyes. "Time spent with you and your family, with those I care about, is never wasted."

She kissed my cheeks like her grandfather had. "Thank you," she said.

I left her on the front step, striding out a few paces before opening the veil. Ahbi embraced me with her power the second I did, but I held off riding just yet.

"Listen up," I said. "I realize you're trying to help me choose, just like everyone else." There was a tint of oops behind her surge of innocence. "But dumping me on Piers was a very bad idea." Well, not so bad. I was kind of over my snit now and the memory of his kiss went a long way to seal my forgiveness.

I really had to get a grip on my hormones.

Ahbi's magic pouted.

"Thank you," I said, softening. "But I need to make this decision on my own."

Her power slipped around me. No apology, not from Ahbi. Even softened by her connection to the Node keeping Demonicon together, my grandmother was a mistress of manipulation. But I could feel the real caring she had for me, caring she had been unable to show while alive and Ruler of her plane.

I stepped into the veil and let her take me home at

last, stepping out into the still-bright kitchen. Traveling great distances always screwed me up when it came to time zones and night versus day. Still fighting disorientation, I almost missed the feeling of Enforcer magic in the house.

Almost. But I knew it wasn't his. Not Quaid's. This power was distinctly feminine.

Which meant it could only be one person. I went to Gram's room, pushing the already ajar door wide to find Varity Rhodes standing at the end of the bed. The former Enforcer leader looked up as I entered, a deep scowl on her face, gray hair pulled back in a tight bun, black robe hanging from her tall, thin body.

"She refuses to talk to me." Varity's deep voice dropped further into disapproval as she went back to glaring down at Gram who still sat on the floor, now in darkness, her friendly sunbeam long gone.

Gram grunted and swatted at her old friend before crossing her arms over her chest, sullen expression as closed as her door had been lately.

"She's just cranky," I said, keeping it light even as my heart twisted inside me. "You know. Typical."

Varity snorted a half-laugh though the worry in her face mirrored mine.

"Whatever," she said, turning and striding past me out into the hall. "Let her sulk. I have better things to do."

I followed her out of the room, reached for the knob. Only to have it slam into my back as Gram's thin remaining power pushed it shut with a bang.

Varity's face crumpled the moment the door closed, but she didn't say anything until we reached the kitchen.

"I've never seen her like this." Varity wrung her thin, wrinkled hands, crisscrossing scars on the backs making me wonder what caused them. "I don't know how to help her."

Not much to say. I sat in the same boat.

"The stubborn old bat." Varity stomped one booted foot. "I want her to attend conclave with me. Engage her in something else. But she won't even say a word."

The door behind me creaked, both of us turning to find Demetrius watching from the top step of the basement. His huge blue eyes brimmed with moisture as he snuffled and wiped his nose with the palm of his hand.

"Poor Ethie," he said. "All used up."

And whose fault was that?

"I realize you can't yet," Varity snarled around her clenched jaw, "but the moment you can kill that little bitch, Ameline, you do it. And give Ethpeal back her power."

"On the agenda," I said.

Varity nodded once, a sharp tip of her head, before stomping out the front door. I felt her Enforcer magic flare as Shenka pounded down the stairs and rushed into the kitchen, out of breath.

"What did I miss?" She spotted Demetrius as he pulled out a chair and perched with a hopeful smile on the edge. I'm pretty sure my second's reaction was automatic as she spun and immediately began to fix him something to eat.

I watched her deft hands make him a giant sandwich.

"Varity was here," I said. "Just Gram stuff."

Shenka nodded sadly. No explanation required.

Demetrius's feet swung, a charming grin on his face, ignoring us as Shenka's food prep continued.

"What did Oleksander want?" Shenka licked a line of mayo from her thumb after cutting the sandwich in quarters and transferring it neatly onto a plate.

"To hug me," I said, a grin pulling at my lips. "He's just so happy, you know?"

She beamed at me as she crossed to Demetrius. The damaged sorcerer clapped his hands as she set the plate in front of him before going to the cupboard again for a glass. Funny how she used her hands when it was one person but her magic for multiples.

Efficiency, your name is Sashenka Hensley.

"I told Mom about Tallah," I blurted. Because blurting things to my friends was the way I rolled.

The glass she retrieved for Demetrius rattled as it dropped the last inch from her grip, circling on its base a few rotations before settling down.

"What did she say?" Shenka didn't meet my eyes as she turned to the fridge and fetched the pitcher of water. I noticed she held it in both hands as she poured, the small fall of liquid shivering from her trembles.

"We're going to talk to Tallah tonight," I said. "It's going to be okay, Shenka." I didn't bother telling her I mentioned it to Piers. Not after my second managed a lip-wavering smile.

"It's for the best," she said, setting down the pitcher, wiping both hands on her thighs. "Does Miriam want me there?"

"Do you want to be there?" Much better question.

Shenka nodded. "I do."

"Then you're welcome," I said.

Demetrius mowed through his snack as we talked, taking giant bites of bread and meat and veggies, rolling his eyes in bliss as he chewed with his mouth open. Shenka refilled his glass when he emptied most of it into his mouth, ignoring the dribbles trailing down his chin and the front of his spotted t-shirt. She sank down next to me and watched him eat.

"Found her." He spit a small piece of sandwich out onto the table. Though I was slightly grossed out, Shenka simply scooped it up and disposed of it with magic as though he were a toddler.

"Found who, Demetrius?" Because with him, one never knew. We'd been talking about Tallah. Did he think she was missing?

"The echo," he said and my heart stood still.

"You found Alison?" Holy. Crap. I had to destroy her, the taint she stole from the vampires.

From me.

Before I could leap to my feet and rush off in a blaze of vengeance, Shenka asked a question.

"Where is she?"

Right. Good information to have if I was going to dash off half-cocked.

He shrugged, stuffed in another bite. "Doesn't matter," he said through chewing. "She's busy."

"With?" I ground my teeth together, hands fisted on the table in front of me as I waited. And waited. While he chewed, swallowed, drank some water. Fixed me with a sweet smile.

"Demetrius." My voice came out in a low growl, my demon pushing behind me while my vampire hissed in my head.

He set down his sandwich, eyes glinting with hints of lucidity. "She's trying to make more," he said. "Like her."

Oh. My. Swearword.

"We have to stop her." Didn't we? Why did he look so unconcerned?

"She'll fail," he said before picking up his dinner again, examining it carefully for a place to bite. "But she keeps trying, yes indeedy doodle dandy." He blinked slowly, a demented owl, grinning with bits of food in his teeth. "Keeps her weak and occupied."

That might be fine and good in Demetriusland, but I was responsible for her. For the echoes she gathered.

"Besides," he said just before taking another calm, massive bite. "She's with the Brotherhood."

She was—

With the—

"Demetrius!" I slammed both fists down on the table, his plate and glass both jumping in response. "You found them? Where are they?" Now I had a mission, and I'd be damned if his stupid sandwich was getting in the way.

Belaisle was mine.

My hitchhikers all roared in agreement, the family magic surging in answer even as the small sorcerer sighed and focused on me.

"You can't," he said. "Not without *her*."

We both knew who he meant.

Ameline.

Oh, *hell* no.

"I don't need anyone," I snarled.

He stuffed in the remains of his sandwich while Shenka laid a calming hand on my arm, though her eyes looked a bit wild around the edges.

I could just imagine how I appeared with Shaylee, my demon, my vampire and the family magic all fighting for freedom and the chance to go after Belaisle.

"He's using the echo girl," Demetrius said. "Dear Liander found a way to siphon from her, didn't he?" His blue eyes misted over, hands pressing to his cheeks. "All those poor ghostie mosties, through her, just another means to a power source."

I sank back in my seat, horror driving bile to the back of my throat. "That's sick." Okay, this was Belaisle we were talking about. And yes, Alison wasn't the girl I remembered. She'd been corrupted, lost the light of her soul. She had only the dark of her ego left, now tainted by power beyond her. Still, she didn't deserve to be fed on by a pack of leeches.

Demetrius's feet swung harder, his cherub face full of sadness despite the grin pulling at his mouth. "Yup, yup," he said, soft and sad.

But it made me think and remember what I wanted to ask him as my temper cooled and the girls chilled out. "The wild magicks I freed, the ones from the crystals in Miami." I grasped his hand a moment before letting him go. "The Brotherhood used to control them, used them as a source, correct?"

He tilted his head to the side, more owlish than ever. "Bingo," he said. I could feel him slipping away from me, back into insanity. I had to act fast.

"They've been coming around," I said, leaning toward him, trying to support him with energy.

He perked, snapping his fingers and wriggling in his

chair. "How are they?"

Oh boy. I was losing him.

At least, I thought I was. I watched as he physically grasped hold of his lucidity, black sorcery sliding over his eyes before he shuddered and focused on me again.

"They must remain free," he said, voice low and steady. "Protect them, but they need to be wild."

"Why?" I thought of Piers, played devil's advocate. "Wouldn't it be better to capture them myself?"

Even as I said it, I shuddered. He shuddered. The whole world seemed to shift as he grabbed my hand.

"Light and Dark come together," he said. "But random wins."

He slipped again, shivering with the effort it took to keep himself present and with me.

"They are trying to tell me something," I said, desperate to hang on to him. "How do I figure out what it is?"

He shuddered, pulling me toward him, the black oozing across his eyes one last time as his sorcery butted against mine.

"Listen," he said. Blinked and sagged with a goofy smile. "Glisten. Pissing rain, what?" He giggled, high pitched and girly, before shimmying back and forth in his seat. "Sing halleluiah, sisters. Sing it!"

I let him go, insides clenched tight. Shenka reached for him with sympathy on her face, but he dodged her, slipping from his chair with sharp cry.

"Time flies!" He clapped his hands abruptly together and fell backward into a puddle of black, like a kid falling into a pond, before it closed around him and he disappeared.

Shenka turned to me, concern on her face, but I shook my head, anger and frustration warring with compassion.

"Just let him go," I said. "He'll come back when he has more info."

"Or when the crap hits the fan," Shenka said.

Yeah. Or then.

"In the meantime," she said, "at least we know someone has a line on Alison. And the Brotherhood."

I just wished it was me and not the half-baked Demetrius Strong.

"You, on the other hand, have a job to do." Shenka swept to her feet, magic sending his dishes to the sink.

Crap. What had I forgotten now?

She grinned as she poked me. "You have to choose who you're taking to conclave."

Right.

Damn. Half the coven wanted to come and I could only pick three.

I could hear the screams of disappointment now.

Sometimes my job really sucked.

chapter thirteen

I set down my small suitcase in the center of the tented room and tried to feel okay about leaving the family under Galleytrot's protection. And yes, that of the six Enforcers now patrolling Wilding Springs.

Still.

Not easy to just walk away.

And yet, I was still inside my own territory, felt the hum of the family magic from its place in the basement of my house. I would know in a breath if something went wrong, could leap into the veil at a moment's notice.

Still.

Unease was a way of life now, I guessed. Even surrounded by the Council's Enforcers, even with all this power at my disposal. At least the small bedroom constructed inside the giant pavilion was nice enough, not stuffy or dark. And thanks to the shielding Mom and the other witches of the Council placed around each sleeping area, I had privacy. Which I immediately reinforced with my own magic, thank you very much.

The pavilion was divided into a number of sections, twenty-nine covens invited from across the continent as the representatives of our territory of North America. Like me, each leader was only permitted three witches as an entourage. Not as a trust issue, but as a way to control the sheer numbers of bodies about to descend on the site. Mom estimated hundreds, but I fully expected over a thousand witches, werewolves, vampires, Sidhe and demons to show up, not to mention the Steam Union.

The only contingent not represented were the maji, though technically I qualified. I sighed as I sank to the soft mattress of my bed, trying to appreciate the lovely, airy feel of the room, the delicate white and floral décor Mom chose. I was really hoping to have Trill to lean on during the conclave.

The young blood maji informed me in no uncertain terms weeks ago she had no intention of attending in an official capacity.

"You and Miriam can handle things," Trill said over a cup of hot chocolate. Her brothers slept in the caravan they used as a traveling home, tucked away in my back yard out of view of the street while the dark-haired beauty joined me for a drink in the middle of the night. "I have other worries at the moment. And I'd rather keep an eye on the proceedings from a safe distance."

No amount of conversation could dissuade her. Or make her stay longer than it took to finish her cup of cocoa. I waved as she drove off in her rusting motor home, gone as quickly as she'd appeared.

Just like Trill Zornov, budding blood maji. And yet, I sensed a change in her, maturity she'd only begun to develop the last time I saw her blossoming and growing inside her. She'd clearly seized her power and embraced it. And though I worried, as I did about everyone I cared about, I knew she and her brothers would be fine.

And watching. Waiting for their chance to strike at the Brotherhood. Knowing Trill was out there actually made me feel better, even if I preferred she be at my side.

"Delightful." Estelle Lawrence peeked into my space, gently parting the heavy fabric hanging over my doorway. "Your mother did a splendid job."

"Just splendid." Esther agreed with her sister, not a shocker, as the twins looked around my quarters with their normally pinched expressions softened, matching glasses shining in the soft witch light, twinsets and skirts as prim and proper as ever.

I dutifully followed them to the room they shared, oohed and ahhed as genuinely as possible while Shenka giggled behind her hands at me. The only one who seemed completely at ease was Sassafras. He'd parked his fat body on the low sofa in the main area we'd been allotted and proceeded to clean himself thoroughly with his rasping tongue.

It was actually hilarious to see the twins acting almost girlish as they gushed over their quarters. I could only imagine how excited they were for this event. Was shocked by their eager acceptance when I ventured to their small house to ask them.

Esther practically pushed Estelle out of the way in her haste to say yes when I broached the subject.

The typically quiet but powerful twins immediately fetched their packed bags and joined me at the door that second.

Okay then.

I ignored the disappointment from the rest of the family, let Shenka deal with it and assigning Gram a coven babysitter—hopefully more than one—as we stepped into the veil and emerged on the other side at the old coven site. Just as long as it wasn't Penelope Anders. Gram despised the blue-haired old lady with the watery brown eyes and penchant for gossip.

Maybe I should have checked after all. I had no idea the reaction Gram would have, in her present state, to being nitpicked and irritated when her power wouldn't allow her to escape.

Shenka's magic touched mine as she sensed my anxiety.

She's safe, she sent. Was I really so transparent? *The*

Happerns are moving in.

Big tension release. The fallen demon Talee, her husband and their two sweet kids might be just what Gram needed to come back to the real world.

I released a big breath and sent Shenka a hug of gratitude as we touched down in the short grass.

Mom greeted us personally as we arrived, showing us to our space while the twins thanked her over and over again.

Nice to see them so enthusiastic, but if they spent the next few days like this, I was going to have to kill them both and hide the bodies.

"So lovely of your mother to insist we arrive first," Estelle said. I used to have trouble telling the twins apart, but now could feel the subtle difference in their magic. Estelle's felt rougher around the edges, just a little, while Esther's had a hint of milkiness.

"So lovely," Esther agreed. "Delightful to be the first, don't you think, Sydlynn?"

Sure, okay. I bobbed a nod, all they needed, because they both smiled at me with their pinched little faces, patted my cheek on the way by and left our area, arm in arm, chattering away to each other partly out loud, partly in their minds.

Shenka laughed when they'd gone. "I just love those two," she said.

The feeling wasn't always mutual between me and

them. But they'd learned to like me and vice versa.

"I need air," I said, restlessness taking over.

"I'll finish getting us settled," Shenka said. "Go." She drew a breath, smiled. "Let me know when you need me."

The Tallah talk. Right.

Sassafras paused in his grooming to stare a moment. "Maybe I should come with you," he said. "Keep you out of trouble."

"We're the only family here," I snapped, my tension buttons pushed.

He grunted softly and rolled his shoulders. "Whatever you say, Sydlynn."

Smartass cat.

I stomped my anxious way through the large main area of the pavilion and out into the warm night air. Two gulps and I already felt better, even as I paced between our giant tent and the one dedicated to Africa. The deep shadows of the looming constructions enveloped me instantly.

Gave me a clear view of the pair of Enforcers standing at the other end of the tunnel.

It would have to be Quaid and Payten, wouldn't it? And she'd have to be clinging to him, whispering in his ear while he bent his head to listen. I froze, everything inside me going still. Even my demon went quiet as we held our collective breath and watched the girl kiss him.

On the mouth. Our mouth. His. Wait—

I choked on my breath as I let it out. And while Quaid didn't turn, didn't notice, Payten did. He was already striding away, back into the light. But she smiled at me, raised her hand to wave.

The bitch.

It was so hard to turn my back on Payten, to walk away, to refuse to acknowledge the fact she knew I was there and rubbed my damned face in it.

No. Syd. Stop.

I pulled myself to a halt, hands clenched into fists.

He wasn't mine. How many times did I have to remind myself? No matter the trysts we enjoyed, the nights he came to me, Quaid wasn't going to marry me. He wasn't going to leave the Enforcer order. And I had no claim on him.

Zero. Zilcharoony.

Didn't hurt any less. Just as I knew it had to just kill him knowing I had to make a choice.

At least, I hoped it did.

My mind went to Gram, to what she'd said. About Grandfather Ivan and how she'd always believed in him. But men lied, didn't they? Quaid insisted he and Payten weren't together. Told me over and over again despite the fact she seemed to act differently. And after that kiss, well, it was pretty clear they were a couple after all.

Then again, I kissed Piers all the time. Liam

occasionally. And we weren't together.

Shut up, logic. You suck.

I felt Mom's power near the center pavilion and went looking for her. For comfort? Maybe. Though I preferred to use the term "distraction".

And got one. The moment I entered the giant central tent, Mom swept toward me, grasping my hand.

"Thank the elements," she said with an exasperated laugh. "I'm starving. Come have dinner with me."

And so, moments later, I found myself seated at a small table in her private quarters in the center pavilion, stuffing a forkload of chicken curry into my mouth.

Heart hurting? Smother it in food. Tha'll do ya.

Mom must have known something was bothering me, but she had the decency to let me eat first before her motherly instincts prodded.

"Need to talk about it?" Her blue eyes shone over the rim of her wineglass.

"No," I said. "I really don't." Sighed. "I do have some updates, though, for what they are worth."

She listened with her usual calm as I explained Demetrius's cryptic little lucidity session and told her about Alison and the Brotherhood. Mom swirled her wine when I finished, frowning down into the red depths.

"He didn't seem concerned?" She took a sip, set it aside. Drummed her fingers on the table, a sure sign of Mom agitation.

"Nope." I rubbed my face with both hands before dropping them with a thud. "And as much as I'd like nothing better than to run off and deal with this mess, he's right." I hated when other people were right. "I can't go after Belaisle without Ameline."

Stupid prophecy.

"And Alison?" Mom's right foot bobbed over her crossed knee.

I shrugged.

Mom finally leaned forward on her elbows. "All right then," she said.

Didn't get to go on. Not when a burst of magic just outside the door announced the arrival of a large group of witches. Mom frowned a little, but went to the tent flap just as Maurice hurried inside with a pinched look of disapproval.

"The Australians are here," he said like they'd personally insulted him by daring to show up.

I didn't need Maurice's announcement to identify the witches milling around in the large open central area of the main pavilion. Their powerful accents and loud voices made it crystal clear their origins.

A short, skinny woman with light brown hair bleached by the sun and a dark tan grinned at Mom as we exited the small dining area. Her bright green eyes stood out against her skin as she strode forward and seized Mom's hand in hers, power flowing between them.

"Miriam Hayle," the woman said in her delightful accent. "Bloody nice to meet you."

Mom laughed softly, bowed her head. "Council Leader Braylen," Mom said. "The pleasure is all mine."

The Australian witch spun and gestured at her people.

"Sorry about the bother," she said. "Damned time zones. We meant to arrive tomorrow, not in the middle of the night."

"Not at all." Mom oozed cordiality as I found myself grinning at the woman's enthusiasm and attitude. "May I introduce my daughter, the leader of the Hayle Coven, Sydlynn. This is Bindi Braylen."

Bindi pumped my hand with equal enthusiasm. "So you're the shelia we all have to thank for the ripples in the world's power." She winked and shrugged like it was no big deal. "Good on ya."

I quickly retreated as Mom took over, a small army of her witches herding the Australians out of the main pavilion and to their own. It still amazed me how good my mother was at her job and prayed to all that was good and holy I would never, ever have to try my hand at it.

Shudder.

Head down, mind on the problem of Alison and the Brotherhood, I was almost back to my tent before I realized someone was following me. Power pulled tight, I spun to find Payten hovering just beyond my physical reach, the Enforcer hood pulled up over her hair, though her face was clear in the softly bobbing witch lights glowing overhead.

She wasn't smiling anymore. I was so shocked she approached me I didn't say anything until she spoke.

"Do we have a problem?" Her voice hung low in the night air, hands twitching at the blue piping hem of her trainee robes. "If we do, I'd like to know about it."

My head exploded. Rage surged, my demon throwing herself at the borders between us, fighting to escape even as Shaylee howled her rage, sending a rumble through the ground between Payten and me. The family magic answered, coiled to attack.

Only my sorcery remained quiet, watching. Hungry.

And my vampire.

Harming her will serve no purpose, she sent. *But you must put this child in her place, yes?*

"I beg your pardon," I said, hating the vibration in my voice as I seized on my vampire's support and spoke through the tightness in my chest.

Payten frowned, coming closer. "You heard me," she said. "Do we have a problem?"

On the other hand, my vampire hissed, *we could allow demon to eat her alive.*

Would probably give me heartburn, my demon snarled. *But I could make other arrangements.*

"Trainee Orter!" A shadow detached from one of the pavilions, the shaking form of Pender Tremere saving her ass from demonic snacking.

She blanched and turned to her commander, eyes wide. "Sir?"

"You will address Coven Leader Hayle with due respect, trainee!" His anger flared in blue fire, slamming into her. Payten staggered backward, face now bright red as she gaped at me.

"My apologies, Coven Leader," she breathed. "Forgive me for my impertinence."

Not very bloody freaking likely.

"Have I made a mistake entrusting you with this assignment, Trainee Orter?" I'd never seen Pender so angry, felt my own rage subside as he dressed her down. His power crushed hers, forcing her to bow her head, her shoulders, hands shaking.

"No, sir," she said with tears in her voice.

Crybaby.

"I think I may have," he said, hovering over her, voice dropping to depths filled with power. "I think you may not have what it takes to be an Enforcer, Trainee Orter. What say you?"

She pushed back a little, her magic rippling around her as she slowly raised her head. "No, sir," she said, tears tracking down her face. "I'll make amends, sir."

"You'd better." He stepped away, magic easing up, releasing her. "Now, offer an official apology to the Coven Leader and be on your way before I have you cast from the ranks."

Payten fell to one knee before me, hand on her heart.

"I overstepped all boundaries, Coven Leader Hayle," she said in a shaking voice. "My most sincere apologies. You are, and shall remain, my superior and I will from this moment forward treat you with only the respect your position commands." She looked up, met my eyes. I looked for anger, vindictiveness. Saw only sincere regret in her face. "I am your servant, ma'am."

Damn her. Why couldn't she just be evil or something?

I waved her aside, turning my back on her, unable to speak past the confusion, frustration and remains of my own temper.

I caught her bow to Pender out of the corner of my eye, her flight. He swept toward me, bowing to me as she left, face pale, brown eyes flaring with magic.

"Please forgive her," he said. "She assumed too much, even considering you attended Harvard together. But such behavior will never be tolerated as long as I am Enforcer leader."

I sighed, tension leaving me tired and sad.

"It's okay, Pender," I said, patting his arm. "Really."

He nodded stiffly. "You are too kind, Coven Leader."

Okay, that made me even sadder. "You can call me Syd," I said. "I'm fine with that."

"I must present an example," Pender said in his stiff

way. "As I am clearly not doing so sufficiently to guide my trainees."

He snapped off a salute, a fist over his forehead, before striding off.

Poor Pender, my vampire sent. *I wonder if he is up for the tasks ahead.*

Not our call, I sent back. Thought about Payten. *Think she meant it or are we being played?*

My demon growled. Like I didn't know her vote before I asked.

As much as we wish things were different, Shaylee sent, *Quaid is not an option for us.*

The memory of the night before twinged in my stomach. Seeing him in the kitchen just this morning, thinking maybe, just maybe...

Unhealthy, my vampire sent.

Impractical, Shaylee agreed sadly.

Let's kill her anyway, my demon snarled. *Just a little.*

A giggle escaped. *You can kill someone just a little?*

Totally, she sent. *Track her down and I'll show you.*

But the anger had run out of me.

What if you make a mistake? I turned away, heading for our quarters. *Kill her all the way.*

Now that would be a shame, wouldn't it? My demon's laugh echoed in my head.

Was it wrong we all laughed with her?

ChAPTER fOURTEEN

I approached the entry to my pavilion when the familiar feeling of the Hensley magic arrived at the site.

Shenka. I reached for my second, just as she barreled out of the tent and ran right into me.

"Syd." Breathless, anxious, she hugged me in quick apology. "Tallah's here."

"You don't have to join us," I said.

"Yes," Shenka said, pulling me along, "I really do."

Part of me suddenly felt sorry for her sister. The look on my second's face told me she'd come to grips with turning Tallah in and was about to tear the older Hensley apart for being such an idiot.

I didn't bother trying to reach Mom, just followed Shenka, still tugging, right to my mother's office. Where we both came to an abrupt halt.

Tallah turned, already scowling, to find the two of us

staring back and forth between her and Mom.

When her eyes landed on Shenka, they widened a little. "You promised," she said.

Shenka shook her head. "You asked," she said. "But I never did."

Rebellion crossed the older Hensley's face and, for the first time, I understood how young she was. Only in her early twenties, older than me, sure, but untempered by the pressures I'd been under and as idealistic as they came. For the first time I felt like our roles were reversed and I was the elder of the pair of us.

Tallah turned to Mom. "Since my sister clearly gave you the impression I've broken law," she said, voice barely containing her anger, "might I be permitted to state my case?"

"There have been no accusations made against you," Mom said. Her kind tone soothed the tense air in the room. "I merely would like to hear what you have to say, Tallah. And to assure you my door is always open to you, no matter the issue."

I don't think Tallah was expecting Mom to be reasonable. Then again, considering the bulk of the time she'd been leader Mom was under the control of the Brotherhood, this new and improved Council Leader must have been a bit of a shock. I was used to the real Mom. Tallah and the others were just getting to know her.

The Hensley coven leader sat, stiff-backed, but her antagonistic air eased. "I was approached by a pair of Steam Union sorcerers several months ago. They claim there are branches of that order all over the world."

"Yes," Mom said. "So we've been informed by the Union members we've met."

That seemed to go a long way to ease Tallah's mind because her shoulders sagged slightly. I took the chair beside her, Shenka on my far side and listened as Tallah went on.

"It's long been my wish," she said, "and was the wish of my parents," Shenka flinched, I could only guess from being left out, "that witches and normals could one day live in peace and co-exist as protectors and nurturers of power and this plane."

Mom's sweet smile shone in her eyes. "A wonderful dream," she said. "But one I'm afraid may never come to pass."

Tallah leaned forward, face eager. "We don't know that for sure," she said. "No one has tried."

Um, Inquisition. Witch burnings. The deaths of the blood of the maji...

"Not recently," Tallah amended.

Mom nodded. "Very true," she said. "So tell me, Tallah. What would be our first step in revealing our true nature to normals?"

The Hensley leader's smile could have lit up the room

without any other assistance. "We would approach their leaders," she said. "Offer alliance, assistance. Once they saw what we could do, surely they would be willing to open dialogue."

She was totally deluded. "Right after they bombed us and dissected us to see what made us tick," I said.

Should have kept my mouth shut. Just couldn't.

She didn't watch enough movies. Or read the news for that matter.

Tallah scowled, but didn't respond.

"Tallah," Mom said. "Such a move would, unfortunately, leave us vulnerable and exposed. Without knowing if we could trust such officials, we would be revealing the existence of our kind to those who have traditionally seen us as a threat."

"I still say we won't know until we try," she said. "Am I the only one who is tired of living life like I've done something wrong? In the fear I'll have to pick up my family and run?"

"Of course not," Mom said. "We all have that fear, those worries, are weary of our forced disguises. But for the good of all magicks and their users, for now, until we can find a way to expose ourselves without generating negative interest, we must remain cautious."

Tallah's face closed off, a mask of blank as she sank back into her seat. "And this is why I didn't bring it to you," she said. "I knew you'd say no."

Mom's jaw tightened. "I'm not saying no," she said. "I'm saying it requires study and discussion. Will you allow me that?"

Tallah's head jerked in an ungracious nod. "And now you're going to order me to stop talking to the Steam Union."

"No," Mom said, eyes flickering to me and back to Tallah. "You are welcome to befriend anyone you like." *Well? Anything?* Mom's mental voice broke into my head. "As long as those friends don't endanger witchdom or other races." *Syd? Are you paying attention?*

What? I was so wrapped up in the conversation and my own incredulity it took me a moment to snap out of it.

I believe she wants to know if Tallah is tainted by Brotherhood sorcery. The wryness in my vampire's mental voice prodded me into irritation.

Right.

Crap.

It only took a second to check, a soft flowering of my sorcery to feel for the touch of the Brotherhood. To my relief, I shook my head at Mom just a little before closing the black blossom again.

Mom stood, offering her hand and a kind smile to Tallah. "We will open this dialogue here at conclave," she said. "If you would be kind enough to lead the discussion?"

The shock on Tallah's face, morphing into a smile of her own, hit my gut with a fist of shock.

Are you thralled again? I threw my words at Mom as she guided the Hensley coven leader to the door.

Shenka joined her sister, held out her hand. Tallah took it, smile fading to a resigned smirk.

"Okay, kid," she said. "You were right."

Shenka laughed and hugged Tallah with enthusiasm. *I'm going with her for a while,* she sent to me as she and Tallah left, the Hensley leader waving at me, her animosity seemingly dissolved.

While I was pleased for Shenka, I was furious with Mom.

Who met my anger calmly.

"What do you think," she said as she crossed to me, "the assembled conclave will say when Tallah broaches the subject of exposing us to normals?"

The heat of my rage froze over and cracked, shattering into glittering shards.

Oh. Wow.

"You're turning her over to the wolves," I said, my mercurial temper now feeling sorry for Tallah and making Mom the bad guy.

I really had to make up my mind.

"She will be shot down," Mom said. "But in her mind, she will have had her say."

Brilliant.

"Fine, smarty pants," I said, grinning all of a sudden. "What about her Steam Union friends?"

"You did ask Piers about them?" How did she know I'd seen Piers?

Blushing.

"I did," I said.

"Then time will tell." Mom sank into her chair again. "And I refuse to worry about it until he tells me otherwise. Tallah isn't thralled. And has what she wants—her voice and permission to speak. So bomb diffused."

This one, anyway.

chapter fifteen

I barely managed any sleep thanks to the almost constant arrival of witches from that moment on. Conclave didn't officially begin until right around lunch time the next day, but the flurry of activity prior made it impossible to ignore the excitement flowing through the gathering magicks now filling the old coven site.

By the time I dragged myself, cranky and sandy-eyed, from bed, the rest of the High Councils had arrived, with just a trickle of their connected covens disturbing the hum of activity now dominating the space. Enforcers swooped overhead, some in black robes, others in a variety of colors, including one group in what looked almost like hand-woven tapestry. Their very dark skin and rhythmic accents made me assume they came with the African contingent.

I wasn't surprised, as I wound my way through the

chattering mass of witches now crowding the passages between pavilions, to find Europe's stood empty and unoccupied. Mom had naturally sent invites to Margaret Applegate, but we both assumed the Council Leader would either ignore us or find a way to create some kind of disturbance. And yes, I realized it wasn't her in control. Liander Belaisle and his vile sect ran her particular show. Still, I'd met the woman when she wasn't under thrall, or was at least partially herself, and hadn't liked her much then, either.

The fact she'd allowed me to be devoured by a vampire queen didn't endear her much.

I marveled at the sound of so many languages spoken, of the different races and faces, mostly women, though a few men wandered the grounds outside the Enforcer ranks. It wasn't long before my idle wandering was noticed and I was corralled into something more productive.

My mother pulled me to her side and took me on a whirlwind tour of the witching world.

"Council Leader Ife Maalouf." Mom bowed her head graciously to a large black woman with gorgeous blue eyes and hair shorn tight to her scalp. The African Leader extended her hand to me when Mom introduced us, her warm, smooth skin soft on mine.

"Coven Leader," she said in a thick accent, white teeth vivid against the darkness of her complexion. "It is a great honor to meet you at last."

I shared a little magic with her even as her brilliant eyes widened. "Council Leader Maalouf," I said.

With a rich laugh of delight, she sent back a fraction of her own magic, thrumming with powerful earth energy and the heat of the sun.

Mom led me away a moment later to the sound of the African witches chattering at each other like excited, exotic birds, shaking her head though her smile remained fixed.

"What was that?"

Crap. I'd screwed up already. "What was what?"

Mom poked me with her power. "You just told her you were equals," she said. "And Ife accepted."

Oh, damn it. "Was that bad?" Images of insulted packs of witches swooping down to hail fire and fury on me flashed before my eyes.

"Considering she is a Council Leader and you a lowly Coven Leader, normally, yes." Mom's blue eyes glittered. With what? Anger? Irritation?

I sucked at this so much. "I was trying to be nice," I said.

"Try harder," Mom said. And laughed.

Teasing me. Amusement, then.

Relax, Syd. No witch apocalypse.

Yet.

I couldn't let Ife think she was the only special one,

could I? My offer of power to the Asian Council Leader, Sumiko Himura, was met with a gasp of shock and a deep bow. She rapid-fired something in her native tongue before bowing to me again.

"Our honor, *megami*," she said in perfect English.

I bowed back as best I could, really wishing I understood what her people said during the introduction.

Finding out when Mom led me away.

"That was interesting," Mom said. "They think you're some kind of goddess."

Choke. "Sorry?"

Mom flicked her fingers at me. "Let them," she said. "It may prove useful."

Oh. My. Swearword.

"I am not going to pretend to be something I'm not," I spluttered.

"Yes, dear," Mom said, patting my hand. "Ah, look who's next."

Yamini Dhavan, the Indian Council Leader, blinked like I'd hit her when I shared magic, the small red dot between her brows pulsing with magic. The lovely sari she wore quivered around her feet. It took her a long moment to respond, and I began to wonder if I'd overstepped with her.

But when she finally did act, it was to grip my hand in both of hers and kiss the back of it.

"Maji," she said in a lilting voice. "I am touched by

your blessing. Please accept mine in return." Her power, soft and sweet, segmented and joined my family magic.

Mom practically hummed with happiness as we continued the circuit.

"Oh, stop that," I snapped at her.

She just winked at me.

We'd reached the front end of the site, back where I'd started near my own pavilion and the entrance to the South American tent. Mom led me forward, smiling broadly at a small, round woman with dark gray hair and deep brown eyes who took Mom's hand and squeezed it in welcome.

"Ana Maria Diaz," Mom said. "May I present Coven Leader Sydlynn Hayle."

The South American Leader repeated her greeting with me, offering me energy before I could do so.

"Maji," she said with a slow wink. "Thank you for hosting us."

"My pleasure," I said, returning power to her. Her eyes widened, mouth opening in a small 'O' as she slowly released my hand.

"Marvelous," she said.

Okay, they were seriously creeping me out.

Before I could find an awkward response to her greeting, I felt emptiness form behind me and turned with a gasp of my own, my sorcery surging in answer.

But it wasn't the Brotherhood coming to attack as my

over-anxious mind feared. Instead, Eva Southway stepped through the gaping hole of blackness, a tall, dark-haired man beside her. And, behind them, strode Piers, and his little sister, Clover, along with a handful of other Steam Union members I'd met before. Mom hadn't specified to me how many each of the magic races were bringing, but from the two dozen or so sorcerers who stood around talking, I could guess.

Ellis Lowsley grinned and waved at me, red hair catching the morning sun as his round glasses threw back the light. He'd served as Piers's second in command during the werewolf fiasco.

I was kind of surprised to see the rest of Piers's ill-fated posse among the Steam Union, and could only assume Eva either wanted them with her because they'd proven brave and cunning or to keep an eye on them.

I was voting for the second option.

Eva and her group weren't alone. In a second surge of sorcery, a line of werewolves marched into the light. Yup, two dozen burly and/or sinewy werewolves. They felt so few compared to the witches piling up on each other to have a peek at the new arrivals. I left the South American Council Leader and went right to Charlotte, hugging her first before sharing a bowed head and kissed cheeks with Oleksander.

And felt the pressure of witch displeasure on me the entire time.

"Miriam," Ana Maria Diaz spoke, voice heavy with indignation. "What is the meaning of this?"

Wait a second. Mom didn't tell the other Council Leaders what she was up to? Wow. That took a cast iron pair. Then again, this was my mother we were talking about.

She was a Hayle, after all.

Mom simply smiled and gestured as the gaping black holes collapsed in on themselves.

"Our compatriots of other magicks have come to join conclave," Mom said at her most diplomatic with power behind her voice. "Under my invitation."

A ripple of anger ran through the watching witches, descending over us from above as the visiting Enforcers joined their territory leaders in their silent protest.

Syd, Mom sent. *Now is the perfect time for you to say something.*

Me? Okay, now I knew she'd lost it. The very last thing she needed was me screwing up everything my opening my big mouth.

She sighed in my head. *Why do you think I've just led your introductions? That I was so pleased they adored and respected you from your reputation?*

Choke.

Just do it, sweetheart. Trust me.

Gulp.

Must you be so stubborn? My vampire sighed as a further

poke from Mom's magic, a tiny needle spiking into my mind, forced my mouth open. And my vampire took over.

"I, for one, am thrilled the Steam Union," my vampire moved my arm, gesturing to Eva who bowed her head , hoping no one would see the little tremor in my hand as I fought to take back control, "and the newly formed werewolf nation," Oleksander saluted, "were kind enough to join us."

Very nicely done, Syd, Mom sent as the tension eased. *Perfect.*

Why, thank you, Miriam, my vampire sent. *Delighted to assist.* She retreated with a smug snort while I batted at her in irritation. *What was that all about?* I felt the anger around me lift, at least a little.

Where has your head been all morning? Mom's exasperation was tinged with amusement. *The maji has spoken, Sydlynn. They will not stand against you.*

Ah. Um. Wow.

There were still mumblings of rebellion, but the gathering of unhappy witches broke and went their own ways as Mom's Enforcers guided the two new races to their pavilions, leaving me standing there with her while she smiled and waved.

I seriously thought I was going to throw up.

While that was fun, my vampire sent, *you really need to take charge of things.*

Piss her off first, my demon chuckled. *That always does the trick.*

Unfortunately, Shaylee sent with a hint of disappointment.

Oh shut up, I sent back.

Mom was suddenly swarmed with her people and I took the opportunity to leave, dodging smiling witches who pointed and stared. I barely made it to the entry of my pavilion when someone caught my arm, turned me around.

Piers smiled down at me, tight in my space, the scent of him filling my world.

"Nice to see you finally pushing your weight around," he said. "Though I really am getting sick of you rescuing me."

My lips quirked. "It's a curse," I said.

Piers laughed even as my eyes drifted over his shoulder. Landed on a darkly scowling face.

Quaid glared while my tall companion turned and noted the angry Enforcer watching.

His gray eyes returned to me, narrowed in understanding. "I see," he said. "So this is the one you pine for, Sydlynn Hayle."

I swatted his arm, temper piqued. "Piss off, Southway," I said.

Piers bent and kissed me. Not a quick peck, either. Slow. Lingering.

And damn it if I didn't kiss him back.

While Quaid watched.

Was it wrong an evil little part of me enjoyed the fact Quaid was forced to stand there and see what he was missing?

I was going to hell.

"You could do so much better." Piers breathed into my mouth as he pulled away, languid, my body tingling from the contact. My demon sighed, torn between the handsome man before us and the one she really longed for, still staring, only a half a tent away.

Piers waved a jaunty salute to me before bowing deeply and spinning, his longcoat swirling around him as he strode off. Whistling.

I met Quaid's stormy gaze, emotions hardened against him.

Turned my back and walked into my tent before my traitor heart could force me to run back outside and beg him to change his mind.

chapter sixteen

My foul humor lingered long past dusk, only the tingling touch of vampire magic shaking me loose from my bad mood. Shenka was smart enough to keep her distance, the twins and Sassafras out and about doing who knew what. So when I felt my undead family arrive and rushed to greet them, my second trailed after me.

"Syd." I stopped at the sound of her voice. Turned and met her knowing smile as she poked me with magic. "Smiling is usually a great way to show other people you're not going to tear them in half and feed them to your demon."

I wanted to be angry, to stay inside my little shell of pissed off, but something about the tone of Shenka's voice, the tickling way her magic prodded me, shattered the hold my temper had over me all afternoon. I hooked my arm through hers with a regretful little smile.

"Sorry," I said. "Guys suck. Did you know that about them?"

She feigned innocence, one hand pressed to her heart in shock. "I had no idea."

I loved my second.

It didn't take much effort to find the vampires. Not because I felt them through our undead connection, which I did. But because of the gathering crowd whispering and gaping at the stunningly gorgeous pair standing next to the main pavilion.

I had to jab ribs to push my way through, though most of the witches who fought me only did so until they realized who I was. Funny to see their irritation—anger even—turn to a pulse of fear.

What did they think I'd do to them?

At least my reputation cleared a path for me so I was able to join Uncle Frank and Sunny without being forced to ride the veil a few feet. I knew Ahbi wouldn't mind or anything, but I wanted the royal vampire couple's arrival to carry more weight than me popping out of a slice of amber fire, ruining their moment.

As it was, I could hardly contain myself as I approached Sunny. Sure, I'd seen her just a week ago. We had dinner at Castle Wilhelm despite Margaret Applegate's almost continual interruptions. But no matter how often I saw the lovely queen and her consort, they were still my uncle and his girlfriend—regardless of their current married status—who practically raised me and used to live in my basement.

I tried for regal and all that proper garbage, but Sunny wasn't interested. She hugged me before I could make a fool of myself trying to curtsy, kissing my cheek with her warm lips.

She'd eaten before coming to join us. Awesome. Not that she'd have the bad taste to snack on anyone present, considering it was illegal. Besides, Sunny was too classy for random snacking. But this way she would feel less threatening to the witches, her spirit magic calm and in balance.

"Syd." Sunny's stunning smile always cheered me up.

"Hey, Sunny." I turned to her companion who swept me into a big hug. "Hi, Uncle Frank."

He grinned down at me, boyish handsomeness all the more attractive thanks to his vampireness. Yes, I was his niece. But he was still a hottie.

Mom appeared as if by magic—imagine that, no pun intended—and the greetings continued. I left her to introduce the vampires to various dignitaries, dodging Mom's hand gesture urging me to join her.

Uh-huh. No way.

I was so out of there.

Almost made it. Only to feel a rush of Sidhe power in the distance, the only warning I had the Gate had opened, just before a rippling wall of green fire appeared to the gasps of the gathered crowd.

And Aoilainn, Queen of the Seelie, rode through on her big, white horse.

She and I had our issues. Shaylee's mom was a bit of a self-centered bitch, truth be told. And had tried to steal my Sidhe ego from me once. Still, I had to admit she was stunningly impressive with long, white-blonde hair hanging to the ground despite her height on the horse, thick ringlets curved to perfection, laced through with tiny braids and sparkling with beads of gemstones like dew.

The witches parted for her as she rode, face impassive, green eyes glittering, into the center of the main pavilion. I grinned at Prince Thalion as he leaped from his own horse, eyes meeting mine a moment in greeting, before assisting his queen from the saddle.

There was a time Thalion and I were enemies. His pining love for Shaylee made him try to trick me into staying in the Sidhe realm. But he'd since come to his senses after I freed his people from the Brotherhood and he'd seen, for the first time, just how cruel and self-centered his queen could be.

All eyes turned as two giant black horses, snorting fire and pawing the ground with feathered, dinner-plate feet trotted through the wall of Sidhe power, pulling an elaborate black lacquered chariot. They thought Aoilainn and her Seelie were impressive. My grin widened at the sight of Odhran and Niamh in flowing robes of deepest ebony, standing at the reins. The Unseelie ruling pair waved at me, Odhran nodding his head while Niamh blew me a kiss.

Mom had her hands full, yup yup.

Thankfully, Sunny and Uncle Frank were kind enough to stop and wait for Mom to greet her new guests. I held my breath as Aoilainn, her tall, slender body towering over my mother's, locked gazes with Mom in this plane for the first time.

This could go two ways: not a disaster or the collapse of the known Universe. After all, Mom didn't appreciate how the Seelie Queen treated me. But she was a diplomat, a politician. I trusted my mother to keep her crap together.

"High Council Leader Hayle," Aoilainn said in her voice of music and sunshine.

"Your Royal Majesty," Mom said without a hint of temper.

Aoilainn looked around, spotted me. "My darling Shaylee."

Grrr.

"Mother." Shaylee spoke through my mouth before I could stop her. "Please address Sydlynn as is polite."

Oh, she did not just zing her own mother in front of everyone?

The Seelie queen's sharp green gaze tightened just a

fraction. But she didn't have time to freak out and go all high and mighty Fey on my ass. Not when Odhran and Niamh descended from their incredible ride and came to bow their heads to Mom.

"Council Leader," the Unseelie queen said. "It is a great honor to finally meet the mother of Sydlynn Hayle."

Blush.

Mom dipped into a flawless curtsy, the implications of her honoring the Unseelie as clear to me as any spoken insult. Niamh laughed out loud, leather body suit creaking, spiked black hair shining with sparks of green light, and bent from her own height. A head taller than Mom, she gripped my mother's face between her long, slender hands sheathed in fingerless lace gloves and countless silver rings before kissing Mom's cheeks with her black-painted lips.

"Delightful," she said.

"The pleasure is all mine, Your Royal Majesties," Mom said with the faintest trace of humor in her words.

Thalion actually cracked a smile at me as a long line of Fey continued to exit the wall of green flame. Seelie and Unseelie marched through, twice as many as the weres and sorcerers, though I imagined Mom's negotiations with Aoilainn included her allotment be separate from the dark Fey. The willow-like forms of the Seelie court appeared as lusciously beautiful as they were heartless, just as nature herself. The Unseelie, in their imperfection, felt more real to me, and I found myself smiling and nodding to many of the creatures, shapes and oddities, some of whom I'd already met in my past two visits to the Sidhe realm.

"Your invitation was most gracious," Odhran said, voice booming like an earthquake, the ground beneath my feet trembling under his presence as he swung to look around, heavy leather coat sweeping over the ground. "And your permission granted so we might join you on this plane once again, however temporarily, was kindly given."

Mom curtsied again, though when she straightened, it was clear to me her gesture was only a courtesy. What she had to say next confirmed it. "You are welcome here," she said. "For as long as you and your folk abide the rules of this conclave." Mom had turned as she spoke, meeting Aoilainn's eyes.

The Seelie Queen didn't acknowledge a word Mom said, instead wrinkling her nose at the gathered, staring crowd.

"I assume I will be offered suitable accommodations."

I had accommodations for her, all right. Stuffed in the darkest, nastiest hole I could find—

Shaylee. I had to snap at her to break her hold on me.

Sorry, she sent, still irritated. *That Fey gives me hives.*

While I'd had my own problems with my mother in

the past, they were nothing compared to Shaylee's with Aoilainn. So I let it go. Because, frankly, I agreed with her and had to be content my Sidhe princess had grown up as much as me.

Not to be outdone, the moment the center of the pavilion cleared, Thalion leading the two horses away with a soft word to them, I felt Ahbi's power surge just as the veil tore open.

Oh. My. Swearword. Did it tear. The largest hole I'd ever seen, gaping so wide I could have driven a train through the gap and had tons of room to spare.

The view on the other side even made me gasp, impressed, and I'd seen it before from a variety of angles. The veil opened onto the Parade, filled with rank upon rank of demon Guards, two large thrones set to the right side of the opening. On the smaller sat my sister, looking all regal and together with her hair in a fancy rope-like style tied in intricate knots around her head and draping over one shoulder, her shining black dress beaded with a million star-like jewels.

Oh, hello, envy. Nice of you to show up.

But it was the occupant of the other who held my attention, mostly because of Mom.

Dad sat rigid, sheathed in heavy robes, the power of Demonicon crackling around him. Meira stood and bowed her head to him, holding his hand a moment as Dad rose to join her. He approached the gap, but didn't cross as Meira waited, a line of demons crossing, each dressed as elaborately as she, massive, red-tinted bodies crowned in impressive horns polished to a shine, their amber eyes glowing with fire.

Twenty demons came to a halt, flanking the opening, waiting for my sister to cross.

"Council Leader." Dad's voice rippled across the veil.

"Ruler," Mom said, chin up, back straight, voice firm.

And that was it. No expression of lost love, no mad dash to hug each other. Just ceremony and stiff formality.

Broke. My. Heart.

"Our daughter, Princess Meira of the First Plane, speaks for the Seat in this conclave." He turned to my sister, releasing her hand. "Have fun, honey," he said.

Ah. There was my dad. And no way was I letting him get away without a hug from me. Screw the pomp and circumstance.

I pushed my way forward again, much easier this time, bowing to Dad before stepping over the veil. Ahbi's power embraced me as Dad bent and kissed my cheek.

"Love you," he whispered.

"Oh, Dad," I choked, wanting to cling to him, to beg him to come and see Mom.

When he pulled away, the pain in his eyes was almost more than I could stand.

Meira broke the hold of Dad's grief, stepping across to join me.

"Council Leader," she said, "I am most pleased to be invited to such an historic event. I hope I can serve my people's interests well in this endeavor."

Totally envious. Where did I go wrong?

The veil snapped shut with a final hug from Ahbi, the witchlights overhead seemingly dim compared to the bright glow of the Demonicon sky.

Meira squeezed my hand before hugging Mom as the gathered witches, vampires, Sidhe and sorcerers all broke and started to dissipate, the show over for the night. There was no sign of Pannera Sthol, but I honestly never expected the thralled vampire queen to show.

As for Europe and Margaret... we'd see.

Amid whispering excitement Ruler himself came to wish the conclave well, and speculation about the Sidhe and vampires, Mom, Meira and I took a moment to connect.

Thank you both for being the most amazing daughters a mother could ever ask for. Mom's hand tightened in mine, and I had no doubt she squeezed Meira's as much with the other. *We face a monumental task, but I have no doubt the Hayle family women are more than up to the job.*

I snorted mentally. *Worked out so far.*

Meira's white teeth flashed against her red skin. *I'm totally in.*

Our moment didn't last. They never did. Not with Mom's eager witches clamoring for her attention, for

Meira's entourage looking for their pavilion. How she'd found so many powerful demons—and yes, I could feel their power, not a one under Seventh Plane among them—with effigies here I had no idea. But it was nice to see Demonicon well represented.

I drifted for my pavilion, pleased to note I was now being ignored as bigger and shinier distractions now abounded. Hell, I was dazzled by the gorgeous figures the Sidhe cut, the echoing boom of demon laughter, the rumble underground as the Unseelie made themselves at home. So much easier to duck my head and just be one of the masses.

I took the opportunity to reach out to Galleytrot as I felt him exit the wards surrounding the Gate, the power surge dormant now the Fey had arrived.

Everything good? I stumbled over a small depression in the already-worn path between pavilions.

Syd. Galleytrot's voice took on an edge of panic. *A giant, man-eating snail has broken free from an evil scientist's lair and is rampaging through Wilding Springs. Right. Now.*

Smartass hound. I laughed despite my flare of irritation.

I promise you, he sent, the image of him sitting in my back yard, tongue lolling out in a doggy grin, *if anything happens, I won't hesitate. You'll know the second I do.*

I know, I sent. *Thank you, Galleytrot. I'm just...*

I do understand, he sent. *And you have cause to worry. So I'll let you have this one slip-up.*

Just save me some snail, I sent. *I hear they are great with butter and garlic.*

He barked a laugh, the boom of thunder in his touch, gone when he cut me off.

Grateful he didn't bring up Liam for once, I ducked inside the pavilion, still grinning.

Only to be accosted by a swirling ball of power.

chapter seventeen

Shenka rushed toward me as the wild magicks threw themselves into a frenzy of fluttering, battering me with their power.

"What do they want?" She was calm, at least, though the faces of the other witches, from various covens, now gathered in the large center common room weren't quite so composed.

"I don't know." I gritted my teeth against the constant pecking of the magicks and threw out a soft net of my own power. They stilled immediately, coming to heel almost like trained creatures, though they didn't calm so much as focus.

Again with the images, the shattering crystals, the broken machine. Belaisle, me, and the darkness. I clung to them, my power teasing out more information. The mirror again, cracking in the center, shattering into a multitude of shards.

Why did that image tweak a memory?

But which memory?

The wild magicks shrieked and fled so suddenly I staggered, realizing as they disappeared through the canopy of the pavilion it wasn't they who screamed.

The sound instead came from outside. Shenka and I both ran to see who was torturing a cat, and why, skidding to a halt with the growing crowd of onlookers as a pair of Enforcers man-handled a small bundle.

The bundle was doing the screeching. And when they finally jerked her to standing, her hood tossed back from her face and I groaned in a gut-punch moment.

Mia's caterwauling cut off abruptly as she spotted me.

"Tell them to let me go," she said, suddenly pompous. "I am a coven leader and have every right to be here."

Syd, Shenka sent. *Don't.*

Sigh.

Someone pushed past me, shoving so hard I staggered into a witch in front of me. My temper boiled as Jean Marc Dumont glanced over his shoulder, a smirk pulling his lips, dark brows shadowing his eyes. Fingers traced my cheek as his younger brother, Kristophe, drifted along in his wake. He tossed his long, pale hair, striding along as though on a catwalk as their father, Andre, glared at me on the way by.

I wasn't his target. Not by a long shot.

"I demand this creature be ejected from conclave." Andre crossed his arms over his chest, aristocratic features pinched with disgust. The entire Dumont family shared the same brilliant blue eyes—all, oddly, but for Andre's sons and Quaid—so when coven leader glared at coven leader, icy matching gazes could have set fire to the place.

"You have no right to kick me out." Mia jerked her arms free of the Enforcers. "I am a duly recognized coven leader." She spit at Andre's feet, Jean Marc lunging for her, held back only by a glare from one of the black-robed witches standing guard. Her eyes met mine. "I have as much interest in this meeting as you do."

Maybe if Andre wasn't such an ass. The first male coven leader in, well, ever, had never endeared himself to me. Sure, he'd done me a solid and admitted I hadn't interfered with the Dumont succession when the freed family magic went to him instead of Mia. But that was about where our nicey-nice play time ended. I hated his arrogant guts and he despised me and wished me dead.

All good, in other words.

But when he pointed a finger at my old friend, his magic—her magic—crackling in threat, I had to act.

"Why don't we ask our Council Leader," I said, putting myself between Andre and Mia. "Since she's, you know, in charge and everything." I leaned closer. "The boss of you."

Burn.

Andre's blue eyes glared his hatred. Hurt my feelings, sure did.

Asshat.

And, right on schedule, Mom appeared, face calm, power thrumming so loudly most of the onlookers found somewhere else they had to be.

Oh, Syd, Mom sent. "Coven Leader Dumont," she spoke out loud as though she hadn't just sighed in my head. Turned and faced Mia. "Coven Leader Tinder."

So Mia had taken her father's name like Quaid. Interesting.

Mia pulled her robe around her as the Enforcers standing guard focused on Mom. I knew whatever Mom decided, they would follow through, end of story.

And, frankly, now that I'd spoken up, I really just wanted her to make this go away.

"I wish to attend conclave." Mia's voice shook a little, but she faced Mom with her head high.

"And I wish to have this piece of worthless garbage expelled from my sight." Andre's power loomed.

Funny, Mom's was bigger. Crushed his like a bug even as she ignored him.

"You are a coven leader," Mom said to Mia. "Thus, you have the right to attend. But you failed to express your desire to join us, and so a place was not prepared."

Technicality?

No, Mom sent. *Each and every person must be invited and accepted before conclave begins. It's law.*

Phew. Saved by witch rules. For once.

Mia shook her head as Andre and his nasty offspring gloated.

"Not so," Mia said, pointing at me. "I was invited."

Um, what?

Mom turned slowly to fix her eyes on me. No one else could probably tell I was about to get a butt reaming.

They didn't know my mother as well as I did.

"Do you mind explaining that, Coven Leader Hayle?" Her voice had a definite chill.

I was in so much trouble.

"Coven Leader Hayle," Shenka jabbed me a fast one in the ribs, a sign to keep quiet, "did no such thing, Council Leader."

Mom's tension eased a bit as she turned back to Mia. "A misunderstanding perhaps, Coven Leader Tinder?"

Andre snorted. "Calling the likes of this thing a coven leader is an insult to—"

The council power roared like a lion before slamming down on top of Andre, driving him, breathless, to his knees. Mom ignored him even as he struggled, his not-so-cocky sons staring between their pinned father and my very irritated mother.

"Coven Leader Hayle has invited me to join her

coven," Mia said. "And that invitation, by witch law, whether accepted or not, includes me on her available roster for attendance of conclave."

That was the most ridiculous law I'd ever—

Mom sighed. A tiny little sigh.

Tell me you didn't, Mom said.

That's a real law? I choked out a mental laugh. *Who the hell came up with that stupidity?*

Syd. Mom's power crackled in my head.

I did, I sent, angry myself now. *Back when she first lost the Dumont power. I offered her a place and she screamed at me and accused me of interference. It shouldn't count.*

And yet, Mom sent, *you never once rescinded the offer. And she can now take you up on it at any point. And use it as leverage to gain entrance to this conclave.* Mom's annoyance eased. *Please, tell me you won't make it formal?*

Hell, no. If only because Mia had just officially pissed me off.

"If you accept," Mom said out loud, "it will mean you are giving up your right to lead your own coven. The Tinder coven you've built."

Mia sagged. "What coven," she whispered. "I want to be a Hayle."

I'm going to kick your ass, Shenka sent in a tight, furious thread.

Great. Just. Great.

Mom turned to me, lips in a grim line. "You are to

accept, as with all your people, full responsibility for Mia Tinder. While she may not yet be part of your coven, you are now her guardian during these proceedings."

Oh no, she did *not*.

Mom—

My mother then spun on Andre, magic spinning in a vortex around her, sending what few gawkers remained scrambling for cover. "Andre Dumont," she said in a voice that would have given Odhran of the Unseelie a run for his money, "the next time you challenge your Council Leader will be your last as master of the Coven Dumont. Do I make myself clear?"

He struggled one more moment, as though to show her he could before bowing his head.

"Of course, Council Leader," he said in an oily tone. "Whatever you say, Council Leader."

Barfaroni.

Mom let him go, sending him and his two scowling boys, Kristophe no longer posing, Jean Marc with his head down, scurrying for cover. I pictured three rats as I fought off a smirk.

Good thing. Mom was not in the mood.

You watch her, Mom sent, turning her back on me and striding away. *If anything happens, I don't care if you're maji, coven leader, queen of the known universe—I'm going to ground you for the rest of your life.*

I didn't comment, let her go. Because I had bigger

things to worry about.

Namely, one very pissed-off second who glared back and forth between me and the girl who approached with a smile on her pale face.

And Mia herself. The two Enforcers bowed to me before rising into the air in a rush of blue fire. I didn't have time for them. Not with Mia hugging me.

"Thanks, Syd," she said. "I knew you wouldn't let me down."

She grabbed my hand, pulled me between two pavilions, trembling, grinning, tears leaking from the corners of her eyes. "This is perfect," she said as Shenka kept her distance, still radiating her fury at me. "It has to be you."

Had to be me what?

Mia glanced to our right and left, all covert all of a sudden. Before jerking me toward her, lips pressed to my ear.

"It's time," she said. "And conclave is the perfect venue. Time to take back what's mine."

Ruh-ro.

She leaned away as my heart stopped, skipped. Pounded a painful beat. "With your help, I'll be Dumont Coven leader again before tomorrow night."

chapter eighteen

"We use your crystal." Mia gulped down a spoon full of soup, not even noticing the sad look on Estelle's face as she set bread beside the fallen coven leader's bone-thin hand. Once inside the pavilion, safely tucked into our area and behind wards, Mia shed the heavy cloak hiding her from me. She looked even more emaciated than before, the light showing the thin veins running under her near-transparent skin, the way her eyes sank into dark pits, two shining blue lights the only sign she was in there.

I'd seen pictures of drought victims who looked healthier than Mia. Was she this thin when I saw her only yesterday? And, if so, how did I miss it?

I sat back and shook my head as Sassafras crouched on the edge of the table and stared at Mia with his glowing amber eyes, tail beating a soft rhythm against the wooden top.

"Mia," I said, "I can't interfere."

"You can." She reached for me, faster than lightning, squeezing the bones of my hand until they ground together. Her thin power crawled over my skin even as Sassafras growled low in his throat, Shenka pacing out her irritation behind me. "The Council has given you carte blanche, remember?" To protect witches. Replacing one coven leader with another didn't really fall into the description. As much as I hated Andre Dumont.

I was about to say so when Mia gulped two big swallows of milk before filling her mouth with a giant bite of bread. "But you won't have to," she said around the bits, reminding me of Demetrius. How damaged was she?

"Why is that, exactly?" Shenka's grating words made me wince, but Mia ignored her.

"You can use your sorcery," she said. "Put the Dumont magic in the crystal. But I'll be holding it." She sat back suddenly, hugging herself and giggling. "They'll think I did it. Don't you see? Perfect." Her eyes sparked with blue fire. "And when you have it in your possession, you simply transfer it back to me."

There were so many holes in her plan I didn't even know where to begin.

The Enforcers would stop her. Us. Mom would. Any other Council Leader, I was sure. And Mia didn't have sorcery.

Besides, she was gone around the final bend if she

thought I'd ever let her touch my crystal.

Just to name a few bumps on her road to Crazyville.

We. Need. To. Talk. Shenka spun and left the room, Sassafras hissing at me before following her. I rose as Mia's face crumpled.

"You'll help me, won't you, Syd?" She reached for my hand again, pressed it to her cheek.

Okay, so Shenka said she still harbored hate for me. But Mia had been my friend once.

How could I just let her suffer?

It took a lot to pull my hand free, Estelle waving a plate of chicken pasta under the girl's nose before Mia released me, diving into the food like she hadn't eaten ever. I nodded to the twins as they hugged themselves in matching movements, twin set fronts folding over their thin chests as they watched me go.

What a mess.

Shenka spun on me the moment I entered our little living room, speaking almost before my power could seal us from prying ears and eyes.

"You will go to your mother right now," Shenka said in a voice vibrating with fury, "and you will turn Mia in for conspiring to interfere with another coven."

It was the smart thing to do. Shenka was right.

"Syd." She shook from her anxiety and pent-up rage, waves of it rolling over me through our connection. "You don't owe her anything."

160

"You must think of the family." Sassafras's words cracked like whips, cutting through my half-daze of what the hell. "This damaged child has no place with us, Syd. And her need for revenge will only bring trouble to the coven."

I nodded. Spoke before I could hold my tongue. "Do you both really want Andre Dumont in the leadership of that family?" Was risking everything worth kicking his ass out of power?

"You are totally deluding yourself about her," Shenka spit, sparks flying from her finger tips as she waved her arms around her, temper shattering into motion. "Andre Dumont is a scumbag and a heartless ass, but he is a hundred times better than Mia." Shenka stopped moving, focused on me. "A thousand."

"Agreed," Sassafras said.

Agreed, my demon snarled.

Agreed, Shaylee sighed.

Sydlynn, my vampire sent. *You already know what you must do. And while your loyalty is one of the things well all love about you, as commendable as it is, there comes a time when you must think of the good of the whole, not of the individual.*

Especially an individual as screwed up as Mia, my demon sent.

It was the cringing unhappiness of the family magic that finally sealed the deal. I nodded to Shenka, heart heavy. Left her there as she watched me go, Sassafras following me to the exit of the main pavilion before his power touched mine.

We've taught you to protect those you care about, he sent. *No matter how they feel for you. Time to let go of young Mia, Syd. And let her fate unfold.*

He didn't follow. Let me walk away, my power reaching out, searching for one who needed to know, to hear from my mouth, what I was about to do.

I found Quaid with two full Enforcers. They bowed to me though he glared. But he must have felt the sadness in me, because his anger faded to concern.

"Might I have a moment with Trainee Tinder?" I held out my hand to Quaid while the two Enforcers grinned.

"Of course, Coven Leader," the tall woman said. Her companion, an older man with a thick blonde beard, winked.

Let them speculate. I only wished I was here to steal him away for a tryst.

Quaid and I walked the edge of the perimeter while I gathered my thoughts.

"Is this about earlier?" He kept his head down. "That Steam Union sorcerer. Is he good for you?"

I so wasn't having this conversation with him. "Mia's here," I said, surprised by the crack in my voice.

Quaid paused in mid step before squeezing my hand. "I heard," he said.

I pulled him to a stop, staring out over the dark trees,

flares of Enforcer power trailing across the night sky as they patrolled the area. A quick weaving of magic gave us privacy as I ran my thumb over the back of his hand.

And told him everything.

Quaid didn't speak, move, even seem to breathe until I finished telling him about Mia and Shenka and the plan his damaged sister brought to me. When I stumbled to a halt, my words breaking at the end, he exhaled softly before turning to me, pulling me to his chest, his warm robe draping around me as he slipped me inside, next to his hard body. I felt his heart beating against me, the heat of his skin through his t-shirt, taste the chocolatey deliciousness of his magic in the back of my throat.

This was his sister we were talking about. His last family. The Moromonds killed his parents, under orders from his own grandmother. Mia was all he had left.

And family, while important to me, meant everything to Quaid.

"You have to turn her in," he said, shocking me to the core.

I looked up into his dark eyes, saw the pain in him, felt it through our twining magic as my demon embraced him, begged him to stay with us.

"Quaid," I whispered. "If I do, Mom will be forced to arrest her."

He nodded. "I know," he said. Stepped back from me while my demon whimpered her loss. "But why am I doing this," he held out his robe, shook the front of it, "why am I working so hard, giving up so much," choke, "if I'm not willing to uphold the law?"

"I'll keep an eye on her," I said, words rushing over themselves as I realized I'd hoped he would feel as I did, that he would convince me to keep his sister safe.

"No," he said. "We have to bring this to Miriam. Now." He reached for me, face grim, magic crawling with anger. "Tonight."

It was so hard to take his hand, to follow him, my reluctant feet dragging as though I were headed to my own doom, not sending an old friend to hers.

ChapTER NINETEEN

I could tell from the look on Mom's face she wasn't so happy to see me. But when she realized Quaid was with me, her tension rose to a whole new level. So high, she practically shoved her aides out of the room before slamming up a shield around us and drawing a deep breath.

"I'm ready," she said through gritted teeth. "Hit me."

Quaid did most of the talking. I was grateful, considering my traitor throat closed over, misery eating at my insides to the point I doubted I could fit two coherent words together. Sass said he and Gram instilled this sense of loyalty in me when I was a baby.

Now I wished they'd just minded their own damned business.

Mom sank into a chair, her anger gone as she passed a hand before her eyes while Quaid wrapped up. Far more succinctly than I could have. Her blue gaze traveled from him to me and back again while she nodded.

"I've been watching young Mia," Mom said. "And I suspected she might try something like this."

Nice of her to tell me.

You're really surprised? My vampire sighed. *Oh, Syd.*

Grunt.

Mom swept to her feet again, hands reaching for us. "I don't want this incident to flavor the conclave," she said. "Quaid, you are now assigned to Sydlynn. The pair of you will keep an eye on Mia and make sure she's contained until this weekend is over."

"Do you think that's a good idea, Council Leader?" Quaid shook his head. "I don't mean to question you but... maybe she should be taken into custody." He glanced at me. "Quietly."

What? I could do quietly.

My alter egos all snorted in chorus.

Jerks.

Maybe it would have worked out after all. Perhaps containing Mia would have solved the problem.

We didn't get the chance to find out.

As Mom opened her mouth to respond to Quaid's suggestion, the flap to her office lifted and Andre stepped through. Accompanied by his sons.

And Mom's nasty little secretary, Maurice.

The turncoat little creep.

The worst part? The same two Enforcers from earlier dragged Mia through behind them, pushing her to her knees on the hard ground.

Mom's shields solidified, no longer just blocking sound, but trapping all of us in the room with her.

"Council Leader," Andre said in his icky voice. Not even a very cool French accent could make him sound good. "I've uncovered a plot against my family." His blue eyes settled on me. "By the Hayle coven."

He just had to try to push his limits, didn't he? Andre Dumont was about to see what his insides looked like splattered on the pretty white walls of Mom's tent.

"Your proof, Coven Leader?" Icicles dripped from my mother's words.

Andre had the sense to back off a pace, but he had no trouble pointing the finger at Mia.

"Mia Tinder," he sounded like speaking her name gave him pain, "plots to steal the Dumont family magic from its rightful place." He then jabbed his little digit at me. "And use the Hayle leader to do it."

"I can assure you right here, right now," I snarled, pushing back with a spike of power to his stomach, hitting him so hard he grunted, "if I wanted your ass dead, you'd be dead, Dumont."

Mom's mental sigh reined me in.

Temporarily.

"We will get to the truth of this," Mom said. And

turned the Council's power on Mia.

Why did the former Dumont leader suddenly focus on me? All the hate and rage Shenka told me about radiated from Mia's trembling body, aimed with sharp precision at yours truly. As Mom drew out Mia's thin remaining magic, she clawed the air between us.

I appeared, from her point of view, in a projection hanging over us all. I heard the conversation again, my denial. Mia's argument. When it was over, when her memory watched me leave the room, Mom released Mia's magic.

"It is clear," Mom said, "Sydlynn had nothing to do with Mia's plan. In fact, she was here reporting it." She nodded to Quaid. "With the assistance of Enforcer Trainee Tinder."

Jean Marc looked like he wanted to argue. I wished he'd open his damned mouth so I could shove something large and jagged in it.

No such luck.

"Very well," Andre said, "I will accept the fact the Hayle leader was not planning to attack my family." How very generous of him. "But I demand satisfaction against Mia Tinder."

Not a blessed thing anyone could do about it now. Not me, not Quaid. Not my mother. Faced with Mia's clear guilt, we were trapped into what I'd hoped to avoid.

What Mom wanted to avoid.

She sighed deeply, nodded. "Agreed," she said. "Mia Tinder, you are hereby under arrest and will be tried for the crime of conspiring against another coven leader."

Mia's howl of fury bounced back from Mom's shields. She lunged to her feet, toward me. I reacted instantly, my power throwing her back, but she never intended to hurt me, I don't think.

She just needed room to act.

And my power toss gave her that room. The two Enforcers took the brunt of the impact as she flew backward, the three of them bouncing from Mom's wards. Both Enforcers fell to their knees, but Mia was saved the worst of the recoil thanks to the protection of their bodies.

Had enough time to pull something dark but sparkling from her pocket before any of us could act.

"He said this would happen," Mia said. "And now I know who to trust."

A gaping black hole opened at her feet as her sorcery—damn it, how did I not know?— poured through the crystal in her hand, the emptiness of it butting against mine as she released it at last for me to feel. Quaid's power lashed at his sister, Mom's coming to bear, but they had nothing, their magic only feeding her as she dove for the darkness.

My own power lunged, caught the edge of the black hole, too late.

It snapped shut behind her.

Mia was gone.

Andre Dumont looked terrified suddenly, pale and shaking as he stared at the place she'd been.

I cursed myself for not paying closer attention, for missing the fact Mia had sorcery, but I couldn't help but toss him a dig, just for old hate's sake.

"Guess you didn't see that one coming," I said with a nasty grin. "You sleep alone, Andre?" He gaped at me, still in shock at his own miscalculation. "Want to bet she'll be coming for you some night?" I laughed, unable to help myself. "Have fun with that, won't you?"

Mom's magic snapped across mine. "I have no choice but to declare Mia Tinder a fugitive from witch law." She released the shielding around her office. "We will do everything we can to capture and contain her until such time as she can be tried for her crimes."

Andre scuttled from the room, his evil sons a whole lot less sure of themselves.

My tremulous giggles wanted to come back, fed by my fury with myself. How did I miss it after all this time?

Because the one who owns her taught her to hide it from us, my vampire sent.

Belaisle.

One more infraction to add to his tally.

Quaid's anger reached out, but I knew the moment I touched his hand it wasn't aimed at me.

"She made her choice," he said. "She could have come to me." A sharp comment rose in my mind, about just how available he'd been lately, but I pushed it down. "Instead, she chose the enemy." His dark eyes held me in a trap of molten temper.

I reached up, touched his cheek, my heart swelling open, my own anger fading in the face of his rigid fury.

"Quaid," I whispered.

"Quaid," she said.

I turned to see Payten at the door, eyes traveling over the two of us, lips in a thin line.

He stiffened, pulled away from me.

"Leader is looking for you," she said. Bowed to Mom. "Council Leader, Enforcer Leader Tremere is on his way."

I let Quaid go, hating he didn't look back.

And that Payten did.

Nice of me to leave Mom to mop up the mess, wasn't it? But I'd had enough, couldn't take any more. Shoulders slumped, heart heavy, I drifted my way back toward my pavilion, wishing this whole damned conclave was over already so I could hide under the covers of my bed and never come out.

A warm hand took mine, empty power nudging me as Piers slid in beside me, matching my slow gait.

He didn't speak, just escorted me to the front of my tent. When I stopped, turned to face him, he kissed me.

But not the hot, hungry kiss I was used to. Instead, his lips moved slowly over mine, nose stroking my cheek, fingers light in my hair, sliding over my neck.

The tingle was there, but subtle, kind and caring, and for a moment a lump rose in my throat.

"Syd," he whispered over my mouth. "I know where your heart lies." His gray eyes were soft, full of compassion. "And I know you're out of time." Nice of him to remind me. "And while I realize you may not have taken me seriously in the past, I'm asking you now." His hands slid down and grasped mine, lifting them to press my open palms against his chest. "Choose me as your mate. I swear you'll never regret it."

He didn't wait for my response, just kissed me softly one more time before turning and leaving me there. Vulnerable, damn him. Wondering.

Quaid picked duty over the magic binding us together, the love I knew would never die. Liam was honorable, if too kind, according to those who thought they had a say.

And while I knew I didn't love him, not like I loved Quaid, nor even as I loved Liam, I adored Piers.

Was his the strength I needed? Was love just a liability?

Sadder now than I'd been before, I turned and went inside the pavilion, knowing I wouldn't sleep a wink.

Chapter Twenty

True to my expectations, I paced the night away and I wasn't alone. After a long talk with Shenka about Mia, Sassafras adding his lecture on top of hers, the three of us took turns either circling the small main room or sitting morosely staring into space.

Because sleep was overrated.

Breakfast turned out to be a giant affair, large tables and massive amounts of food spread out in the common areas of each pavilion. I found myself dining with a pair of witches from the Hensley coven while Tallah cornered her sister, still struggling to meet my eyes. Whatever decisions Mom had reached about the Hensley leader, I was still nervous about her particular need to expose us to normals, but even more so her contact with the supposed Steam Union.

Had to remind myself to prod Piers later to see if he'd

heard anything from his contacts.

From the irritation on my second's face, the way she crossed her arms over her chest and refused to look at her fast-talking sibling, Shenka wasn't regretting leaving the family coven and had given up completely the guilt she'd carried telling me about Tallah's conspiracy, not only with the sorcerers, but her constant badgering to return to her family coven.

Conclave didn't officially begin until lunchtime, but it didn't stop the gathered witches from finding advanced seating in the giant center pavilion hours early. Tiered risers now lined the inside of the space, a large section in the lowest row set aside for each of the visiting Council and race leaders. Otherwise, segregation went out the window, werewolves sitting next to Sidhe, witches mingling with Steam Union while the large center space remained open, reminding me of a circus tent waiting for the show to start. Though the vampires were notably absent during daylight hours, I spotted a beautiful woman speaking to Mom and, recognizing her from Sunny's group the night before.

And went to find out who she was.

"Sydlynn Hayle." The tall, buxom redhead shook my hand with firm pressure, handsome face mature though her pale green eyes sparkled with good humor. "I've been wanting to meet you for some time now, but my queen has kept me busy."

"Syd, this is Chambrelle Strait," Mom said. "Sunny's human representative."

Ah. Gotcha. "Nice to meet you, too."

"We need to find time to get to know each other," Chambrelle said. "When life isn't so crazy."

"You mean this isn't normal?" I laughed, liking the easy way she joined me.

"Then again," she said. "If lack of crazy was a stipulation, we'd never meet again."

Someone blew a horn, the tooting joined by a second, a third, until a ringing chorus of music summoned us to conclave.

Chambrelle followed Mom, waving to me as they left. I had a good vibe from the woman, and if Sunny trusted her, I trusted her. Still. Getting to know her better was a great idea, if only to make sure.

I'd been a terrible judge of character lately.

Part of me felt a little sick as I searched the crowd for Shenka. The last conclave I'd attended had been a trial. Mom's. And though things all turned out for the best— eventually—being here still brought back memories.

At least the feeling around me was more festive than somber, the gathered magical races excited to be here. Their enthusiasm, like walking through a wall of childish delight, lightened my mood until, when I finally sank onto one of the elevated benches next to my second, I was actually smiling.

Sassafras left Shenka's lap and stood in mine, thick tail winding around my wrist.

Keep your senses open, he sent. *If the Brotherhood is planning an attack, it will be while we're in session, I'm thinking.*

Way to pop my bubble, smartass cat.

Still, he was absolutely right. And, thanks to his reminder, I was acutely aware, moments, I think, before anyone else, we were about to have company.

But not a sorcerous invasion. At least, not overtly. Just as Mom and her Council settled into place, the other Leaders already seated and surrounded by their own members, the air in the center of the pavilion ruptured into blue flame.

And Margaret Applegate burst through.

I respected my mother for a lot of things. Her ability to hold her temper under pressure was at the top of the list. Even as my alter egos fumed, my anger surging inside like a rampaging bull in a glass factory, Mom faced the sudden appearance of the European Council Leader and her members with calm and absolute poise.

So. Jealous.

Still, Mom's poise left me the freedom to poke around while she dealt with Applegate.

Because she wouldn't have liked how I wanted to handle it. Nope, nope.

"Council Leader Applegate." Mom's voice rang in the space. Magic powered, clearly. No way she made herself sound like she was inside an empty marble hall instead of a soft-topped tent full of people without it. "Welcome to conclave. So happy to see you've accepted the invitation after all."

Um, weren't there rules, Mom? Hadn't she just brought up those rules to me last night over Mia?

I'd have booted the arrogant old biddy's ass out the front side of the tent and back across the Atlantic with a very sharp shoe.

A rumbling undercurrent raced around the tiers of seating, the other Council Leaders and heads of races scowling at Applegate and her posse as they hung in the air over the empty center of the pavilion. Only a handful of witches arrived with her, but at least fifty Enforcers made a protective semi-circle with just the front end open for her to face off with Mom. I poked and prodded among them, searching for a particular pair of witches I'd met in Ukraine last winter, but came up empty.

Neither Gwendolyn Ravensdale nor Finlay Wright were part of Applegate's war party.

Seriously, that was what it amounted to. Strong witches, a bundle of Enforcers... made me wonder what the Brotherhood was up to now.

And worry. Lots and lots of worry as my maji power opened fully in response.

"I believe," Applegate said in the most insulting tone I'd ever heard from a human mouth, "you're in my seat,

Miriam."

Oh *hell to the tenth degree* no.

But Mom's reaction to the arrogance of Applegate—Liander Belaisle, in other words—was lost to me. Because I had a more important discovery to slice bits of anxiety from my already tense coil of magic.

Applegate had a sorcerer with her. The gaping emptiness was impossible to miss. And not just a thralled witch, either. A full-blown, power sucking Brotherhood member right here, front and center.

Mom. I felt her catch my thrown thought even as she responded to Applegate.

I'm a little busy, Syd. "I'm afraid you're mistaken," Mom said out loud. "As host of this conclave, the head seat falls to me."

You're about to be busier, I sent. Let her feel the sorcerer.

Her face didn't register her reaction, nor did her outward feeling of magic. But I was inside her head when she began to swear, so I knew better.

Taught me a few things. My demon, even. She flinched from a few of Mom's choice curses, mumbling to herself about Mom going over the line.

I was pretty used to focusing on two conversations at once by now, absorbing the mutterings and noddings of the other Councils, the general consensus in Mom's favor even as she stopped cursing and grumbled a growl in my head.

Pinpoint the scum, Mom sent.

Her wish, my command.

It wasn't hard to find him, floating with a grim smile next to a vapid looking woman with overly bleached hair. As one of the Enforcers shifted position, I caught a clear look at his face.

And starting swearing myself.

We know him? Good thing we were taking turns losing our crap. I didn't want to think what would happen if Mom and I both snapped at once.

I do, I snarled. And did my best not to throw myself at Vasyl Krajnik, the former second of the Czar of the Black Souls.

I heard Oleksander's roar of fury before I remembered I wasn't the only one who had a grudge against the sorcerer. The werewolf king surged to his feet, Charlotte next to him, Raoul, her father, standing behind with Maksym and half the werewolf nation. All shaking, bodies vibrating, partially shifting as a people, wolf snouts and eyes appearing in tandem as Oleksander lifted one clawed hand and pointed at the smirking sorcerer.

"Vasyl!" The werewolf didn't have Mom's power to back his voice. Didn't need it. "*Ви мрець!*"

Uh-oh. I recognized the murderous tone in his voice enough to know what the big were just said was a clear threat. I threw up a shield around the werewolves as Applegate smirked at the fuming king and his gathered people. As if expecting this very reaction and anticipating the outcome.

Charlotte. I dove into her mind, slapping her firmly with my power as she howled in blind fury. *Snap out of it.* She tried to jerk free, but I was stronger. *Listen to me,* I sent. *This is what they want. Do not under any circumstance shift into full wolf form.*

I could see her shudder even from across the pavilion, but caught her sharp nod, the tightness of her agreement. Charlotte spun on Oleksander, hissed in his ear. He tried to fight her, as she fought me, but her claws dug into his arms, turning back to fingers as his anger dulled and retreated.

We were going to have to keep a very careful eye on the werewolves.

Sucked so much.

"Your little dogs seem upset by something," Applegate turned to Mom. "Hard to paper train, are they?"

Wow, she was really pushing it. And not just with Mom. From the angry expressions on many faces, this whole "let's try to get along" thing Mom had going was working out okay. To the point no one had Applegate's back.

Belaisle must have sensed his slip up, because he abandoned his attack of the werewolves and focused on Mom.

"Very well," Applegate said. "We'll see what kind of leader you are when all is said and done, Hayle." The European witch swooped toward one side of the tent, her power rudely pushing aside some of the gathered witches and other races watching the spectacle. Mom didn't move to stop her, to my surprise, as Applegate made herself a little podium of her own, chairs and a table appearing out of nowhere, as the European Council Leader settled in with her army around her.

Bindi didn't have Mom's reserve, her people grumbling around her as she stood and scowled at Applegate.

"Your contingent seems a bit off weight," she said in her strong Australian accent. "No covens wanted to come play?" She eyed the Enforcers inside the European Leader's section. "And we all agreed when this began our Enforcers would remain outside."

"I agreed to no such thing," Applegate said. To Mom. Ignoring Bindi completely. Nice. "And these witches are my support staff." Yeah, right. Buying it.

Not.

Bindi spluttered, glared at Mom.

Who simply nodded to the Australian Leader with more respect than necessary, probably in an effort to diffuse the growing unhappiness in the pavilion as other leaders started to shift and mutter.

Nothing like stirring up a sense of entitlement in a

group of witches to start a party.

"We will accept Margaret's assurances," Mom said in a velvet voice backed with steel, "that her support staff," she said that with a straight face? Wow, "will maintain the expected decorum."

Margaret just sniffed, looked away. Bindi looked around, for support, obviously. And this could have dissolved quickly into mayhem. Mom was just a figurehead after all. The Councils were here of their own accord.

But the others quieted, shrugged, leaving Bindi no recourse.

"I formally lodge my displeasure of this ruling," she said. And sat.

Mom was already moving on, smoothing edges with her power.

So was I.

Who is the woman with Vasyl? I sent the message to Mom, but it was Sassafras who answered with so much sadness in his voice I actually looked down at him to find his amber eyes brimming with moisture.

That's Eloise Brindle, he sent. *How far their coven has fallen.*

Brindle. I knew that name... snapped my mental fingers a moment later. Didn't Mom help my friend Beth with a scholarship named after a Brindle?

Kate, Sassafras sent. *She would be horrified to know her descendent has thrown in with the Brotherhood.*

There wasn't much I could do to comfort him except stroke his fur and cuddle him close when he turned to hide his head against me.

My tension held a tight hold as Oleksander addressed Mom.

"We demand the European Council turn that criminal over to justice." He pointed right at Vasyl and I realized then why Applegate chose the place she did for her entourage. Nice and close to the werewolves.

Applegate yawned and gestured to Vasyl herself. "He is under my protection," she said. "Come and get him."

The crowd stirred, fell silent. While most of them clearly had no idea what this was about, there was enough animosity floating around they had to be aware this situation could blow wide open at any moment.

"Vasyl is my second," Eloise said. Voice dull, eyes empty, as though prompted. "The family magic has accepted him. And I can prove it to you." No one asked her to, but she turned to him, a puppet on very short strings, opening her power for us to see.

There it was. Family magic, blue and glittering, swirling around him. Tied to him somehow. Perhaps he was latent? It didn't matter. Not really. The display was enough for the others.

Just not for me.

Mom's energy dimmed, forced to cave to law.

"Your petition is denied," Mom said to Oleksander.

"And should anything untoward happen to the second of the Brindle family while you are in conclave, you will be held personally responsible."

Oh, Mom.

I understood, I totally did. But she just forced the werewolves to look out for the wellbeing of one of the sorcerers who used to be their master.

The worst part was the feeling of the Brindle family magic, at least for me. Of course it wasn't fighting Vasyl. His sorcery kept it so drained and beaten down, the leader so suppressed, I was surprised she was awake.

Maybe she wasn't, for all that.

chapter twenty one

I fully expected the whole shebang to go kablooey at any second. I wasn't expecting, however, to die of boredom.

Not right away, no. Not when Mom stood to give her welcome speech thanking the supernatural races for attending while I fumed and connived and tried to come up with a way to kick Vasyl's ugly ass without getting the werewolves in trouble.

And certainly not when I finally came back to the present from a sharp prod of Sassafras's magic.

You're supposed to answer her, he sent.

What? Who? Nobody said there would be a test.

I looked up and met Mom's eyes as she waited patiently, arm held out toward me.

What the hell did I miss?

Get up. Sassafras's voice grated in my head. *Now.*

I scrambled to my feet, almost dumping him on his head, handing him off instead to Shenka. Okay, so she grabbed him from me before I could drop him. And stared at Mom, frozen.

Syd, she sent. *Your speech.*

My—

Just repeat after me, my vampire sent. *Welcome, most revered of all magic users, to my humble home.*

I mumbled what she told me, Mom's power amplifying my words. When I stumbled over "revered", Applegate's snort of derision drove my temper into a spike and brought me to life.

None too soon.

The speech my vampire unfolded made my brain numb. Worse that Sassafras dove in from time to time to tweak the message.

—in my power to—

No, no, say, in my purview—

Don't listen to him.

She has no idea how to frame a speech.

I made it through. Somehow. And sank to the bench dripping in a cold sweat.

Who was the smartass who failed to mention I had to speak in public? I aimed my renewed anger at Mom, Shenka and Sassafras, including my egos along for the ride.

Mom chuckled. *You did fine, sweetheart.* "We will now

hear from Council Leader Diaz."

I thought I told you, Shenka sent, her distress clear in her mental tone.

I've been preparing for weeks, my vampire sent.

Sydlynn, Sassafras snapped. *When will you learn to pay attention?*

At least it was over. And I didn't cause an international incident, blow anyone up or anything.

Called it a win and settled in to calm my nerves.

All the way down to dull and lifeless as, witch after witch, speech after speech, my soul was sucked out through my ears and devoured by the deepest boredom I'd ever felt in my entire life.

I caught myself wishing Belaisle would show up just so I had something to do. Or Galleytrot's giant snail. But picturing it sliding its slimy way over the assembled witches and magical beings just led me to sigh and shift in my seat.

There was only so much I could do with a man-eating gastropod to keep me amused.

Who knew the opening day of conclave was mind-numbing exploration of each and every Council and attending coven's rewind of the last one hundred dismally wretched years?

Mom. You're killing me.

Her mental laughter barely hid her own weariness. *You mean you're not enjoying yourself? But Syd, this is the best part of conclave. Day one is always about boasting.* Her chuckle turned to false disappointment. *I thought you knew that?*

Gripe.

And day two? I dreaded the answer. Why hadn't I asked? Because I didn't bother with boring details, did I? That was Shenka's job.

I really had to learn to pay attention. Sass would love to hear me say that.

Oh, day two, Mom sent with so much enthusiasm I couldn't miss her sarcastic undertones. *Yes, we make laws on day two. Big ones, little ones. All in a bundle. But day three, that's the best.* Okay, this was fun, at least. Who knew my mother had such a sense of humor? I could almost see her clap her hands and widen her eyes in pretend excitement. *Day three we pass those hastily and badly written laws that make everyone's lives all convoluted and confusing. Fun, right?*

Snort.

You're kidding me.

Syd, Mom sent, sobering but still amused. *You know witches. Grew up with them. Since when have you known them, as a whole, to do anything with sanity or purpose? Hide-bound, frustrating…*

Job getting to you? Sympathy made an appearance past my need to giggle.

At times, she sent. *I really never knew just how ridiculous we are as a race until I took this position. Even more now.* She sighed in my head. *Not that it matters anyway. Nothing important will be decided here this weekend, I can promise you that.* I thought of Tallah and wondered for a moment. *Our focus is on the Brotherhood. Not silly laws that no one pays attention to anyway.*

Fair enough.

When Chambrelle stepped up to speak about the vampires, I perked. Surely she would provide some sordid entertainment. I had high hopes she might save me with one scandal or another, but nope. More drivel and tedium.

With the following tales of the downtrodden depression of the werewolves, the self-centered focus of the Sidhe and the shirking of responsibility from the Steam Union and I was about to tear my own head off and toss it into the ring to see if anyone wanted to play some noggin soccer.

Even Meira let me down, though I listened to a little of her speech before sighing yet again and squinching lower in my seat, one foot thudding endlessly against the riser below me, drawing an angry glare from the witch using it for a backrest.

Sigh.

Sigh.

Holy mother of all the elementals and everything that could possibly be considered holy—

Trill's laughter in my head was so welcome I latched

onto her. Hard. Caught the image of her sitting cross-legged on the bed it the back of her caravan.

And you wondered why I didn't want to attend conclave, she sent with a giggle.

Bratski. *Save me,* I sent with as much drama as I could pour into it. *I'm dying here.*

You're just going to have to suffer for the greater good. Her amusement faded. *I hear there have been some complications.*

And how did she know that? Still, it was nice to have her to dump my stuff on, if only to keep my mind from imploding.

I have met a few of the Steam Union here in this territory, she sent. *It's possible Tallah's visitors are the genuine article.*

Really. *Piers is looking into it,* I sent. *But can you check for me, too?*

Already on it, she sent. *I'll have Apollo contact his friends. If any of them are involved, they'll know right away if this is legit.*

Thanks. I felt way better. Not that I didn't trust Piers to follow through, but this was Trill.

I take it you have a reason for rescuing me, I sent, *that has nothing to do with rescuing me.*

She laughed. *Just checking in. You know how the Brotherhood's silence makes me nervous. I'm on pins and needles waiting for the other shoe to drop.*

So you're happy they are stirring again. She laughed while I thought about the wild magicks. *Any guesses what the message might mean?*

I could feel her shake her head. *I wish,* she sent. *But the next time, reach for me. I'll see if I can help.*

That would be awesome.

I have to go, she sent. *But have no fear, my brothers and I are close in case you need us.*

You could just drop the cloak and dagger and come join me listening to mindless drivel.

I'll pass, she sent. *As appealing as that sounds.*

Hugged me with her power and was gone.

I was so grateful for the distraction, I almost missed it when Shenka rose beside me, Sassafras in her arms, still managing to clap. I surged to my feet, butt aching from the hard seat, totally missing the applause thing, coming in too late as the horde of witches and others turned and began to leave.

Way to stand out like a sore thumb, Hayle.

Shenka giggled, Sassafras hissing at me.

"You could at least have paid attention," he snapped, "instead of wriggling around the entire time like a petulant child."

Whatever. At least I missed Applegate's speech.

Had to find a silver lining somewhere.

Speaking of which, as I turned to go, flexing my legs to bring feeling back, I ran into Piers. He caught me as Shenka scooted around us with a little smile and a slow eyebrow raise for me, carrying my cranky Persian with her.

"You could have saved me earlier," I said. "Tell me you sat through this entire thing like I did."

He laughed. "Every painful moment," he said. Grinned. "Nice speech. Who taught you to speak, a pack of chimpanzees?"

Hardy har har. "Keep laughing, sorcerer boy," I said. "Let's see you wrangle a demon cat, a vampire essence and my mother all while trying not to pass out from performance anxiety."

Piers bowed to me. "I am merely a peasant in the shadow of your greatness."

Oooh. He was so going to pay for that.

Piers took my arm, still smiling, nodding at the few people still left in the stands. "You do realize," he said, keeping his tone pleasant, "Vasyl is the Brotherhood's eyes into the conclave."

What, did he think I was an idiot? "Duh," I said. "Though why he bothered, I have no idea. Applegate is his already."

"Except," Piers said as we began to descend to the main floor, "he has to fight to hold the Council Leader in thrall." I'd buy that. I'd seen flickers of Margaret behind the facade Belaisle created. "But Vasyl is a sorcerer, his creature through and through. And thus is more valuable."

I almost argued Vasyl had the Brindle family magic to fight, but who was I kidding? He'd drained it into a coma.

"It worries me," I said, realizing it as my feet touched the main level. "It's not like the Brotherhood to be so..."

"Blatant?" Piers nodded, still smiling. Okay, I could play his faking pleasantries game. "I agree. Which means Belaisle has other plans, doesn't he?"

Lovely.

"Or this is just a distraction," I said.

"For what?" Piers paused, turning me toward him, waiting for a pair of witches in quiet conversation with a group of werewolves to pass us out the exit. "Maybe instead a show of power?"

"So out of character."

Totally.

"Any word on the Steam Union friendlies?" Now that Trill was poking around, I remembered to ask him.

Piers shook his head. "Not yet. But I have my doubts still."

Who didn't?

He didn't comment further, gaze leaving me, a small smile thinning his lips, eyes narrowing as he watched something over my shoulder.

"I need to speak to the coven leader." Damn it, that voice. I turned to find Quaid glaring at Piers who just shrugged before bending to kiss my hand.

"We'll talk about this more later," Piers said.

I gave him a little push with my magic, shooing him off as he laughed and strode away.

Leaving me to focus on Quaid who still stared after him with his fury barely contained.

"You don't have the right to be angry," I snapped. "Back off."

Quaid flinched, cheeks paling before he flushed and took a step off. "Are you going to pick him?"

"You didn't need to talk to me." Was he serious? "You're just being a jerkasaurus."

His scowl hurt, not because he was angry with me, but because I saw the pain behind it.

"Besides," I snarled back, so not in the mood for his little jealousy play when he clearly had no intention of following through. "I thought you and Payten had a thing going, Quaid. Go screw your little Enforcer bunny and leave me the hell alone."

Wow, Syd. Where did that come from?

Didn't matter. Because he got the message, loud and clear.

But not in the way I was expecting.

"How many times," he growled, looming over me as he closed the distance between us, "do I have to tell you there is nothing," his power sparked as he cut the air with one hand, "between Payten and me?"

Such. A. Liar.

I turned to go, felt his hands on me, the pull of his magic, how my demon needed him.

How I needed him.

And hated him for it so much, in that instant, my free hand lashed out and slapped him across the face.

I instantly regretted it. But there was no taking it back. Not the blow. Not the hurt. Not the resignation on his face as I backed away before spinning and running away from him.

chapter twenty two

I had no appetite, despite the delicious aromas floating around me. The main pavilion was now full of tables, stuffed with witches serving a variety of foods from all different cultures. I just couldn't bring myself to focus on dinner.

Shenka bullied me into a long, black velvet skirt and silk blouse, my witch's uniform, the replacement pentagram necklace Mom gave me hanging around my neck. My second even put my hair up for me.

"Now you look the part," she said while Sassafras snorted.

Didn't help Meira joined him in laughing. Charlotte, too. Nice of them to come and share in my misery, offering casual suggestions to "improve" my appearance. After the little run-in I'd had with Quaid, the last thing I wanted was to go through the dog and pony at a formal dinner.

"You have to go," Shenka said, Meira linking arms with me despite her height advantage, looking as stunning and scary as usual.

"Mom needs us there," my sister said. "Besides, I hear you're the guest of honor."

Blech.

At least my sister was only teasing me. After a brief introduction yet again, Mom sat at the head table and everyone dug in. I fidgeted on her right, alternating between scowling at my plate and smiling when prompted by my irritated second.

For goodness sakes, Syd, Shenka finally snapped. *Smarten up already.*

But it was Sunny who finally got through to me.

You have so much weighing on your mind, my vampire queen sent. *I'm happy to lighten your burden.*

I wish you could, I sent, toying with my fork and the idea I could just get up and leave and no one would stop me.

I take it this has to do with matters of the heart? Sunny's power soothed me, her spirit magic as comforting as one of her full-body hugs.

How'd you guess? Was I that transparent?

She laughed in my head. *Darling*, she sent, *I've seen you face some of the most atrocious, frightening, overwhelming situations with courage and fortitude. But when it comes to your emotions, you are a little bird nursing a broken wing.*

Thanks a lot, I sent.

It's a compliment, Syd. Sunny's power retreated but she stayed with me. *You care so much, I worry for you. But what could be a weakness is actually your greatest strength. Don't let that change.*

Not what Sassafras thought.

I really do love you, I sent, gushy all of a sudden, biting my lower lip to keep from crying.

And I love you, my most darling Sydlynn, Sunny sent. And gently released me.

I managed a few bites of food after that, but thankfully by the time I managed to focus, dinner was pretty much over. I fled as Shenka took over the niceties of mingling, slipping into the darkness alone, using magic to hide myself.

I just wanted to be alone.

Only to have green Sidhe power embrace me.

I turned into Liam's arms, inhaling the scent of fresh earth and his fabric softener, my entire body going limp with relief just to be held by someone who loved me without condition.

He led me to one of the decorative benches on the site, pulling me tight against him as his power softly engulfed me.

"Nice to see you too," he said.

I smiled up at him, all awkwardness gone. "Sorry," I

said. "It's been a little rough and seeing a friendly face is a good thing."

Liam's answering smile faded, the sparks of green in his eyes dim. "Friend," he said, picking out the one word that made everything uncomfortable between us again.

And then surprised the hell out of me by smiling anew.

"I need to apologize to you," he said, "for being such a loser weirdo lately." I tried to shake my head but he pressed his fingers to my lips, eyes full of laughter. "Don't you dare," he said. "I've mastered moping angst. Don't take that accomplishment away from me."

I giggled. "You're the best I've ever seen," I said.

Liam bent and kissed my forehead, arm loose around my shoulders, safe and warm and gentle. I leaned in, pressing my nose to his soft shirt, allowing Shaylee to embrace him fully as he spoke.

"I saw you earlier," he said. "When I was delivering some last-minute things to Odhran and Niamh." He paused. "I wasn't spying, I swear. But you were with the Steam Union guy."

Oops. My mind raced over Piers's and my last meeting. Did he kiss me?

Yikes.

But Liam's reaction didn't go where I expected it to take him. "I'm done putting pressure on you," he said. "It's your life, Syd. And even though I love you, it's your choice." He pushed me back a little, face no longer sad, though I could feel the softness of his edges, the way his power sank into the ground.

And realized then what I'd never seen before. What no one in my family understood.

Liam wasn't weak. Not in the least. He was an old oak tree, with roots buried deep beneath the ground, massive and stable, able to withstand anything. Sure, his bark and branches and leaves were more likely to be damaged, but the core of Liam O'Dane was as solid as the earth itself.

"I love you," he said. "And no matter what you decide, I'll always be your friend." He patted my knee with his free hand. "I want you to do what's best for you."

Sweet. So. Sweet.

"What if I don't know what's best for me?" I suddenly felt tiny in the massive shade of his power, still seeing him as a towering oak, wanting to lie against him and absorb the quiet peace of his nature.

"You'll figure it out," he said. Kissed me softly, the touch of power sliding between us tasting like a spring morning. "You always do." Liam stood up, helped me to my feet. "I have to get back to the archive," he said. "Can I bring you anything the next time I come?"

There was no way anyone could possibly be as amazingly nice as him and live.

And yet, here he was before me.

I hugged him, let him go. "Thanks," I said. "Just keep Galleytrot in line and check on Gram and I'm good."

Liam's lips twisted. "I'll do my best for the first," he said. "And the second... Ethpeal might not like me, but I respect her, Syd. I'll make sure she's okay."

I watched him go, heart swelling, choices narrowed, still trying to decide if love was worth it.

"How nice to see you again." Vasyl stepped from the shadows, interrupting my joyful moment. Made me instantly cranky. His shaved head shining in the witchlight as I scowled into his shark eyes. My demon made plans to tan his hide for a jacket after she'd killed and eaten him.

"I can't touch you now," I said. "But conclave won't last forever, sorcerer."

Vasyl shrugged, a languid movement, not a trace of concern on his angular face.

"Liander told me you would bluster and threaten," he said, accent smoothed out more than the last time I spoke to him. And, on using Belaisle's name, confirming what I already knew. "I told him you were above that. Alas, I was mistaken."

A string of swears coursed through my thoughts as he went on.

"He wished me to pass on a message." Vasyl leaned closer, lips curling his thin mustache and goatee into a devilish mask. "That he will see you soon and cannot wait to catch up."

"If your main job here is to piss me off," I said, "you suck at it."

I was a terrible liar.

Vasyl laughed, stepped aside. Gestured for me to pass. Which I did, the back of my neck prickling with nerves. But I refused to look back, my feet stomping all the way to the opening of my tent.

Where I found Piers lurking.

Made me think of Liam and pissed me off even more.

"This better be good," I said.

One of his eyebrows shot up, voice mild as he spoke though his words had sting.

"As long as you consider the safety of this conclave 'good,'" he said.

Zing.

"Whatever." I crossed my arms over my chest. "I just got through having a bully wrestling match with Vasyl Krajnik, so bear with me."

Piers nodded. "He has that effect on me, too. But we don't have time for your temper." He stepped closer, real concern on his face. "I've just heard from Els." His friend, Ellis. "His network claims the Brotherhood has finally surfaced."

Okay, good. Very good. And very, very bad.

"What does surfaced mean?" I picked at the velvet of my skirt as my mind churned.

"Large groups are mobilizing out in the open," he

said. "Gathering."

For an invasion? I reached for Galleytrot, felt Liam connect through their power as he approached my house. *Be on guard*, I sent. *Something may be coming your way.*

We're on it, they both sent before the hound spoke up. *Brotherhood?*

I hope not. I cut him off as I returned my full attention to Piers. "We need to tell Mom."

He waited, jaw working, as I reached for her. She listened, intent, as I told her what Piers told me.

No indication of their goal? I could feel her moving, leaving a crowd of other magic, probably going to her makeshift office.

Not according to Piers, I sent. *But his sources seem to think they are preparing for something.*

My Enforcers are ready, Mom sent, though the worry in her voice mirrored mine.

Mom, I sent. *How can they be? They have no defense, remember?*

Her frustration poured over me like a cold shower. *I know*, she sent. *But what else can I do?*

I'm coming to you, I sent. *Call for Eva Southway. It's time witches and sorcerers worked together.*

Mom's affirmative touch ended as she broke from me.

Just as the wild magicks appeared in a swirl of power.

So frantic this time, their touch stung, grabbed my

power, jerked me forward—

—*into darkness, the flash of glass, the sound of marching feet, Belaisle's face. And, in his hand*—

The shard of a mirror. A mirror I'd seen before. Used to travel.

From the Enforcer stronghold.

My chest squeezed tight as I emerged from the vision, the magicks's panic taking over.

I understood their message. All the images fell in to place, even as I turned and ran for the main pavilion, screaming for Mom in my head.

chapter twenty three

I was so freaked out I didn't even think of the veil, instead running flat out with Piers beside me through the front of the large pavilion and to Mom's office.

Almost colliding with Pender as he appeared in a flash of blue fire at her door.

Gasping for air—I really had to start jogging again—I clutched at Pender's sleeve, heart pounding so hard in my chest I could barely think.

"The shards," I said as I pushed the tall Enforcer leader through Mom's door. She rushed forward, eyes locked on me as I panted and spoke again. "The mirror shards. Are they all accounted for?"

Pender's frown of confusion turned to worry as he immediately fished into his robe and retrieved his. I'd seen it before, knew now there were many such shards, doorways to the Enforcer stronghold.

To the place the battle between Dark and Light would be fought.

I showed them both what the wild magicks had shared with me while Piers stood, silent and tense, at my side.

Pender's face paled as the image of Belaisle holding a shard flared a moment before fading. "All of the fragments are in safe hands," he said. Didn't sound convincing to me. "But I'll check in with them all anyway."

"Pender," Mom said. "Are there any unaccounted for? Lost or rumored?"

To that he shook his head. "None," he said. "The stronghold is secure."

For now. But I was certain the wild magicks were warning me for a reason.

Pender left, shoulders tight under his heavy robe, power flaring as he left the pavilion. I crossed to a chair in Mom's office, sinking into it as Piers came to stand behind me.

"Perhaps a meeting of the minds wouldn't be untoward at this point, Council Leader?" I felt his hands settle on my shoulders, the touch of his sorcery following after.

Mom nodded, brows pulled together as she did. "I was thinking the same thing. If the two of you would kindly go secure a place we can talk unnoticed?"

Somewhere not here. Made sense.

"The Steam Union would be more than happy to host," Piers said. "And our power will be more than enough of a deterrent to prying magicks."

Perfect. Except, of course, I'd just run, screeching for Mom, through the conclave grounds. Way to keep things under wraps, Syd. Still, I was sure no one knew why and, hopefully, I could put my panic off to my natural weirdness and no one would notice.

Mom seemed to think along the same lines as me. "Please tell your mother how delighted we are she's invited us to come to your pavilion for a visit." I felt her power relax as she spoke, realized she had to know there were spies among us, giving them enough information to keep whoever needed to know just enough to satisfy curiosity.

She might have seen eavesdropping as par for this particular train wreck, but if I caught anyone snooping they'd be relocating to a new area code.

Two new area codes. Their ass would be moving on alone.

Eva Southway didn't look surprised to see Piers and I and I could only assume he managed to warn his mother before we swept through the front of the pavilion.

"Coven Leader Hayle," she said, spiked blonde hair shining in the witchlight, gray eyes flat, but not unpleasant. "Welcome."

I wondered if she'd still look at me the same way when this little meeting was over.

Mom arrived next, sweeping through the entry like she owned the place—which I did, thank you very much—but with a gracious smile and a warm greeting for Eva.

"You remember my husband, Felix?" Eva gestured to the tall, handsome man with the dark hair and thick beard. He bowed over Mom's hand before doing the same to mine. "And our daughter, Clover." I remembered the beautiful young woman with the thick, black hair, a match for her father. I thought her Piers's girlfriend when we'd first met and almost tore him a new one over the poor thing. Her sweet smile and little curtsy were meant to be endearing, I guessed.

Cute and all, but not distracting enough to take away from the more eager antsy pants dance going on in my stomach.

Meira arrived on the veil, alone, about a heartbeat after Mom shook Clover's hand. Though she'd grown to be far more diplomatic and steeped in politics than me since moving to Demonicon, from the scowl on my sister's face, she wasn't in the mood to play.

"Mom said this was important." She hugged me swiftly, nodded to the Southways. "The Brotherhood?"

I shrugged as the air beside me shuddered into shadow and Sunny and Uncle Frank appeared.

"Thank you for allowing us through your shielding," Sunny said at her most queenly. Eva nodded graciously.

"I assumed there wasn't need for the entire conclave to know we were having this little tête-à-tête," the Steam Union leader said. "We're awaiting a few more?"

A flare of green power answered her question. I gritted my teeth only to sigh in relief as Odhran and Niamh stepped through. Alone. No Aoilainn.

"We thought it prudent to leave our counterpart out of this discussion," the Unseelie Queen said.

Brilliant.

Which left Charlotte and Oleksander, who sauntered into the tent as though only paying a casual visit, their cheerful false greetings turning to grim silence as Charlotte came to my side, her towering grandfather crossing his massive arms over his broad chest.

"We're only waiting on Pender," Mom said.

"I'll seal our shielding anyway," Eva said. "I take it there is information we can have now, while we wait?"

"Exactly." I stepped forward. "Here's what we know." I just reached the part where the wild magicks had a message for me when they appeared in a flurry of fear. I registered the gasps of surprise from the others and reached for the gathered magic users with my various powers, feeling my egos latch onto and connect with their counterparts. The family magic took hold of Charlotte and Oleksander even as the wild magicks began their show all over again.

We all saw it this time, right from the beginning. I had no idea why their freedom was such an important part of the story, but they seemed keenly attached to the beginning, seeing me, the broken machine. And then, the flash of a mirror before being engulfed in darkness. Coming out of the black again.

To Liander Belaisle, smirking, laughing. Holding a shining glass shard in his hand.

They released us in a flare of power. I staggered back, expecting them to flee, but they didn't, instead heading for the front of the tent to swirl around Pender who dashed, panting, into our midst. They spun in circles, touching him, as his anguished face locked on Mom's.

"Talcort is missing," he choked. "He was a fragment holder and I've been unable to reach him."

Mom's pale face remained stoic as she nodded. "How long?"

"I don't know." Pender's hands shook as he pushed his hood back, running them through his thinning hair. "He was fine. I spoke to him myself this morning."

No one had a chance to ask questions. Still connected to me, their magicks woven through mine, the others felt Demetrius reach for me and fell still as the wild magicks wailed softly, musically.

Sadly.

Demetrius's mind locked in place with mine and—

—*I could suddenly see through his eyes, disoriented from the change in perspective. I felt his mind fighting itself, struggling for control over the insanity trying to pull him into darkness. I boosted his power, felt him stabilize, the hug of his gratitude, before I actually paid attention to what he saw.*

The edges of his vision were hidden inside a hood, head down, the sight of many feet before him, all draped in dark cloaks. In a stone room somewhere. The sound of a voice I knew jerked his head up.

Liander Belaisle stood only a few feet away, smiling, holding up the fragment of mirror. "The time has come, my brothers and sisters," he said. "To take what is ours. Are you ready?"

They roared their approval as Demetrius shuddered, fighting the need to press his hands over his ears. I helped him, calmed his heart even as mine, back in my body, fluttered like a dying bird.

The shard of glass flashed, a large opening appearing on the stone wall before the gathered sorcerers. Demetrius looked right, left, as if to show me what was coming.

Hundreds of them. Eager faces, twisted in hate and anticipation.

Oh. My. Swearword.

He marched with them, through the doorway to the stronghold plane, emerging through the giant mirror used as the main entry. Those ahead of him already fought the few Enforcers standing guard, but from the sadness in Demetrius's mind, I knew the outcome was inevitable.

They fell, the guardians left behind, under the power of the invading Brotherhood army.

Demetrius slipped to the left, out of the main line of marching sorcerers, slipping into a side alcove. His view was partially blocked by the doorway he peeked around, but I saw enough.

Enforcers came running and were taken down, their old faces crumpling in despair as they fell. Younger ones too, trainees from the look of them, dragged forward with bloodied and battered wounds, to be corralled with sorcery while Belaisle looked on.

And he wasn't alone, standing there all triumphant. Alison stood with him, a swirling mass of echoes floating above her. And, her pale face covered in her hands as her wide eyes stared in shock, Mia.

"Finally," Belaisle said. "Bring them."

A handful of sorcerers forced the gathered Enforcers forward, shoving them onto their knees to face the leader of the Brotherhood. I felt Demetrius whimper, heart clenching against what I guessed was coming.

Not even Belaisle was that much of a monster. These were old people and kids.

Please, no.

Belaisle's sorcery lashed out, wrapping around the group, pulling at their power. Mia cried out, turned away, Alison watching with dull dispassion as the Enforcers screamed in pain, collapsing under the siphon of their magic.

I watched him drain them of their lives through Demetrius's eyes, saw them crumble and fall to the ground, eyes staring, glazed, empty as, one by one, they died.

In a flash of hate-filled action, Alison lunged and gathered the fleeing echoes to her, forcing their remains into the swirling mass of ghostly shapes she already controlled.

Someone in the room with me at the pavilion choked on a sob, but I was still with Demetrius, locked into him, watching. Assessing past his need to grieve and sink into the black of insanity.

I felt his embrace, lost sight as he ducked into darkness—

—and left me.

I shook my head to clear it, entire body trembling as I looked around at the shocked, horrified and grief-stricken faces around me.

Cringed in agony as Pender Tremere cried out and fell to his knees, sobbing his despair while the wild magicks sang sorrowful counterpoint.

chapter twenty four

"It wasn't the conclave Belaisle was after," I whispered. "It was the stronghold."

Mom cleared her throat, tried to speak. Fell still.

I was such a fool. Idiot, moron. Why had I not considered this? Belaisle knew as well as I did where the last battle of ours was to be fought. And, until now, that battleground was in the hands of my allies.

No longer. If I wanted to fight him, I had to go through his people first.

Damn. It. All. To. Hell.

And I'd been worried, the very first time I'd seen the mirror shard, when I'd been freed from the stronghold prison. Remembered thinking I should ask about the fragments, about how the mirror worked. Why didn't I say something to Mom then?

As usual, my vampire sent, *you are beating an undead*

horse.

Sigh.

In case you've forgotten, my demon sent, *we'd just freed your mother from the Brotherhood and barely avoided being burned at the stake. We had a lot on our minds.*

We are all at fault if any are, Shaylee sent. *Now, can we please focus on what we're to do about it and drop the sorrow show?*

I snorted out loud. Everyone stared at me like I'd shot their dog. "Ego pep talk," I said. Yeah, that made them more confident. Now I saw real worry in their faces.

"When the North American Council first discovered the stronghold," Eva said, crisp and angry, "the Steam Union did nothing to stop you because we assumed it would remain safe in your hands."

Hang on. "Discovered?" Wasn't it the home of the Enforcers? And a prison.

Knew that one personally.

Mom shook her head, but not at me. "Until this point," Mom said to Eva, "we didn't think the stronghold was a target. Why would we?"

Eva's scowl darkened her face, making her look older. "You truly have no idea what you occupied," she said.

Mom stilled, body a statue. "Explain."

The Steam Union leader let out a massive sigh. Relented a little. "I should have been more proactive," she said. "I'm sorry, this is hardly your fault."

Mom continued to stare at her. We all did.

"In case you've missed it," Eva said in tone so dry I instantly wanted a glass of water, "the stronghold is a power source."

Oh. Crap.

Mom nodded slowly. "In a way," she said, tilting her head as if trying to process something on her own. "But yes, I do see that."

"No," Eva said, "you obviously don't. How much of it have you explored?"

Mom glanced at Pender who had finally managed to pull himself together.

"In the three hundred years we've lived there," he said, as if he made the discovery himself, "we've barely scratched the surface of what the stronghold—and the plane around it—have to offer."

Eva nodded sharply, as if to affirm what she already knew. "Whoever made that place," she said, "it wasn't any of us."

Meaning.

The maji.

Pender shook out his cloak and fixed Mom with a steady stare.

"I will raise an army at once," he said, "and retake our stronghold."

Didn't he just hear what Eva said? Not his.

Maybe mine?

Mom didn't say anything. Looked at me instead.

And I... had no choice. Shook my head.

Her shoulders sagged a fraction. "I won't throw good Enforcers after the dead, my friend." She hugged herself a moment before dropping her arms, face flashing from fear back to steady and calm. "We have no defense against the Brotherhood."

"But we do." I was surprised to hear Eva speak up. And, from the startled but happy look on Piers's face, so was he.

Mom turned to the Steam Union leader and nodded once. "I had hoped we could ask for your assistance," she said.

How proper. So clean and diplomatic. And yet, I knew if Mom let go, if we dissolved as a group into despair as Pender had, we'd be lost.

Rigid control it was.

Though I knew it was a good thing Eva was on our side, her explanation didn't give me nearly enough satisfaction.

She turned to her tall, handsome son before I could ask more questions. "Go home," she said. "Assemble the Union. It's time we took a stand against the Brotherhood."

I was almost pissed at him for the surge of satisfaction on his face. Would have been if his expression didn't darken into fierce joy.

"Yes, Mum," he said. And dove through a wall of

black without another word.

I knew how awesome it felt to be able to act at last after being held under tight rein for so long, so I hardly blamed him for his reaction. And, hopefully, with the help of the Steam Union, the Brotherhood wouldn't keep their possession of the stronghold for long.

"Are you saying the maji created the stronghold?" I needed to know what she knew.

Eva didn't look at me. "We're not certain," she said. "But we do know if the Brotherhood now have possession, they also are in control of a vast source of power." She held up her hands before I could attack her with another question. "Here's all I know," she said. "Our scholars tracked our occupation of the stronghold for almost a millennium. Then, we were kicked out. By whom? No idea. Or why, for that matter. The records are light—apocalyptic light." I could only imagine what that "kicking out" looked like that there were so few accounts left behind. "But shortly after that, the Steam Union and the Brotherhood split into their two factions." She finally looked up, met my gaze. "Our power was greatly diminished, our people fewer in number than our enemy. Again, there is nothing in our histories to tell us what caused the chasm. But it exists to this day, a fundamental breach between sorcerers."

The Light and the Dark. Holy, hang on a sec. Up until that point, they were one.

Was their rift the beginning of the prophecy I now chased down toward the very stronghold plane the Brotherhood took into their possession?

A shiver ran down my spine at the implications of these threads of fate running for so long, through so many conflicts. But it made sense, in a way. And helped explain further why Belaisle wanted the place. Not only to control the battlefield, but as a source to feed his sorcery.

So. Not. Good.

"Did the maji kick you out?" But what motivation would they have to do so? And yet, as far as I knew, they were the only ones capable of defeating the sorcerers.

Eva spread her hands before her. "As I said," she let them fall to her sides, "I've told you all I know."

"When we first found the stronghold," Pender said, voice so soft I almost missed the fact he spoke, "it was by accident. We uncovered a coven site, found a mirror shard." His anger had run out of him, despair trying to find its way back in by the trembling of his lower lip. But he went on, tone growing in strength. "The stronghold fought us, fought our magic. It took many years for it to accept us. To welcome us and allow us to live within it."

I remembered Gram's insistence I not use my power inside the walls. Now I wondered if it was less to keep the Enforcers we evaded from knowing I was there than to prevent an attack from the stronghold. I'd felt the protections in the place, knew Eva's assessment of it as a power source was very true.

"Does that mean the stronghold might fight back against the Brotherhood?" Charlotte's eyes lit with wolfish tones. "It could do our job for us."

But Eva was already shaking her head. "They lived there once," she said. "And witnessing what we just did," her shudder was mirrored by the rest of us, "their use of power didn't trigger an adverse reaction."

Too bad. I would have loved to see the roles reversed.

The wild magicks suddenly settled around me, limp ribbons of grieving power. I welcomed them, let my egos soothe them even as Demetrius reached for me again—

—this time I left everyone else out of it as I looked through his eyes. Saw Belaisle standing over the broken machine, the same one I destroyed on the top of the Coterie Industries tower in Miami.

He gloated over it, the parts scattered through some kind of workshop.

"You were right to think they would bring it here, my lord." One of Belaisle's bullies looked around, a hulking mass of a man. So odd the small, slender leader of the Brotherhood liked to keep giants around him.

"Of course," Belaisle said, laughter in his voice. "How could they resist? And, in doing so, they fell right into my plans." He touched the twisted metal that had been the base of one of the crystals. "Once I could track the Enforcer doing the research through the touch of my power, it was simplicity to find him and watch him. And take back the shard and the power that is ours."

The Enforcer he killed. Pender called him Talcort. A scientist? Who made his own trap. So the machine was never meant to succeed, was instead a lure to me to create a beacon inside the stronghold for Belaisle to follow.

Despair woke inside me despite my best efforts. I thought I'd landed a blow against Belaisle. Instead, I gave him exactly what he needed.

How could I defeat someone who could outthink me so far in advance?

"And kill him." The larger sorcerer laughed. "Mortok said he pleaded for his life and gave up the key willingly."

Demetrius hissed in my mind, went dark—

—left me alone in my body again, still draped in the traumatized wild magicks, but with every pair of eyes in the room staring at me.

I had to tell Mom. Pender. Hated to, but had no choice.

The Enforcer leader's shoulders bowed so low when I finished explaining what I'd just seen I thought he might fall to the ground again.

"Miriam," Sunny's grim expression flared with spirit magic. "What do you want us to do?"

Mom's hesitation only lasted a moment. "We must end conclave," she said. "Send everyone home. Now that we know what the Brotherhood came to do, I doubt the others are in danger. But we must deal with this immediately."

Meira's knee-jerk reaction to that plan matched mine to a "T".

"We can't," she said.

"We concur," Niamh said, making me wonder who wore the pants in their particular Sidhe royal family. "The purpose of this conclave was to uncover those inside the Brotherhood's influence."

"That goal hasn't changed, Mom," Meira said. "I think it's even more important now than ever, considering what we just witnessed."

"Margaret Applegate is our main target," Eva said, nodding her agreement. "Freeing her, if such a thing is possible, will at least remove their influence over the witch nation if not help us," nice of her to think in plural terms, "retake the stronghold." She bowed her head to Pender. "For the Enforcers. Of course."

And other equally important reasons. Like me needing access to the last battle site. Something I'd failed to share up to this point.

Oops. My bad. Though I really wasn't looking forward to the reaction coming after my little announcement.

"The big fight Ameline Benoit and I are supposed to have with Belaisle?" I loved blurting. Had all kinds of great things about it. Like shocking the hell out of everyone so they didn't start yelling at me right away. "That's where the maji prophecy seems to think it's going to happen."

Eva blanched, gray eyes snapping with anger. "You planned to share this information at some point without being asked?"

Oh no, she did *not*. "I've been a little busy channeling a crazy dude," I shot back. "Give it a rest."

She shook her head, but backed off.

"So," I said, "anyone want to venture a guess as to why the stronghold is so important for the final shebang? Is it just for a power source? Because, from what I know, Belaisle controlling more power shouldn't matter in the end. No armies, no fancy footwork. Just a little cage match tied to the prophecy and maji and all that juicy stuff."

Eva looked lost, then angry again. "I'm missing vital information, it seems."

Sucked to be her.

Took all of five minutes to reciprocate with Eva and share everything I knew. Her look of frustration turned to shock and then worry as I finished up with the whole prophecy mumbo jumbo.

I had a feeling her opinion of me just took a nose-dive. At least where my involvement with her son was concerned.

"The important thing is we keep this to ourselves at this juncture." Sunny slipped her arm around my shoulders as if to protect me from the stunned and anxious Eva Southway. "If word were to reach the general population of witches the stronghold has fallen to the Brotherhood, we could face mayhem."

"Agreed," Mom said. "We can just be thankful our regular exchange and training programs with the other Councils were suspended in June in preparation for conclave. The Enforcers we lost were ours alone."

Pender jerked as though she'd poked him with a red-hot stick. "My order has been silenced," he said. "I've already seen to that."

Poor Pender. "No one is saying those under your command will speak out of turn," Mom said, coming to his side, laying a kind hand on his arm. "Very well, if this is the consensus. We carry on as though everything is fine. For tonight."

"While working together," I shot Eva a glare, "to make sure by the time this conclave is over, the stronghold is back in our possession."

"And the Brotherhood has been removed—their influence or their persons—from all of magickdom." Mom's grim tone matched my mood exactly.

And my desire to rid us of the Brotherhood. Imagine that.

The Steam Union leader looked like she wanted to argue for some reason. Was she having second thoughts? I just dared her to cross me.

Piers's mother or not, she wouldn't survive the

outcome.

"And if we are unable to reclaim the stronghold?" Someone had to say it. I was just glad it was Uncle Frank and not me.

Mom's shoulders twitched at the exact moment Pender's did.

"I won't accept that option," Mom said.

Neither would I.

chapter twenty five

I sat, knees jiggling, as the gathering of conclave attendees settled into their seats, chattering and smiling, laughing and talking around me. Clueless. While my stomach flip-flopped like a suffocating fish.

Shenka squeezed my hand, even her practiced smile tight around the edges.

Sassafras crouched in my lap, ears down, whiskers sagging.

Of course I told them. As soon as I walked through the door into our little quarters the night before, the pair of them pounced on me, demanding to know what happened.

I almost forgot the wild magicks, now burrowed under my clothing, hiding, their sorrow infectious as I filled the pair in on the latest disaster. Sassafras's soft moan joined Shenka's gasp of horror, the Persian slinking into my lap to press his face against my stomach as his grief shuddered through him.

"He killed them?" Shenka's eyes flooded with tears, dark skin shining with tracks of moisture as she let them fall, unheeded.

The Lawrence twins came to sit silently on one of the low couches, listening, absorbing, hugging each other as I finished the story.

Shenka stood, began to pace. She'd clearly adopted my favorite past time when agitated. "Miriam is right," she said. "We have to end conclave."

But Estelle shook her head. "No," she said. "We must do what we came to do."

"The stronghold can wait," I said. "And as tragic as the loss of those Enforcers is, we have to try to stay logical about this."

Me? Logical? Maybe I'd finally snapped. Lost my heart or something. Because I couldn't bring myself to feel anything past numb.

None of us slept much and, though I was used to going a few nights without rest, my immortality making it easy for me, the rest of my party wasn't so lucky.

Silent and grim, the twins chose to eat breakfast in the pavilion, but I insisted Shenka and Sassafras come with me.

And pretend at normal. Because, that was what Mom needed us to do.

I hadn't heard a word from Piers, and any attempt to connect with my mother was blocked. She had to be working, focused. Still, I could have helped.

Right. By alternating between moping in stunned unfeeling and thrashing around in fury.

Deluded much?

At least I had Shenka and Sass to lean on, to keep me focused. It felt so wrong to have the rest of the conclave carry on as though nothing happened. Because, to them, nothing had. Meira's grim nod to me as she took her seat, paired with the equally dark looks of her entourage, told me she'd filled them in on last night's events.

The Steam Union contingent, still minus Piers, looked equally as out of sorts, though to be honest, Eva never did show much emotion, so I hoped her attitude wouldn't be seen as unusual.

Sunny and Uncle Frank were naturally absent, but Chambrelle's nod to me, soft tilt of her head, told me they'd informed her of the pertinent details.

Only Mom looked calm, politely cheerful, as she took her seat at the head of the Council's box just as the carol of trumpets announced the opening of the second day of conclave.

Margaret Applegate's grinning triumph registered right on time. I held my breath, hating what was coming next.

Wishing Mom would speak first. Pissed she insisted

on allowing Applegate to out what happened last night.

It was our final decision, made together, though I still thought it was a terrible idea.

"If we appeal to the conclave in a position of weakness," Mom said, "we only give the Brotherhood an opportunity to show us as weak. But if Applegate brings it up, I'm hoping we can, instead, appear to be dealing with it instead of desperate."

Everyone nodded, thought it was a great way to go.

"Mom," I said. "That's a lot of hoping."

"Regardless how it comes out," Mom said, hands on my shoulders, face close to mine, "it's coming out, Syd. We might as well see what the Brotherhood might reveal through their delight at our loss rather than try to put a cork in something that's already happened."

Grumble. Mumble. Sigh.

"I've received word," Applegate said, bringing me back to the frustration of the present, voice carrying through her magic, "there was an attack on the Enforcer stronghold last night." The entire gathering fell deathly silent as Mom's pleasant smile remained intact.

She didn't comment, nod her head, anything but keep that smile firmly fixed on her face.

Applegate went on.

"Is it true?" All innocence and fake concern. She turned to Mom with a little moue of shock. "Did the

Brotherhood kill your Enforcers and take control of the stronghold?"

I'd never heard a gasp that loud before, as though each and every person in attendance drew a breath at once. The sides of the tent swayed from the change in air pressure as the focus turned to Mom and crushed down on her like the weight of the entire world.

Mom did nod at last, hands still and silent in her lap as she acknowledged the fear pushing against her. "It is true," she said. "For now."

The sigh following stirred the gathered magicks, woke the wild ones still hovering against my skin as though needing my warmth and presence to ease their pain.

"I see." Margaret frowned, turned to the gathering. "And she claims she is able to keep all of us safe. When she can't even protect her own territory."

Bitch. Bitchy bitchass mother witch of a bitchbag.

Before Mom could say anything, as the gathered magic users absorbed what Margaret said, she smiled. Beamed. Raised both hands.

"Fear not," she said. "For there is another explanation for all of this."

Mom's eyes locked on mine.

Syd, she sent. *I think I know where this is going at last.*

Then she was way the hell ahead of me.

Do not, she sent, *under any circumstances, react. Do you hear me? Just trust this is necessary. And will hopefully show us what the*

Brotherhood is after here at conclave.

There was her "hopefully" again.

Wait. React? To what?

I had my answer a heartbeat later as a gaping black hole opened in the middle of the empty center of the pavilion.

And Liander Belaisle strode through.

Choke. Gasp. Snarl.

Syd. Mom's power slammed against me, pinning me to the back of the bench as my egos fought each other for the right to kill his arrogant ass. *He's not here.*

He. Was. Right. There.

But no. No, Mom nailed it. An illusion stood before us, a projection he sent through the unnatural gash he'd made in the veil.

Coward didn't even come himself.

Fear pulsed through the crowd, but no one moved. Not while he smiled up at Margaret, then turned in a slow circle, his projection spinning until he bowed to Mom.

"Allow me to introduce myself," he said.

"I know very well who you are," Mom said.

"Of course you do." He turned, met my eyes. "Ah, Sydlynn. Delightful."

Just let me go after him, my demon hissed. *In and out, Entrails 'R Us.*

"I'm afraid you've been misinformed," he said to the gathering as though not needing me to acknowledge his greeting. "As usual, my people are vilified, stories told out of turn by a handful of vindictive witches."

My stomach cramped as my demon roared and surged against the confines of Mom's magic.

Remember, she sent. *To most of the witches here, the Brotherhood are just a dark sect of sorcerers, more a myth than reality in their closed-off lives, not the enemy we've come to despise. Only we have had real contact with them and understand the impact they have on our planes.*

Us. And Applegate.

"As it turns out," he went on, "we're not so bad." He ran both hands down the front of his double-breasted suit coat, flashing another smile. "We just want to get along." Tell me the conclave wasn't buying this slick delivery? "And the accusation of our 'attack' is unfounded. As I can explain, if permitted?"

No one argued. I think partly because, if my allies were like me, they couldn't muster a word to say.

Belaisle took the quiet for acceptance. "To do so," he said, "will take a proper address of your fine conclave." His smile turned down to an artful frown. "I can't tell you how hurt I was to be overlooked for an invitation to this lovely get together."

Mom's power retreated. *Okay,* she sent. *Kill his ass. Make it look like an accident.*

Too late, and we both knew it.

Margaret gestured to the gathered leaders. "The

circumstances of Master Belaisle's arrival may be unusual," she said. "But we have allowed other races and magical powers to attend our conclave. Would it be right to exclude the Brotherhood?"

A vote. All righty then. He'd have his ass kicked and I could go after him.

Alone.

And screw the prophecy.

Panic set in as hands rose to contest it. Meira, of course. Chambrelle for Sunny. Oleksander with a nasty expression on his face. Mom. And Odhran.

Not enough. Damn it, what the hell?

Was Mom really right about the witches?

"And all in favor?" Margaret's sickening smile told me what I already knew as hands shot up.

Every Council but Mom's. Aoilainn, I'm sure just to piss off her Unseelie cohorts. And, to my utter shock, Eva Southway.

Belaisle's smile widened, cream and cats coming to mind. "Your faith in me is appreciated," he said. "My party will arrive presently." He turned and bowed his head to Margaret who returned the gesture before he vanished through the black hole.

Which remained, gaping emptiness taunting me.

Maybe this was a good thing. If he was here in person, I could slice and dice without having to chase him down.

Mom, I sent. *Haven't you warned them about the Brotherhood?* What the hell had she been up to all these months?

Of course I tried, Mom sent, her exasperation coming through. Boy, was it. *Might as well beat a brick wall with a soggy noodle for all they listened.*

I'd beat them, all right.

If it doesn't impact their little circles of influence, they bury their heads in the sand and sing nonsense until you go away. Her anger dissipated, turning to disappointment. *We've become so afraid of being noticed, of being discovered, taught so well to hide who we are as a race, we witches no longer can see trouble even when it's delivered to us in a hand-wrapped package.*

My knee bounced so hard the heel of my foot hurt from the impact.

We have to do something. Warn them again.

I wish it were that simple, Mom sent. *I fear our need to go unnoticed is our greatest weakness.*

Maybe I could change that. Peel away Belaisle's skin so the gathered witches could see just what he was made of.

Figuratively. Of course. The real skinning would come later, in private, where my demon could enjoy herself without being interrupted by people screaming and throwing up.

Wouldn't you know, Margaret thought of everything?

"Only one matter to bring up before our

Brotherhood friends join us." Applegate jabbed a finger in my direction. "It is very well known Sydlynn Hayle has a grudge against the Brotherhood in general, Liander Belaisle in particular." From the bemused looks on the gathered witch's faces, it was no such thing. Mom was right. Clue. Less. Applegate went on anyway. "It is my belief his life will be in danger if she is allowed access to him while he attends conclave."

You bet your booties, lady.

I choked on fury while she cornered me as neatly as Mom did the werewolves the day before. "Since there is precedent set," she said, "I order she be held responsible for his safety during the course of this conclave and, should anything happen to him or his people, she be held to the fullest extent of our laws."

"Considering you don't preside over this conclave," Mom said, voice dry and heavy, "your order is denied."

I could feel the argument coming, but was forced to sit there with my mouth shut.

Or blurt something unfortunate.

"We don't want our guest to feel unwelcome or in danger," Margaret said, changing tactics. "Knowing Coven Leader Hayle's power, she is the only logical one at present to ensure Liander's safety."

While the other Council Leaders balked at Margaret's heavy-handedness, they softened to this argument. Which made me grit my teeth in frustration.

Damned witches were all the same.

Mom's power scorched the edges of mine, but in anger at the situation, not at me.

"Very well," she said. *I'm sorry, Syd*, she sent.

Don't be, I sent back, mind churning over the possibilities. *At least this way we'll have him where we want him when the time comes.*

Mom's power withdrew as her lips curved into the barest smile.

I had a feeling I'd have help stripping his skin from his body one tiny piece at a time.

Chapter Twenty Six

Mom broke the conclave for a half hour to have a pavilion erected for the Brotherhood. I held my seat, eyes locked on the gaping hole where Belaisle and his people would soon emerge and struggled to keep my cool over Eva Southway's betrayal.

She reached for me with her sorcery before I could decide whether Piers would still be interested in me if I murdered his mother.

We'd lost anyway, she sent. *And I, for one, would prefer to have Liander Belaisle in reaching distance.*

Except he's coming here with a plan, I shot back at her, hating she was right. *And previous experience tells me whatever he has up his ugly designer sleeves will make your little attempt to corner him look like a sixty-year old pageant queen on crack.*

She laughed softly in my head. *I've had doubts about my son's interest in you*, she sent. *And now I understand what he sees, what I missed.* She paused. *I have absolute faith you will prevail, Sydlynn Hayle. The rest of us are simply at your service.*

I glared at her even as she tipped her head to me and went back to speaking to Felix.

Hrumph.

Mom was just settling into her seat again when the black pit pulsed and Liander walked out, a small group of Brotherhood at his back. I recognized the bully from the lab immediately and, to my shock, another familiar face.

Rupe was with him. Once my friend, the Goth known as Blood, tied to Mia when she was Pain, Rupe had been manipulated by Ameline, and, thanks to Belaisle, uncovered his own sorcery.

And joined the wrong side.

The tall, well-dressed young man waved at me with a grin, and Mia's defection suddenly made all the more sense. Her Pain to his Blood. She'd always thought he was her other half. Was broken when his parents moved and they were parted.

I guess she never did get over him. And now, thanks to Belaisle's conniving, she had to think trading sides meant having Rupe back, too. Though he had to have promised her magic.

A double header Mia would have never been able to resist.

I flashed my teeth, leaning forward until Sass hissed at me, and waved back to the traitor who used to be my friend, hoping somehow, in her broken little mind, Mia would wake and see who she'd chosen to trust. Putting all of my fury for her into my glare at him.

Rupe had the good sense to break eye contact.

The hole closed, Belaisle's three Brotherhood members in keeping with the number permitted. He'd thought of everything, hadn't he? He gestured for his people to precede him as he smiled, the picture of benevolence. Too bad his soul was a gaping hole of nothing.

"If I may," he said, addressing Mom. "My absence yesterday denied me the opportunity to speak on the behalf of my people."

I could tell Mom wanted to squash him like a bug, but her grace was legendary. "Proceed," she said.

Liander stood in the middle of the vast empty pavilion center, as calm and comfortable as a master magician casting an illusion over an audience. "I could tell you about the last century of my people's development," he said, "but the Brotherhood instead prefers to look to the future and our plans for it."

This should be good. I felt Sassafras's body shake as he growled silently, hyper-focused on the sorcerer.

We all were, down to the last of us. Even me.

"Which is part of the reason I wished to join conclave," Belaisle went on. "The future. And our desire to change the way magic is perceived by normals."

Say what?

"Too long have those with power hidden behind shields and false lives, pretending to be who we are not." Holy. Crap. No way Tallah's visit was from the Steam Union, or any kind of coincidence. Now I knew Belaisle was behind it all along. "Even as normals destroy this plane with their greed and industry." Oh, and Coterie Industries wasn't involved? He was such a charlatan. "It is time all magic races work together to enforce our protections and guidance of this plane." He turned to Meira. "Of all planes."

While the other magic races simply scowled, I thought one or two of the gathered witches might dissolve into puddles of panic. A roar of terror raced around the circle of watchers, witches actually clutching each other in fright.

If Belaisle wanted to empty the place, he was doing a good job of it. Way to make friends, loser.

Mom's power took firm hold of the space and shut everyone down.

Just in time for my sister to make a wisecrack.

"Perhaps if you'd come to us before attacking the Enforcer stronghold," Meira said in her best deadpan politician's voice, "there would have been a chance to hold such a conversation."

As if. But the jab hit home.

I hope he bled from it.

"Not so," Belaisle said. "But I'm glad you brought it up, Your Highness."

The scrabbling need to escape the idea of exposing themselves had faded to a soft skim of anxiety so sharp the sides of the tent were in jeopardy. Still, the Asian Council Leader seemed poised as she rose to speak.

"What was your purpose?" Sumiko's face settled into cold composure, soft Japanese accent appearing over her perfect English. "Such an attack goes against the very laws we strive to uphold." While she'd agreed to allow him entry, it appeared she didn't trust him either.

At least not everyone lost their damned minds.

"You may not be aware," he said, "but the stronghold, as you call it, does not, and never did, belong to the North American Enforcer order."

Knew that. Now everyone did. Couldn't keep a lid on this, either, turned out. Liander had all the answers to the unspoken questions weighing on conclave tied up in a pretty bow he handed to the gathering in his silken voice.

"I doubt your Enforcers know who the real creators of the empty plane are," he said. Maji, jerktard. So there. "Nor did they desire to find out." He turned to Mom who shook her head.

"It has long been a question on our minds," she said.

"The empty plane is ours," he said. "Created by the Brotherhood almost four millennia ago. It is, in fact, our home. Was lost to us when the maji attacked during the time of the Egyptian Pharaohs."

Liar. At least, if Eva was to be believed. Could I believe her? *Mom.*

We have no way of knowing if Eva's information is right. She sounded a little desperate. *It could be true, Syd.*

Hell no.

"I'm hearing lots of air come out of your mouth." Yeah. Pot. Kettle. Wasn't shutting me up, though. "But I'm not seeing any proof, Belaisle."

He looked up at me with the most condescending tsk I've ever had the fury to be targeted with. Turned to Mom. "You need to teach your little maji patience, Council Leader."

Splutter. Choke.

Grrr.

"The North American council discovered it, quite by accident, I understand." Liander waited, eyebrows raised, for Mom to respond.

"Three hundred years ago," she said. "A mirror shard was uncovered in an abandoned coven house."

"Not a coven house," he said. "But a *Brotherhood* historic site."

Mom didn't comment. From the feeling around me, the way resistance faded at his words, she didn't have to.

We'd lost the popular vote. If not the stronghold itself forever.

"Your Enforcers repurposed our home," he said.

"Something we only discovered recently." Okay, now I knew he was lying. Belaisle must have known about the Enforcer's occupation ages ago. Why else would he have tricked the order into taking the machine back to the lab? "When we found out our ancestral plane was occupied, we reacted with anger." Regret, so false and overdone, pulled at his face. I wanted to smack it away, tear him open, show the gathering what I saw.

Felt.

The emptiness in his heart matching the nothing of his sorcery.

"We managed to acquire the means to return, only to be confronted with an attack." The memory of Demetrius's experience surged inside me, reminding me how much of a sociopath Liander really was. "And, sadly, we answered with force." He shrugged. "The Enforcers refused to be evicted, leaving us no choice but to answer fire with fire."

Is that what he called it.

"You murdered innocent elders," Mom said, voice steady, calm as though discussing the weather. "And young trainees just learning the Enforcer craft. You call their presence an attack, Liander?"

Maybe it was the cynic in me that thought the stares and whispers from the gathered witches were a little too excited, too titillated by the reveal. Like this whole mess was here for their entertainment. Not something to be taken seriously.

I opened my power to show them what Demetrius showed me. We'd see then what they thought of today's program.

A pair of sharp nails dug into my arm in a tight pinch, shattering my furious intent. I turned, scowling, locking gazes with a pair of faded blue eyes.

Don't do anything stupid. Gram's mind was thin, distant, but there, with me. *Won't get us anywhere. He's telling the truth about most of it.* Varity squeezed in beside her and nodded. *Enough truth the rest of it won't matter in the end. The bastard is a master of lies, but in this instance, he's right. The stronghold was never ours. And the loss… casualties of our little war.*

What are you doing here? I wanted to hug Gram even as I stared at the pair in shock. *How did you get in?*

Gram snorted while Varity rolled her eyes at me.

Just try and keep us out, Varity sent.

We felt the stronghold fall. Gram's eyes narrowed, lips a slash of anger. *Couldn't just sulk in my room and not try to do anything.*

So what about the stronghold? I sent. *There are other ways in.* My excitement started to bubble. *There has to be a way to take it back.*

Gram shrugged her thin shoulders under the borrowed black robe she wore. *Now that he has them convinced,* she gestured at the gathering, *an attack to take it back will be seen as an affront on another magic race.*

I'd had my hands tied before. But this was ridiculous.

I have my doubts the Brotherhood were the creators of the plane, Gram sent, reaffirming Eva's thin information. *I think it's more likely the maji were the masters of it at one point.* Knew it. *But I don't have proof.*

Bummer.

There was one way to find out. "How do we know you created the plane?" I pushed against his power as he turned to me with a smile.

A knowing smile, the bastard.

"Perhaps you should ask your friends," he said. "The real maji."

Oh no, he did *not*. And yet, he might as well have punched me in the gut. Belaisle knew where I was heading with this.

And he already had an answer.

I called Iepa anyway, not expecting a response. Felt her sadness as she responded.

She never responded.

Unless it was to stab me in the damned back.

Why did I bother?

She appeared next to Belaisle, a wavering, soft form hovering over the ground. Her power radiated outward, touching the far walls of the pavilion, leaving absolutely no doubt who—and what—she was. Forget the gasps, this conclave had enough of them today already. I glared at my maji guide/slayer of hope as she bowed her head to me.

"The empty plane was once the home of the sorcerers," she said as her iridescent power floated around her. She didn't say they created it, though, did she? "All sorcerers." Her eyes drifted to Eva Southway. "Before the break."

So they were one big, happy family once, were they?

I almost pushed her about the real creators of the plane until I snagged on the loophole she'd made.

Did she just give me a way to access the stronghold through the Steam Union?

Iepa didn't stay, flashing out again even as the conclave broke into excited chatter. I locked gazes with Eva who only held mine a moment before looking away.

What was churning behind her gaze? And would it work to our advantage?

Anger burned a hole through me as I threw some parting words after Iepa.

So nice to see you, I sent with as much venom as I could muster. *My day wouldn't be complete without you stabbing me in the back.*

She didn't answer.

Exactly as I expected.

chapter twenty seven

A second gaping hole opened and Piers Southway stepped through. From the easy grin on his face, he'd managed to listen in. Alone, towering over the shorter, more slender Belaisle, he saluted the leader of the Brotherhood.

"I think I heard a little birdie," he said. "She mentioned something about the empty plane. How it was once the home of all sorcerers." Piers stroked his chin with one hand before winking at the now scowling leader. "Does that mean I get to pick the paint color for my new room?"

A titter of laughter raced around the tent. I could feel Eva's power pushing against her son, saw the flicker of anger on her face, but cheered inside as the young Southway did what his mother refused to do.

Challenged the Brotherhood.

"Steam Union," Belaisle almost spat at Piers's feet. "You're not sorcerers. When you're not hiding in mouse holes, you're just lapdogs of the witches."

Since when did witches and the Steam Union work together?

Just petty jealousy on Belaisle's part, maybe. I was pretty sure he never meant to let his temper slip. To show his shark-like underbelly. Doing so broke the spell of words and persuasion he held over the gathering, their support retreating in a tangible wave.

Go for the throat, I sent. *Nice and juicy.*

Patience, my pet, Piers sent back.

What was he up to?

At least Iepa gave us something we might be able to use after all.

Piers turned to his mother. "Mistress Southway," he said. "As your representative, I request the right to petition for entry into our ancestral home." Oh, he'd been listening all right, the bratski. His voice thrummed with emotion as he spun on Mom next. "How our hearts have longed for a place to belong, Council Leader. A true home where we can dwell and be at peace with our dear brothers." His hand fell on Belaisle's shoulder.

Liander shrugged it off with a snarl.

I coughed out a laugh, wanting to dance up and down in my seat and only holding still due to the hold Gram had on my arm.

Mom nodded graciously. "We will add the discussion to our schedule," she said. "Now, Master Belaisle, if you will please take your seat, we have proceedings to reconvene."

Oh, snap.

I had to endure staring at Belaisle the rest of the morning, but it was worth it. Just to see him scowl.

Which made me suddenly nervous as we broke for lunch. No way he didn't foresee a snag like this one. Or did he? Maybe Iepa's little pronouncement threw him for a loop.

No way. Wouldn't underestimate him ever again.

I waited for most of the place to empty before turning to Gram and Varity.

"Okay," I said. "Harvard. I'll go kick some ass and you two back me up."

Gram swatted me. "Don't be an idiot," she snapped. "The stronghold isn't going anywhere." She hesitated, jaw set. "Where is Ameline?"

I blinked in shock. "Gram, I know you need your power back, but—"

She whacked me again, anger burning in her eyes. "When in the world will you ever learn to pay attention, girl?"

Ouch. Physical form and feelings hurt, I shrugged.

And got it as Gram sighed.

"You want me to call her," I said. "And go after

Belaisle."

"Ding ding," Gram said. "She finally woke the hell up and got it."

Sassafras's tail thrashed against my thigh. "Nicely," he said.

"No time for nice," Gram shot back. "No time for anything."

Hell in a hand basket.

I fought the urge to leave right then, spent the next several hours arguing with myself and the need Gram saw to pull Ameline into this mess with me. A mess she would, most likely, add to if given a chance.

Tallah, naturally, played right into Belaisle's hands, giving her address as Mom had encouraged her to do. Before we both understood just how manipulated the Hensley leader had been.

How we all had been.

I hated Belaisle with a passion so powerful as I listened to Tallah speak in a clear, ringing voice, her hope feeding the conclave he'd buttered up, it was almost impossible to hold still.

And, coming from one of their own, they began to buy it, these silly witches. Her initial mention as she stood to address them raised the expected response.

"Council Leaders," she said in her ringing voice, stunning with her glowing dark skin, long, straight hair to her waist, bright red dress standing out like a rose among a black garden of witches, "though perhaps his message might not be trustworthy, I would ask we at least consider enough time has passed for us, as a nation, to reveal ourselves to normals and take our place at their sides in ruling this plane."

They didn't have the same excessive reaction they did when Belaisle brought it up, but close. In fact, I think a pair of old witches down two rows from me might have almost expired from shock at the mere mention.

This was giant, taboo, holy crap run away stuff Tallah was talking about. Witches had long memories, especially when they were connected to burnings and stakes and Inquisitions. Normals hunted us, weren't prepared to share their little lives with those who would always be more powerful.

And yet, they didn't run, the conclave of witches. They fanned themselves after shrieking and covering their ears. Finally stilled enough Tallah could continue.

"The modern world is far different than the one we fear," she said, turning in a slow half-circle, as though addressing each and every witch. "Technology has done much to dull their superstitions, to making us legend." She bowed her head to the scowling werewolves. "All of us legend."

Aoilainn looked bored, bless her. The Unseelie King and Queen refused to meet Tallah's gaze.

As for Chambrelle, she shook her head, face grim.

"You're a fool," the vampire representative said, red hair glowing in the light as she stood to face Tallah down. "My queen and her people haven't had the luxury of hiding as well as the witches. They have been hunted by normals throughout the ages. It is only through sheer force of will and absolute caution they have been kept safe from exposure and I, for one, will never allow those I guard to fall under the horrors of normal's attention." She sat, arms crossing over her chest.

Tallah's smile faltered as Oleksander pounded the thin rail in front of him and shouted something in Ukrainian. I could only imagine it was in support of Chambrelle as she nodded to him with gratitude on her face.

Considering both Odhran and Niamh continued to ignore Tallah, their vote, and that of the silent and petulant Aoilainn, were answer enough.

"Coven Leader Hensley," Mom said. "Revealing ourselves to normals isn't our decision to make alone. Other magic races must be in line. For, once normals are aware of us, surely they will go looking to see if there are those with power beyond our ken."

Tallah bobbed a nod of agreement. "I only ask we discuss it," she said, her disappointment clear in her voice.

After centuries of fear, of hiding, the witching nation, steadied by the distrust of the other magic races, did what they always did.

Refused to change while pretending they might, maybe, someday, if pigs flew and unicorns pooped rainbows.

Didn't mean they weren't going to talk it to death, though. Because, what would be a discussion they planned to do nothing about if it wasn't picked to death down to the dregs of its meaning?

The debate ran from Council to Council for the next several hours, a ring around the rosie from should we to hell no.

And all through it, Gram poked. Prodded. Jabbed. Snarled.

Until I just couldn't take it anymore. So, as the sun began to set that evening, I finally tossed up my hands when conclave ended, the gathered witches—if only the witches—chattering in excitement about the possibility of revealing their power for all the world to see. I spun away from Gram's steady pick-pick-picking that hadn't eased up all afternoon and went in search of my enemy.

I left them all, Sass safe with Shenka, waiting until I reached the outside of the pavilion before tearing a thin hole in the veil and stepping into Ahbi's embrace.

I guess I need to find Ameline, I sent, grumpy.

My demon grandmother grunted. And dumped me in the trees just outside the conclave site.

Testy old bat was in as bad a mood as I was.

"I was wondering when you'd get around to looking for me."

My stomach knotted further as I realized Ahbi hadn't abandoned me there out of pique, though I almost leaped out of my own skin as the wild magicks, no longer content to remain hidden, shrieked in fury and fled in a flare of power.

Ameline emerged from the dark trees, pulling back the hood of her stolen Enforcer robe, watching them go with speculation before meeting my eyes. "Nice to see you, Syd," she said. "Ready to do things my way yet?"

It was only sheer will keeping my hands from closing around her slender neck. Her ice blue eyes told me she found it funny.

I was not laughing.

"When this is over," I said, "when Belaisle and his people are toast, I'm going to kill you for what you did to my grandmother."

Grandmothers.

But Gram, most of all. I could feel her power crawling around inside Ameline. Felt the contact, the familiar connection. My demon howled her pain and need to jerk the bitch's heart from her chest.

Ameline laughed. "We'll see," she said. "Now, if you're through with your little show of force, we need to talk."

I shoved her back into the woods as an Enforcer

patrol went by. Ameline didn't seem worried about being caught, which made me nervous.

"About the stronghold," I said.

Ameline's frown of pity fired up my temper again. "Irrelevant for now. His seizure of the site means nothing to us. Not in the end. We will arrive at the appointed time and place when fate decides no matter what Liander Belaisle's plans to the contrary."

Was it wrong she actually made me feel better with that pompous little speech?

"There will only be four of us in the end," she said. "And all will be decided one way or another."

True. Okay then.

She leaned toward me. "You are correct, though," she said, like it hurt her. "This must end. It is in our power to bring the prophecy to fruition, not his."

Good to know. "How?"

Ameline shrugged. "I have almost all I need," she said. "Only two are missing. The first I think I can handle on my own. But the second is more problematic."

She was talking about power. She already had a baby soul from the Sidhe, born of Bronagh, Aoilainn's main advisor, and Cian, the Gate creator, which still gave me the creeps. Like Liam and Ameline had a kid. Shudder. And with Gram's witch magic tied to the Enforcers, Ameline's power there was set, as far as I could tell. She was born with creation magic, like me, and her sorcery was growing, I felt that much.

Which left vampire.

And demon.

"This could all be over tonight," Ameline said in a reasonable voice, "if you're willing to give up your sister."

chapter twenty eight

My demon reacted well before the words Ameline spoke made it through my stunned mind. She lunged forward, taking control of me, driving my right fist toward the other witch's face.

Ameline was clearly ready for my reaction, dodging to the side, though she underestimated my demon's speed. My knuckles impacted her shoulder as she twisted to the side, sending her spinning as my right foot lashed out and caught her in the ass, propelling her forward into a tree.

Ameline spun, snarling, power surging.

"If we fight," she said, "it will attract the Enforcers. And this will be over before it began, the Brotherhood the victors. Is that what you want?"

"You." I cut the air with one hand, back in control as my egos boosted my fury. "Stay." I lashed at a tree, sending a vibration through it so powerful the top of the evergreen shook and swayed. "Away." A deep, rumbling tremor made Ameline stagger while Shaylee held me still. "From. My. Sister." I ended with a pulse of spirit power that took her full in the chest.

She absorbed most of it, but the attack left her gasping even as Galleytrot's desperate mind reached for me.

Syd. Thunder rumbled in his voice. I felt him running, covering the miles, heading for me.

Stop, I sent back. *It's fine. Protect the family.*

He skidded to a halt. *You're sure?*

Nothing you can do, I sent as I faced down my opponent, both of us panting a little. *Just having a chat with Ameline.*

Ah. Galleytrot paused. *Have fun, then. Don't break the plane, okay?*

No promises. I let him go, grateful for the aside. Talking to him calmed me enough I was able to speak without hurting someone.

"You heard me," I said. "Touch one hair on Meira's head and the prophecy can wait for another dark maji to come along."

"Fine," Ameline snarled. "Fool. But when you change your mind, when you realize this is the only way, I'll be waiting."

Blue magic flared around her, the power of the Enforcers as she drew on Gram's magic, and vanished.

I cursed a long string of vile words in a variety of languages while stomping a useless circle in the spread of fallen pine needles. That's how she'd managed to avoid notice, set off the wards. She felt like an Enforcer.

And I was an idiot, for real.

I finally cooled enough to stop and evaluate.

We can't let her have Meems, my demon growled.

Never. *Cold day in hell*, I sent.

And yet... I hated it when my vampire said that.

There will be another way, Shaylee sent.

We can hope, my vampire sent. *Though perhaps we need to ask Meira herself before we choose for her.*

There's nothing to choose, I sent in a snarl before jerking open the veil.

What a ginormous waste of time.

Ahbi hugged me fiercely as though agreeing with my determination to keep Meira safe before depositing me just outside my pavilion. With a whisper of warning.

Didn't take long for me to figure out why Ahbi spit me out here. Not while Belaisle and Vasyl stood talking. With Celeste Oberman in their midst.

They spotted me before I could overhear, Belaisle's fake smile widening as he waved for me to join them. Vasyl's shark eyes watched me, cold and silent as the tall vampire clan leader glared her hate for me.

"Look who decided to make an appearance," Belaisle said as he turned to Celeste. Full dark had just settled. She didn't waste any time. "As a representative of Blood Clan Sthol and her majesty, Queen Pannera."

I was so over the show, he had no idea.

"How nice for you," I said before turning my back on them and walking away.

Not the response Belaisle was expecting, I don't think. It took him a few trotting strides to catch up to me, smile still in place.

"I just wanted to thank you for such a lovely event," he said. "Though I've enjoyed my time among you all, duty calls."

Leaving so soon? Damn, I knew he had more on his agenda than aggravating me.

I stopped and turned to face him, seeing Celeste and Vasyl watching from the corner of my eye.

"I'll see you soon," I said, pouring sunshine and rainbows into my tone. "Oh, Ameline says hello. She's looking forward to it."

His smile flickered, hardened around the edges. "I'll be waiting," he said.

Opened a hole in the veil. And stepped through it with a small salute.

I ignored Celeste's laugh at my expense, refusing to acknowledge her at all. She was a minor player in this. It was Belaisle I had to worry about.

What the hell was he planning?

That man was giving me an ulcer so big it was about

to eat my liver for dinner.

The touch of Mom's mind, almost desperate, broke the nasty spiral of my thoughts and spun me around. She wasn't calling for me or anything. In fact, I think the connection was a mistake. But there was no way I was leaving her to face whatever it was that freaked her out.

I didn't run.

Not quite.

Her office was crowded with Enforcers, Pender right in front of her desk. I had to push my way through, saw Quaid glaring in fury. But not at me.

Their anger bubbled like a volcano waiting to erupt. Mom met my eyes as I joined her in facing down the need of the order.

Pender's gaze flickered to me, determination failing him for a fraction of a second. "We are ready to reclaim our stronghold, Council Leader," he said, voice vibrating and crackling with power. "Just give us the word and we will fight to the death."

A murmur of agreement ran through the watching Enforcers.

And I thought I was bad.

"My hands are tied," Mom said. At least she held steady, reasonable. "With the supporting information we received from the maji Iepa, it is clear we no longer have a right to the stronghold or the plane in which it rests."

Yeah, they took that well.

Mom squashed their furious response with a dose of Council magic. "Listen to me, all of you." They fell silent, all that duty and honor stuff shutting them up. Good for something, at least.

Oh, Syd. So cynical.

Mom went on. "There will come a time our people will stand again in the halls of the stronghold." They swayed like saplings in a strong wind at the formality of her words while I choked on how much she sounded like a bad epic fantasy novel. "But that day is not today. You must believe I will do everything in my power to restore our honor." There it was again. Stupid word, really. Foolish sentiment. What good was honor when all it got you was a pack of mindless drones hell bent on throwing their lives away for nothing? "For now, I ask you," her tone shifted, voice throbbing with power, "I order you, my Enforcers, to stay the course and have faith in me."

They shuddered as if she'd scratched them behind the ears and nodded as a group. All but Pender who jerked himself around and led them out.

I spotted Quaid leaving, head down and, on impulse, went after him.

Thank you for coming to my rescue, Mom sent softly as I ran after him.

My power hugged her in answer.

He was easy enough to corner in a dark alley between pavilions, my magic sliding around him, my hand on his arm turning him around. The guilt of the slap I'd delivered returned in a flare of hurt, but Quaid didn't seem to hold it against me.

Though he held something against me. The full length of him, crushed to me as he wrapped his arms around me and pressed his hungry mouth over mine.

I kissed him back, wanting to devour him, opening my power to his fully. Thoughts of Payten, of Piers and Liam, of Belaisle and the poor, dead Enforcers left me as the bond we shared, the link to our destiny, smothered my will and swallowed me whole.

When he came up for air, I panted against his throat, the heat of him the warmth I craved. Such an odd understanding. I'd lost the ability to feel heat and cold, at least environmentally. Had always showered in the hottest water I could, missing even that small joy now. But standing there, in Quaid's arms, in the circle of his devouring magic, I finally understood what I'd been longing for all along.

"I have to go," he said in a voice coarse from emotion. "My leader needs me."

I grasped his arms, anger flaring. "You promise me, Quaid," I said. "You swear to me you won't go to the stronghold."

He shivered. "Syd."

"It's your duty," I said, using it against him, "to uphold the command of the Council Leader." Quaid tried to look away, agony on his face, but I shook him from my hold on his arms and he met my eyes again. "You must protect your leader and your Council. And that means keeping Pender—and your sorry ass—away from the Brotherhood. Do you hear me?"

Quaid wavered, groaned softly. Bent his head over mine and touched my lips with his, the softest kiss, hot breath trickling over my skin and down into my lungs.

"I love you," he said. And left me there.

He might as well have just ripped out my heart.

"You believe him?"

I shrieked and spun, both hands pressed to my chest, to find Piers watching me from the shadows. His face showed no expression as he came to my side, looking up to where Quaid had gone before sighing and meeting my eyes again.

"You scared the crap out of me." I swatted his arm.

"Do you?" Piers's intensity freaked me out. "Do you believe him?"

"Yes," I whispered. Bit my lower lip.

The tall sorcerer nodded. "So do I," he said. "But that doesn't mean he's going to do the right thing."

I hugged myself, not wanting to have this conversation. I had enough going on, didn't I?

Piers didn't seem to care what I wanted.

"Love can only take you so far," he said. Paused. "You love another, too?"

I nodded, feeling miserable. I couldn't believe I just stood there, allowing Piers to strip my heart raw.

Oh, wait. Quaid did that already.

Right.

"Sometimes love isn't the important thing," Piers said. "Not at first."

I just stared at him a moment before speaking. "I don't love you."

He nodded. "I don't love you either," he said. "But I adore you. And I know we are compatible." He didn't try to kiss me. Far too practical for that at the moment. "And I have enough of a backbone to stand up to you when necessary." Damn him. He'd been talking to Sassafras. "Your Sidhe suitor doesn't have that quality."

That cat was a pelt for my floor when I caught him.

Piers backed off, blonde hair rippling in the light as he stepped out of the shadows. "Time does wonders," he said. Opened his mouth as if to say something else. Shrugged. "I spoke to Mum," he said, his abrupt about face making me twitch. "She's willing to try an infiltration, but fears we don't have the power to stand against the Brotherhood if they choose to expel us."

"Even if this conclave agrees you are part owners of the empty plane," I said, "Belaisle is under no pressure to allow you in." In fact, would probably enjoy crushing the Steam Union and laugh at the wails of anger from the Councils and other magic races.

"We need proof the Brotherhood are as evil as we know they are," Piers said. "To show the conclave they aren't to be trusted."

Because Belaisle had effectively hamstrung us when it came to warning the others.

Grrr.

"There's only one way," I said, knots loosening in my stomach as I finally decided to act. Funny how my tension eased when I was about to walk into danger. "We need a demonstration. And a willing witness to testify."

"Care to fill me in?" He followed as I strode off.

"I'm surprised you haven't thought of it yourself," I said. "We're out of options and, risky or not, we need to free Margaret Applegate."

chapter twenty nine

I picked up Shenka and Sassafras on the way to see Mom. Neither of them questioned my reasoning or asked where we were going until we sat in Mom's office. And not alone. Our little group had assembled yet again, Eva Southway's sorcery blocking off the room for privacy.

Because it didn't really matter at this point if the rest of the conclave knew we were talking. Belaisle's little show and Iepa's matching tell had blown the lid off everything.

When I laid out the way I saw things to Mom and the others, my mother sighed and sank back into her chair.

"While I agree with you," she said, "what you're suggesting is complicated."

Uncle Frank snorted. "That's a nice way to put it," he said. "Syd's about to start an international witch war in front of every High Council on the plane and you think it's complicated."

I rolled my eyes at him. "It won't be seen as interference if it works," I said. "Margaret will be free to say so."

"Wherein lies the issue at hand," Sunny said. "I don't mean to counter you, Syd, but what if you fail?"

No one said anything, though the ground under my feet trembled as Odhran and Niamh both scowled.

When the silence broke, it was the Unseelie Queen who shattered it. "There is no success without risk," she said. "I agree with Sydlynn, in this instance. It's worth trying, if only to ensure the Brotherhood no longer has control over one of the High Councils."

And all the witches underneath her, even without direct taint. An entire territory owned by the Brotherhood, able to act and react within our race, within our governing bodies, unchecked.

And ready to spread, if I knew Belaisle. To take over all witches, exactly what he wanted. Subtle and under the radar. Because someone like him would rather slip his way through a crack like a cockroach than actually attack head on.

The idea we could lose just by our own race's fear of taking action made my stomach ache.

It was then I understood why he brought up the idea of witches coming out. Not to encourage them. But to ensure they burrowed deeper into their private little groups, segregating them further as they ensured their coven's safety by minding their own business, secure in the fact they'd talked it out.

Oh. My. Swearword.

Evil and brilliant. He knew witches better than they knew themselves.

Mom said they were complacent, more interested in their petty little lives than the grand scheme. My job wasn't to destroy the Brotherhood. Though that would come.

My job was to make the witches pay attention.

How often had I heard that particular pair of words used together, aimed at me? Gram. Sassafras.

I was as guilty as everyone else of losing my focus. Sure, my problems and interactions were big picture. But I still didn't see the forest for the trees. My disasters kept me so wrapped up in what was happening to me and my family—and to the planes—I failed to recognize I was losing the real fight.

To wake up the witch nation. Before it was too late.

Okay. So how to manage something no one had ever done, not in the centuries since covens went into hiding?

Lost in me me me again. So much I almost missed it when Meira spoke up. "Have we managed to examine the others?" My mood lifted a little as Mom's smile appeared.

"We have," she said. "Thanks to Eva and her people."

"Surprising," the Steam Union leader said. "Europe is the only territory the Brotherhood affected."

Well, not exactly true. But Mom and her Council were free now, weren't they?

No time for personal back pats.

"The most dangerous part of this," Shenka said, voice quiet as though nervous to interrupt, "is the fact some of the younger witches are actually buying into what Belaisle is selling."

Hang on. Didn't I just have this conversation with myself?

"They'll back down," I said. "Witches always do."

Shenka's frown told me she disagreed. "Our coven has long been indoctrinated in radical ideas," she said. "It was my grandmother's wish, and my mother's, that witches be free." Shenka's voice rose in volume as her courage increased. "And they will maintain that goal. As will some of the more forward thinking."

A few rebels. I had to love them, wished I could make every witch like them, even as the desire to take them and shake them swamped me with need. "Thanks to Tallah," I said.

Shenka flushed, red tint flaring under her dark skin. "I'm well aware of my sister's faults," she said. "But we were raised to believe we could be liberated to use our magic in the open one day. And while I understand such a wish is foolhardy—as long as the Brotherhood is involved—it's still something I hope for myself." She paused as I let my magic hug her, apologetic. "She is motivated, has Miriam's blessing to pursue it during conclave."

Mom's hands settled on her desk. "If only I'd known the monster I was making. Even a few voices, a handful to step outside the boundaries, can reveal us to the normals and set off a chain of events we aren't prepared to face."

"That's Belaisle's fault," I said. "But now that it's out in the open, we need to cage it up again."

"Do we?" Shenka spoke up again. Hesitated. "We've been underground for so long, suppressing who we are. But this is the twenty-first century. The Dark Ages are long gone." She chewed her lower lip. "And the days of the Inquisition and the power of the Brotherhood over the church."

"My dear," Oleksander said, leaning over to pat Shenka's knee. "I can tell you, without a shadow of doubt, the moment you expose yourself to normals, you will be hunted and trapped, enslaved." He nodded his big head. "Studied and bred for more power. You understand?"

She sighed, sagged. "I know," she said. "But not if we used magic against them as defense."

Against normals? I shuddered. "You realize any plan of Liander Belaisle's is a bad one, right?"

Shenka's dark eyes were full of sorrow. "I just... I'm worried, Syd."

Mom stood and gestured to the others who rose. "I'll deal with Tallah," she said. "And I will speak to the other leaders about this nonsense." Shenka looked hurt. "I'm sorry," Mom said. "It's not nonsense, Shenka. But it is unthinkable."

My second backed off, head down, while I did my best not to storm off, find Tallah Hensley and beat some freaking sense into her.

Seriously.

"For now," Mom said, "our focus is on Margaret Applegate." She fixed me with a steady stare. "You have a plan?"

I didn't, not really. But Piers was way ahead of me.

"We do," he said, stepping to my side. "The sorcerer second of Eloise Brindle is the lynchpin to Belaisle's hold over Applegate." He smoothed his long, blonde hair with one hand, the other falling on my shoulder. "Syd gave me the idea to check." I did? "The power core of control, over Applegate, is no longer Belaisle's, but sits with Vasyl Krajnik."

That was good news, wasn't it?

Eva looked irritated to the point of snapping. "You are to ask permission before acting."

"Leave the boy," Oleksander said. "He's done well."

I'll pay for it later, Piers sent to me. *But it's worth it.*

"If we can free Eloise," Sassafras said, "you think Applegate will follow?"

"I know," Piers stressed the word as he addressed my demon cat, "if we break Vasyl, the controls over the entire territory will fall."

Big responsibility Belaisle laid on the other sorcerer's shoulders.

Meira's amber eyes glowed with fire. "You're thinking this is too easy?"

Fear crawled through me, not just about this, but about her. Ameline's face flashed in my mind as I stared at my sister.

Piers hesitated. "Perhaps," he said. His hand tightened on my shoulder. "If so, we're walking into a trap."

So what else was new?

Mom stared at her desk top for a long moment before looking up, face set. "Do it," she said. "But Syd must stay out of it."

I opened my mouth to protest, but she shook her head.

"The Steam Union are sorcerers," Mom said. "And have their own laws. Which means they are technically outside the witch network."

"I'm a sorcerer," I started.

"You're also a witch," Mom finished. "You can try sophistry all you want with me, missy. I refuse to give anyone reason to charge you with anything. All of your excuses and attempts to section off who you are and what you mean to different races is a smoke screen. You're on thin ice and you know it."

"She's not the only one stretching things, Mir," Uncle Frank said. "The sorcerers are at conclave, have agreed to follow conclave law."

Eva shrugged and smiled. "What's the worst that can happen? You all kick us out?" She nodded to Mom. "We'll do what we can."

"I can suppress my family magic," I said, fear tingling stronger, like a premonition of disaster waiting to happen. "It worked before." In Europe. Well, kind of worked. With a lot of talking and blustering and people who loved me threatening to blow up part of the Ukraine.

Mom's blue eyes held, not a scrap of softness in them. "You," she said, "will stay out of it. And that, Coven Leader Hayle, is a direct order from your Council."

Damn her.

We can handle it, Piers sent.

He had no idea.

chapter thirty

Piers walked me back to the pavilion alone. Shenka was already gone, chasing after Tallah, and Sassafras stayed with Mom. I wondered where Gram and Varity had gotten to, worry spiraling into a normal tornado of "holy crap what now" and "sigh".

"I hope you think about what I said earlier," Piers said as I stopped at the entry.

Huh?

Oh, right. The love thing again.

He bent, kissed my forehead, warm and tingling as his sorcery nuzzled against mine. It was the first time my normally hungry power blossomed and woke without trying to devour everything around it, instead accepting the touch of his magic.

"We make a great team," he whispered against my skin. "When you wake up, I'll be waiting." With that, he strode off into the darkness.

Guys were always doing that to me, damn it. Kissing me and leaving with some stupid line for me to mull over.

Jerks.

The twins fluttered around Demetrius who shoveled food into his face like he hadn't eaten for a week. I gaped at him a moment before rushing forward and falling into the chair beside him.

In a swirling mass, the wild magicks descended, settling on me once again, though they seemed to have recovered from their excessive grieving.

"Demetrius." I touched his arm as he smiled at me, blue eyes wide and staring.

"Yummynom," he said through the mouthful. "Jolly belly, Syd."

Oh boy.

He'd held it together long enough to return to us. Well, good enough, then. Even though I had a million questions for him, he'd earned his peace. And dinner.

But he shuddered as I pulled away, the strand of wild fire magic prodding him gently. I watched the life return to his eyes, awareness even as he gasped and almost choked.

I patted him on the back as he gulped a drink of water before sagging in his chair, food forgotten.

"Syd," he whispered. "Oh, Syd."

Tears leaped into my eyes. "I know," I said. "Thank

you for showing us. We needed to know."

His head bobbed, chin on his chest. "Hurts, owie," he said.

I just bet.

"Listen," I said. "There's more. Piers and the Steam Union are planning to go after Vasyl tomorrow and try to free Applegate." Why was I telling him? Because, even broken, even reduced to this tiny man who wore stained t-shirts and often had food in his teeth, Demetrius Strong suddenly reminded me so much of Gram I couldn't help myself.

I trusted him.

Imagine that?

He shivered, turned sideways in his chair, laying his head on my shoulder. "Won't be easy," he said.

I hugged him, cradling him like a toddler, rocking a little as the wild magicks slipped over him, cooing softly. "Will it work?"

Demetrius sat up abruptly, pointed at my chest.

"You might," he said.

I sighed. "I can't. Mom ordered me not to."

His sigh was long, drawn out, chest collapsing. "Then," he said, "dunno."

I sat back as he dove into his meal again. And focused on the wild magicks.

"You lot," I said. "Any help from the peanut gallery?"

They actually meeped as a unit. Froze in place.

Hmmm. "I need your help," I said, wondering how much they understood.

Twitch. Spark.

"Can you do anything to free the witches?" Applegate, Brindle, the Enforcers...worth a shot.

With a sob of compressing air, the wild magicks bundled together into a shining ball and vanished.

Cowards.

Still, it made me smile for some reason. Like a pack of bad kids running off when there were chores to be done.

Which meant I only had the hard way left.

Everything in me rebelled as I reached out to Ameline.

She answered immediately.

Here's the deal, I sent in a whip crack of magic. And told her what Piers had in mind.

She listened quietly until I was finished.

He'll fail, she sent.

Cynic, I shot back. But yeah. I already knew that, didn't I? *Fine*, I sent. *We work together*. I'd have to find a way around Mom's order.

Wait a second. Considering she'd given me total autonomy, did I have to follow her order?

Worth arguing with her about after the mess was sorted out.

But? Ameline's mind rang with amusement.

You keep your grubby paws off my sister, I snarled. My

demon pushed against her to add her own threat to my words. *We'll find another way to work this out.*

Ameline's artful sigh made my teeth ache. *So stubborn,* she sent. *As you wish. I'll be in touch.*

Cut me off. And no amount of screaming at her did me any good.

I really, really, really hated her guts.

Really, really.

Demetrius passed out on the couch, Shenka arriving home with a grim expression to cover him with a blanket after the twins retired to their beds.

She refused to talk to me about her sister, which I took as a bad sign. But I didn't push her. I wasn't the only one with problems I wasn't willing to share.

The next morning dawned bright and beautiful, warm even as the sun rose. The kind of day I used to love when I just wanted to be ordinary, a perfect day for soccer, hanging out in the back yard with some lemonade and a sappy romance novel and lying under the stars with Meira and Sassafras, making up stories about what we saw in the night sky.

Maybe I'd have days like those again.

I could only hope for that kind of peace.

The last day of conclave would be filled with policy arguments, new law and territory dispute rulings and any wrap-up needed from the last two days. Would be nice to have the issue of suddenly exposing all magic users to normals swept under the rug for another one hundred years. I laughed to myself, sipping a strong cup of coffee as I realized I was so wrapped up in what was going on behind the scenes, I'd paid little attention to the actual reason most of the magical races were here.

Let them make their rules and solidify their treaties. Live their lives in peace with their heads stuck in the sand. I had their backs.

And, honestly, wouldn't have trusted anyone else to the job anyway.

The air of excitement was back, despite the rapid arrival of the Brotherhood and Belaisle's equally swift departure. I guess that meant the gathering was a success. The Council would be happy, at least.

As I sat in my usual seat and tuned in to what was going on, I realized something. The speed at which the gathering made their changes to the order of things was in direct conjunction to the importance of said order. When items really mattered, needed deep discussion and input from all sides, they flew ahead full steam. And yet, the pettiest things, inconsequential, were assigned time at a later date to be hammered out and chewed over.

Snort. Witches. At least the wild idea to jerk back the curtain and say hiya to the unmagic world was forcing them to slow down.

For now.

I spotted Charlotte as she rose, circled the bleachers.

Welcomed her as she sat beside me. Her wolf's spirit slipped over her eyes as she met my gaze with her typical blank expression.

We are behind you, she sent, hesitant but more powerful as she got the hang of it. *No matter what happens.*

Nice to know, I sent back. *You're growing stronger, I see.*

She smiled a little. *Your lessons are helping.*

The very idea I was teaching her how to use her magic always made me giggle.

You know what's coming? I squeezed her hand.

Miriam told us the final plan this morning, she sent. Looked upset.

Don't worry, I sent. *I have my own plans.*

Charlotte perked immediately. *I knew you would.* She tipped her head to one side, eyes narrowing. *There's more.*

Sigh. I hated how easy it was for her to read me.

I have to use Ameline, I sent.

Her mind growled, wolf showing up again. *Nothing good comes of her*, she sent.

Tell me about it.

And yet, Charlotte sent, *I trust you, Syd. I know you will do only what is best for all of us.*

No pressure or anything.

I just hoped her total support wasn't unfounded. Or I'd be in a whole heaping pile of doodoo without a shovel.

CHAPTER THIRTY ONE

If I had to sit through the creation of one more silly law, I was going to attack Applegate openly just to get the party started.

"Surely you agree," a portly witch with a strong Spanish accent, a coven leader from the South American territory, appealed to first her Council and then to Mom. "Adding this clause to present law will ensure the purity of witch blood."

I rolled my eyes, lower lip aching from all of my irritating chewing. At least they weren't talking about the power reveal yet. Petty lawmaking could go on all day as far as I was concerned. Anything to keep the gathering from passing legislation on exposing us to normals.

Mom's sigh was unheaved, but I heard it in her voice. "I understand your concern," she said while I tossed my hands in the air before I could stop myself. "And though

I really do believe your worries that dogs and cats," snort, okay, it was kind of funny for all that, "will rise and try to seize power from our kind, I'm comfortable accepting your addition to law that will deny them power and the ability to evolve into magic users."

The witch beamed at Mom while the gathering chittered like a pack of nosy monkeys.

Was this chick really serious? And how was Mom keeping a straight face?

How offensive, Sassafras sniffed. *As if cats would care.*

Snort.

I tuned out again, grateful for the distraction when Piers's mind brushed over mine.

It's time, he sent. Just as Tallah stood up, beaming, surrounded by smiling witches.

Was it ever.

Finally. I sat up straighter, Sassafras perking, pointed ears twitching in response to my movement.

Wish us luck. Piers's magic embraced me, wrapping me in emptiness. An emptiness that changed as my sorcery blossomed beneath me and welcomed him in. Suddenly he was all richness and depth, heat and coffee touched with mint. I let him hold me a moment longer before breaking the contact.

I take it they are ready? Sassafras's mental voice crackled in my head.

As they will ever be. I shot a very thin line toward

Ameline. *You'd better be here when I need you.*

Her mental laughter was my only answer.

"Council Leaders," Tallah said. "We now bring before you the proposal to begin our contact with normals in power and open dialogue between our people."

Piers was already slipping around the back of the benches, heading for the European contingent, while Tallah spoke. My stomach clenched, made worse when I felt a different mind latch onto mine. A mind filled with panic.

Syd! Trill's maji power zapped me like a lightning bolt. *Stop him!*

I tried, trusted her absolutely. The panic in her wasn't something I could ignore. But the moment I reached for Piers, I felt it, too late, as his sorcery lashed out and impacted Vasyl's.

This time there really was lightning, thick white bolts of it, streaking from the former Black Soul sorcerer. The gathered witches cried out, Tallah ducking as the lightning ricocheted against Piers and, through him, in a cascade of protections, thundering across the short distance to strike each and every Steam Union member in attendance.

I jumped to my feet as three people fell from the bleachers in front of me, realizing then Eva secreted her people throughout the pavilion as, en masse, they all collapsed.

The snap-crackle-boom died away, flashover of light

forcing me to blink several times to clear the tears of pain from my eyes. By then, the whole pavilion had fallen deathly quiet.

All but for Vasyl Krajnik's laughter.

Fools, Ameline snarled in my head, even as a black-robed Enforcer spun, her hood falling back, power lashing at the amused sorcerer.

Why wasn't I surprised Ameline was here all along?

Whatever protections Belaisle left with Vasyl, they pushed Ameline away, too, though she was spared the sizzle of super-charged electric retaliation.

Syd, Trill sent, *listen to me. Vasyl isn't alone. He has all of the power of the stronghold at his disposal.*

Um, what?

That's why Belaisle was here, she sent. *To test the connection, to make sure it would work. He wanted you to attack. I'm sorry*, her voice wailed in my head as the gathered witches finally shattered their trance-like silence and roared in sudden reaction. I ignored the mayhem, focusing on Trill. *I found out too late. I should have warned you, but my connections inside the Brotherhood didn't tell me until just before I reached for you.*

Not your fault, I shot back. Wait. She had Brotherhood connections?

Since when?

You must attack together, she sent. *You and Ameline. It's the only way.*

She's not full maji yet, I sent, teeth gritted as I reached for my rival even as she leaped into the air on a ball of blue fire while a handful of Enforcers rushed toward her. *Besides, attacking him with power will only feed him.*

Not if you're together, she sent. *You already know this, you've seen it with my brothers and me, how our combination rejects Brotherhood attacks.* She sounded irritated to have to be explaining things to me. *Because you both have sorcery, and you're maji, he won't be able to draw on your power. He'll have to fight you or fall.*

Okay then. Good to know.

Gram's hand suddenly latched onto my arm, her mind interjecting, cutting through into our conversation.

And Vasyl's connection isn't perfect, she sent. *Feel it.*

We both did, Gram along for the ride. The empty darkness was vast, massive. But the edges felt rough, cracked and warped.

There's weak spots, Gram sent. *Focus on those and you'll sever the connection.*

Did you do this? I turned to her, eyes wide.

Varity helped, Gram sent. *She's in the stronghold now, hiding. But she won't be able to hold on much longer without you.*

She was what? *Is she out of her mind?*

Gram's eyes sparkled with a hint of her former self.

Crazy old ladies.

We're coming, Trill sent, the image of her running for the pavilion in my head. *Just do what Ethpeal says and we'll back you up.*

I lashed at the Enforcers, sending them back, eyes locked on Ameline's. *Will this work?*

Trill gulped. *It has to.*

Lovely.

Well, I wanted a way to show the witches exactly what they were up against. The means to shake them free from their complacent, apathetic need to mind their own business.

Time to see if I could wrangle me some attention.

Sassafras squawked as I twisted and dumped him on Gram, rising into the air myself, drawing Ameline to me, linking my power with hers yet again. I could feel her weaknesses, like blank spots inside her, not the emptiness of sorcery, but more like unfulfilled potential.

She had enough of each I knew we could manage. Hoped.

Mom's mind crashed into mine. *Don't you dare*, she sent.

You should have thought of that before you told me I could do whatever I wanted, I sent. *Let me handle this, Mom.*

Vasyl was on his feet by then, facing me down while Margaret Applegate pointed at me with a shriek of fury.

"If she touches him," she cried out for all to hear, "I demand her death!"

I felt Trill arrive, knew if we were going to act it was now or never. Before the other Councils decided to throw the weight of their Enforcers against us.

Syd, now! Gram's mind reached me, a flash of Varity Rhodes in my head, crouched in a dark corner, her power undermining the magic keeping Vasyl linked to the stronghold. I only had a second to realize the old Enforcer leader had sorcery before Trill's power flared, the touch of darkness in her creation energy calling to the sorcery beneath me. I opened wide to my maji magic and fed her even as Ameline's power siphoned from me to fill in her own gaps.

A quick glance down and to my right showed me the maji girl and her brothers, Owen on the far end with his brilliant blue eyes flat black and Apollo in the center, his body swirling with light and shadow.

You must be the focus, Trill sent.

Naturally. I funneled their considerable power into path with mine, Ameline's darkness joining me as we aimed our attack at Vasyl.

At least he finally had the good grace to look scared. "You will allow them to attack me under the protections of conclave?"

Could I do this? What if we failed? Even as I committed to what we were about to do, I doubted.

Until I spotted Sassafras bounding over one of the risers to land in Eloise Brindle's lap. The coven leader shuddered as he head-butted her, his demon power flaring. She immediately sagged to the side, shook her head and looked up at me, pale face full of rage and hurt.

"This sorcerer is not my second," she screamed as her family magic surged around her in outrage, my demon cat snarling in her arms. "My coven is under attack!"

Syd, Mom sent. *Now*.

Awesome.

Eloise cried out, swayed as Sassafras screamed in what had to be pain, the Brindle family magic collapsing in a spiral of blue, even as Margaret Applegate, her lips twisted in hate, slashed at the coven leader.

But the damage was done.

Together, I sent. And crushed Vasyl Krajnik with all the power at my disposal.

chapter thirty two

Tried to.

So. Much. Resistance. The very plane fought me, the feeling of the stronghold pushing back so powerful I gasped for air. But held on, poured everything I had into it, and more.

Much more.

Mom fed me magic, a living stream of it, joined almost immediately from Bindi Braylen and her people. The Australian Council Leader nodded to me scowling at her counterparts.

"What are you waiting for?" She stood, swaying as we pulled on her Council power. "A witch is under attack. Defend her!"

They did, at last, their power joining us, though much slower than the Sidhe who leaped to assist, even Aiolainn, though I was sure only because Niamh sat beside her, hissing in her ear. The werewolves offered what they had, the soft iridescence of their power golden around the edges. And Meira, my sister, tore a hole in the veil and offered me Ahbi.

Meems, no, I sent. *The Node.* And opening herself like this made her vulnerable to Ameline.

Will be fine, she sent back. *Crush him like a bug.*

I tried. So. Hard. Felt everyone around me giving and giving even as Vasyl's laughter grew and Applegate's screaming ceased as she realized we would fail.

Damn it, if Trill was right, how could we fail?

At least she'd hit on one thing. He couldn't take our power, not through Vasyl, anyway. So that was a bonus. Still.

Double damn it.

Varity's mind touched mine. *I've given all I have*, she sent, faint, so faint. *But I will give the rest if it will mean they fall.*

No. I cut her off, forcing her to back out. I caught a glimpse of her panting, hands over her face, in the dark of a quiet room in the stronghold. *Get your ass home. Now.*

I'd find another way.

There had to be one.

And there was. Because random wins.

They appeared in a swirling ball of light, diving for the Black Soul sorcerer, threads of wild magic coiling into a spear of attack. Vasyl's laugh turned to a shout of fear, but they didn't hit him, turning at the last moment, coming right.

For.

Me.

I only had a heartbeat to draw a breath before they hit me full in the chest.

Right in the heart.

My insides exploded, power erupting from every cell in my body. I felt my consciousnesses meld, merging with the wild magicks, the others magic races falling away, still feeding me, but no longer needed.

Only Ameline, who had no choice but to join me.

Images flashed around me, shared with those who watched, fed me energy, images the wild magicks tried so hard to make me understand.

But this time, when they reached the flash of Belaisle holding the mirror shard, they didn't stop. Instead, they wound on and on, showing us the future.

What was coming.

Death. Destruction. Fire and earthquake and the demise of our plane. Normal cities falling to plague and volcano, continents shifting and sinking into oceans boiling from the exposed magma beneath the Earth's crust. The sky tinted orange, the very air burning as the last magic of our plane exploded in a massive exodus of energy.

But they weren't done, not even close. With Earth

gone, they turned to Demonicon, the Node crumbling and collapsing, the planes broken apart, colliding, rupturing into massive chunks of debris until demons were no more. And the Sidhe realm, the green dying, withering, the waters drying up before darkness swallowed it and its shining people whole.

Other planes, ones I didn't recognize, races I didn't know, burning up in a fiery end while Belaisle's voice laughed.

And laughed.

And laughed.

The images cut off abruptly, my body compressing as the wild magicks left me in a pulse of power, a weapon against the darkness.

This time when they flew toward Vasyl, they carried my power with them. Mine, and that of all the magic users gathered to stand against him.

Varity. I reached for her, felt her answer. *Now.*

With a soaring song, the small, glowing ball of power punched through Vasyl's chest and exploded out the other side. While Varity Rhodes, her sorcery boosted by mine, cut the line between the Black Soul sorcerer and the stronghold.

For a long moment he sat there, staring at me in utter shock before keeling slowly over onto his side, toppling from the bench with a fist-sized hole in his sternum I could see through.

We'd hoped for a chain reaction when we freed Applegate.

And boy, did we get one.

In a clap of thunder so loud I was sure I'd never gain my hearing back, a giant black hole flared into life around the dead sorcerer, sucking in threads of emptiness from every single person in Applegate's party, including her assembled Enforcers. They shook as a unit as the taint of the Brotherhood left in a rush, slamming home into the black hole before it shrank with a sucking noise and popping out of existence.

Applegate staggered, catching herself on the back of her bench, looking up to meet my eyes.

"Sydlynn Hayle," she said in a shaking voice, "thank you."

And collapsed.

chapcer chircy chree

I released the others, not needing them any longer, feeling Trill linger the longest even as I shoved Ameline away from me when I felt her trying to siphon more power.

The dark maji shrugged and offered a little smile like she had to try.

I'd give her something to siphon.

I tried not to think about the charred remains of Vasyl as Enforcers rushed forward and removed his body or the paleness of Applegate's face when Mom rushed to her and bent over her prone form.

Instead, I focused on the quiet in my mind where Varity had been. Grasped for Gram's hand. Felt the old Enforcer leader's heart beat on the other side, just enough, her connection to Gram telling me she was fine.

Better, was there, safe and sound, when she burst

through into our plane and her energy hugged me.

Awesome. Gram sank down to the bench, still clutching Sassafras. I sent her a magical kiss on the cheek before facing off with the silent, shaking and finally clued-in witches who watched in horror.

"Darkness is coming," I said, not in the least bit self-conscious about using formal language, feeling as though this was right and necessary. "And now you've seen the face of that darkness."

"The Brotherhood are your enemy," Ameline spoke up, voice ringing in the stillness as everyone stared, too stunned to speak. "You must guard against them and their lies, their insidious ways. Or they will use you as they did Margaret Applegate."

"Every witch, were, vampire, demon, Sidhe and all others must stand against them," I said. "Any thoughts you had perhaps the Brotherhood really meant what they said, about wanting peace, must be purged if we are to survive." I fixed my gaze on the Hensley leader. "His desire for us to expose ourselves to normals was only part of his aim to destroy us and take possession of our magic. And now, we've seen where such an act will lead."

I shivered inside at the images, still raw in my mind, the wild magicks burned into my brain.

Tallah sank into her seat, head bowed. I felt terrible for Shenka's sister, but at least it looked like she got the message.

"Your houses may be dirtied with the touch of the Brotherhood," Ameline said, a trace of disgust in her voice. "But you are not alone."

Wow, was this really her speaking? Self-centered, all about me Ameline Benoit?

"We will help you," I said, spotting Trill helping Apollo from the ground, Owen bent in half with his hands on his knees, panting for air. "Darkness might be coming, but we are the Light."

Trill looked up at me and saluted.

Tallah stood, turned to Mom. "I propose a law," she said. "The Brotherhood and all of their members are now to be considered the mortal enemies of every magic race represented here, and we will act as one to eradicate their presence from our planes forever."

I didn't condone genocide, as much as I would have liked to see the Brotherhood fall. But no one was listening to me anymore. Not while they all surged to their feet with a roar of approval, Mom nodding in acceptance.

Oh, so now they wake up and smell the decaying pus bag that was the Brotherhood.

Typical.

I released my power, still levitating me over the proceedings, sinking to the floor of the pavilion, Ameline beside me, as Mom gestured for silence.

"From this day forward," she said, "any witch, were,

demon, Sidhe, vampire or Steam Union member who is found to harbor the Brotherhood or forward their aims will be charged with treason and punished to the fullest extent of the law." Another roar. "Further," she went on when their *hell yes* died down. "Any Brotherhood member caught in any plane or territory of the above mentioned races will be arrested and brought to trial."

"No," Tallah said, fury making her voice vibrate. "They will be arrested and summarily executed without trial."

Uh-oh. I spun on Mom. *This could get out of hand very fast*, I sent.

Too late for that.

The wave of approval was so powerful I almost missed Ameline's mental chuckle.

Witches, she sent. *How delightful.*

Can Tallah actually propose something like this? I looked up at Mom who didn't meet my eyes.

Any Coven Leader can propose new law, she sent, tight and angry. *You really haven't been paying attention.*

Damn it.

I turned to scowl at Ameline, just needing something, someone, to focus my frustration on. The wild magicks suddenly appeared again, skipping and dancing happily over my head.

You did wonderfully, I sent to them.

They hummed in joy, dive-bombing the ground as

they celebrated their victory.

The fact they'd just killed someone didn't seem to put a damper on their mood any, and considering they were wild magicks...

I just couldn't bring myself to feel bad for Vasyl.

Ameline's power snapped out before I could stop her, snatching at the spinning ribbons of energy. Their joyful song turned to a snarl of rage as they slapped her back. She staggered, choking on a nasty laugh, blue Enforcer power snapping as she dodged my grab for her.

Worth a try, she sent. *I'll see you soon.*

And was gone.

No time to think about Ameline. Not when I looked up at the worry on Mom's face to the cheering sound of the law granting us the right to destroy an entire race being passed.

chapter thirty four

"This could be very bad," I said as I sank into the chair across from Mom. "You realize this will probably blow up in our faces."

My sister snorted as she reclined in another chair, huge platform boot bobbing on the other end of her crossed knee. "I don't see how the downfall of the Brotherhood is that big of a deal."

Mom sighed. "It's not the Brotherhood we have to worry about," she said as her eyes tightened. "I'm all for wiping their asses from every plane permanently."

Vicious.

"But it's not the guilty who I'm concerned for," Mom said. "We've effectively passed a law allowing witches and the other races to kill anyone they even suspect might be Brotherhood."

Eva Southway squirmed in her seat, skin drawn and

pale, both eyes ringed in black as though the power of the Brotherhood punched her in the face. At least she was alive after the backlash of Piers's attack knocked out her and her sorcerers. "My people will be at risk," she said. Sounded very unhappy, not that I blamed her.

"Not to mention every person out there who has sorcery, but might not know it," I said.

Meira's smirk of triumph faded. "I didn't think of that," she said.

Funny how quickly I forgot she was just a teenager in the body of a mature demon. Sure, she was fabulous at her job, but her youth added to the burning need for revenge all demons possessed and I wasn't surprised she was so bloodthirsty.

Or had missed the deeper point.

"Surely you can temper this law somewhat," Sunny said. I was so relieved when day finally faded to night and we had access to the vampires again. The mess of conclave's end wasn't the smooth and ceremonial process I was sure Mom's people planned, wrapping up more so in a rush of exiting witches, all flashing off to their own territories after a brief farewell to my mother.

And me.

Groan.

At least one thing was certain: the Brotherhood were no longer welcome on our plane or any known one. Which meant they were about to have a very uncomfortable transition from power-hungry, underground players to hunted fugitives.

As long as we managed to keep the innocent carnage to an absolute minimum, I guessed I could live with this outcome for a little while.

Mom sat back as she pondered Sunny's question. "I'll reach out to the Council Leaders in the next few days and attempt to do just that," she said. "But what they saw, after being lulled into almost believing Belaisle... I think it's frightened them into overreacting."

No, really? Understatement of the year.

"At least we're all on the same page, for once." Uncle Frank bumped fists with Charlotte whose calm expression didn't alter. "That's a victory in itself."

I knew it couldn't last, but yes. I'd take that, too, thank you very much.

Niamh and Odhran stood, his Sidhe cloak sweeping the floor, the soft vibration of earth magic following them as they bowed to Mom.

"We will return to our realm," Ohdran said. "And though I am certain we are free of Brotherhood influence thanks to Sydlynn's assistance last year, we will do a thorough sweep of our plane to ensure our continuing freedom."

Mom stood and bowed to both of them, all of us silent as they left. I felt the rush of Sidhe power as they departed, taking their people with them while Oleksander leaned forward, hands on his knees.

"There is the case of Margaret Applegate," he said. "How will she be dealt with?"

Mom tapped her fingers on the table top, a small sign of her agitation. "I don't know," she said. "She's free now. And if I tried to interfere, we'd be right back where we started."

"No need." We all turned to find the small woman standing in Mom's office doorway. The Margaret I'd met at Wilhelm Castle had been partially in thrall to the Brotherhood, but I thought I'd seen her true character after she was freed the first time. And the woman I'd interacted with then had been strong, strong enough, I thought incorrectly, to stand against the sorcerers.

This Margaret was a broken vessel, her round face sunken, skin the color of gray paste. The power she used to radiate felt contained, compressed, as though the Council magic grieved for her.

No, wait. She didn't feel like Council power. Only personal. What had she done?

Mom came through her captivity stronger for it. Margaret Applegate wasn't so lucky.

"I've stepped down," she said, voice barely above a whisper. Paused while Mom stood, reached for her, but shook her head. "No, it's for the best. They don't trust me anymore." She shivered, a tear tracking down her cheek. "I don't trust me anymore."

I stood, went to her. "Now that you're free," I said, "you're exactly who they need." The same argument I'd used on Mom. Only I wasn't so sure I believed it this time.

Margaret smiled a little through her tears, patting my arm in a kind gesture. "You're a dear," she said. "I can't tell you how it ate at me, what they did to you." Her eyes settled on Charlotte. Oleksander. "To your friends." She turned to Eva. "To my friends." The Steam Union leader bowed her head. "The European Council needs new leadership. Someone who they can look to for guidance." Margaret stepped back half a pace. "I'm not that leader anymore."

I looked up as a tall, blonde woman with strong features and pale blue eyes strode through the doorway, her hand settling on Margaret's shoulder.

"It's already done," she said with a faint accent I didn't recognize. "Margaret's choice will be honored among our covens."

"This is Femke Svensson," Margaret said. "She will tell you what I can't." The woman choked, a soft sob escaping. "And now, if you'll excuse me, I must return home to bury my best friend."

My heart constricted as Margaret turned, her eyes meeting mine.

"Elliot," I whispered.

She sobbed again. And left.

Damn it. I knew her Enforcer Leader had to be dead. I just didn't want to admit it.

"I would like to make a suggestion," Femke said, crisp but kind. "That each Council be assigned a Steam Union representative, as a show of good faith with their order, as well as an early warning system in case of Brotherhood attack."

Brilliant. I saw Eva's face perk despite her obvious pain from the bruises.

Mom's smile told me she was as relieved as I felt. Why hadn't I thought of that?

"Excellent," Mom said. "And will go a long way in keeping our sorcerer allies safe from false prosecution."

Okay then.

I felt the air behind me stir, glanced over my shoulder to see Piers slip inside the office. No one else noticed him as they gathered around Mom, Meira discussing the possibility of finding a sorcerer with demon blood to take home with her while Oleksander argued his people would have trouble accepting such a watchdog.

I left them to argue, went to his side. He looked like hell, blonde hair charred at the tips, face marred by scorch marks and bruises matching his mother's. He hunched over a little as if in pain and, when I touched his arm, flinched from me.

Silly, I sent. And let my vampire, sealed to my spirit magic, explore and heal him while I fed him power.

Thank you, he sent as his cracked ribs healed over, seared flesh under his clothing softening and renewing with fresh skin. By the time I let him go a few moments later, he looked himself, if tired, even his gorgeous locks restored.

Because I may not have loved Piers that way, but I really adored his hair.

"Piers." We both turned to find Eva watching. "Femke, this is my son. He would be the perfect candidate to advise your Council."

I looked up at him in time to see his brow knit. "Actually," he said, "I was thinking the North American Council would be a better fit." He bowed to Femke. "My sister, Clover, would be an excellent choice."

Eva's jaw worked just before she winced. Man, that had to hurt. "We'll discuss it," she said in a tone of voice that said they would do no such thing.

I'll work on her, he sent to me. *If you wish.*

And left it hanging there, between us.

I pretended to listen as Mom and the others continued their conversation even though I didn't hear a word they said.

You don't love him, my demon growled. *But he's good for us.*

As good as Liam? Shaylee's heart was in the obvious place.

Perhaps better, my vampire sent softly. *And yet...*

306

And yet.

I squeezed Piers's hand. *I'm looking forward to getting to know your sister*, I sent.

His sigh reached through his magic and touched my heart.

Ruled by love, he sent. *So much power, so little sense.*

If you say so. I let go of his hand as he grinned at me.

So it matters that much to you.

It does. I hugged myself as he nodded. *It might be dumb and romantic and deluded, but.*

But.

He bent and kissed my cheek, the tingle of contact sweet, full of warmth.

Watch your back, he sent. *And, if you insist on thinking with it, your heart.*

With that, he left me standing by the doorway and went to shake hands with Femke.

Amazing how such a simple gesture could mean goodbye.

chapter thirty five

I left them to hash it out, no longer feeling like they needed me. Mom would fill me in later and I really needed to just get out of there, catch some air.

The giant central tent was already being disassembled, the walls on one side coming down. I skirted a group of witches folding and compressing the fabric into small squares which then vanished in pops of blue fire.

Time to go home and sort through what happened here. Make a plan.

Or curl up in a ball in my jammies with a carton of ice cream and a funny movie.

Perfect.

Except perfect wasn't about to let me have my retreat moment. At least, not yet. Not when I was cut off as I strode for my pavilion, wondering if Shenka had finished packing up yet.

Trill grabbed me, pulled me into a fierce embrace. "Thought we lost there for a minute," she whispered.

I grinned at her brothers, as Owen came to hug me. He'd grown a lot, as tall as I was, now, at height with Apollo. I released the younger Zornov and accepted a kiss from the older as he winked at me.

Made me snort.

"Couldn't have kicked ass without you," I said. "Thanks for being here."

Trill shrugged. "I wish it could have been different," she said. "Would have been nice if it was Belaisle who took that hit to the chest and not his lieutenant."

We all knew Liander was headed for a different fate.

"You're staying a while?" I didn't mean to sound so plaintive, but I missed their young faces, their energy.

Trill shrugged, Owen looking suddenly excited.

"As long as Ethpeal's making waffles," he said, voice cracking from soft soprano to more manly baritone.

I laughed. "We'll see." Hopefully this little bout of excitement had roused Gram from her funk.

Time would tell.

"We'll meet you at the house," Trill said. "I have some things to tell you."

I waved, let them go. Stood there and absorbed the fact things were done. Over. At least for now.

Someone nudged me from behind. I turned, found Gram, supporting Varity, the pair grinning at me like they'd had the time of their lives.

I said it once and had to say it again.

Crazy. Old. Ladies.

A quick hug for both, a shot of magic to help Varity recover, and I pulled away, trying to scowl, smile fighting its way to the surface.

"You pair," I said, "are more trouble than I'll ever be."

Gram grunted. Sure she was offended. Right.

Varity leaned in, squeezed my shoulder with one long-fingered hand. "Well done," she said.

"Back at you." I let my sorcery brush hers, felt her section it off even as I tried. "You could have told me you were a sorcerer, too."

Varity and Gram exchanged a look that said there was a whole world of things they knew I didn't. "Wouldn't have mattered," she finally said. "I never intended to use it."

"Well, I, for one, am glad you did," I said. "Don't be so quick to wall off your power, Enforcer. Some of us won't judge you for it, at least."

I was guessing her reasons for hiding. Must have hit the nail square from the way she scrunched up her face.

"Old habits," she said. "And I had to choose, a long time ago."

Foolish, in my opinion. "If they were smart," I said, "they'd start training their own who have sorcery."

Syd.

Ding. Freaking. Ding.

Made a note to mention it to Pender even as Varity's eyes widened and she chuckled.

Turned to Gram, slinging an arm around her shoulders. "Brilliant," she said. "You done good, Hayle."

Gram blew a raspberry with her thin lips. "She's a work in progress."

The pair snickered as they left me.

I was just thrilled to see Gram smile.

Started to head out again. Quaid's hand squeezed my elbow as he came to my side, shattering my good mood all over again. "Are you going to marry him or not?"

Holy hell. Talk about sudden conversation shifts to give me a headache.

I stared up at him, drawing a breath to setting into this thing between us a little before blowing his head off. Realized Sassafras was right. Magical connection or not, I had to deal with this once and for all.

"For the last time," I said, freeing myself from his grasp, "that's none of your damned business." Hesitated. Finally drew a breath before my chest collapsed from lack of breathing. "Or are you making it your business?"

Syd. Syd. What are you doing, Syd?

Did I really just—

I did. I had to.

Time to know the truth even if it broke my heart

forever.

Quaid's face crumpled, body shaking as he lifted his hands, imploring or warding me off, I wasn't sure. But for one aching moment of possibility I stood there with him and wondered.

And hoped maybe I didn't have to choose after all.

With a strangled cry, he turned from me. Hung his head. Shook it.

Walked away.

And that, as they say, was that.

Or so I thought. Even as I trembled from the backlash of my own shattered hope, a hand settled on my shoulder and turned me around.

And Payten met my eyes. Tears stood in hers as she looked up, watched Quaid go, before turning back to me.

"Are you sleeping with my boyfriend?" Such a soft sound, her voice. Such a horrible, painful question.

On so many levels.

He'd lied. And I had done as she thought.

"I love him," she said, voice thick and heavy. "I have since we met at camp that first summer." She let out a breathless laugh around her tears. "I knew you and he were a couple. But we clicked, he said you were over." She shook her head. "Did he lie to me?"

To both of us.

"There are times I know he loves me, too," she said. "But other times I wonder where his heart really lies."

No. Way. I would not believe she was like me. Would. Not.

I just couldn't give her that.

Cold swept over me as my demon mourned, Shaylee sighing her sadness, my vampire softly sinking into silence even as the family magic wept for my loss.

I was done. Now and forever. To hell with fate or destiny or the damned magic keeping us together.

He'd broken my heart for the last time.

"Trust me," I said to her, putting every last scrap of conviction I had in me into my voice, my power, my words. "Quaid is all yours."

She backed off a step as I pushed past her.

Crossed over the border of the site and tore at the veil. Ahbi tried to hug me, but I wasn't in the mood for comfort.

Not from her, anyway.

It was inevitable, wasn't it? Wasn't he always the one I went to, the shoulder I could cry one? The only one who loved me without wanting something in return?

Weak or strong, right for me or wrong, I emerged from the veil just outside the wards to the Sidhe cavern with one thought in my mind.

I had a choice to make. And the answer was obvious.

The moment I stepped through, Liam came running, his arms wrapping around me, lips next to my ear as he whispered his love for me. Kissed my forehead, my lips before letting me go.

My oak tree. Stronger than I ever gave him credit for.

"You are amazing," he said, a little breathless, the scent of his fabric softener and the earth all around me. "Syd Hayle wins again."

I stared up at him, frozen, unable to smile in return, to breathe or speak.

"Syd." Liam's relief faded into worry. "Are you okay? Talk to me." He shook me a little even as the heavy weight of Galleytrot's power joined us, the big hound sitting down behind Liam to watch me with eyes burning with red fire.

You love him. My demon's pain hurt me, too.

She does, Shaylee sent.

And he will do just fine. My vampire hugged me as the girls came to join her, even my demon finally relenting. The family magic stirred as I drew a ragged breath and kissed Liam with desperate need.

He kissed me back, answering what I demanded with his own want, lifting me into his arms and carrying me in a few short strides to his bedroom door. I pulled away from the intensity of his kiss, holding his face between my hands as he paused on the threshold.

Do it, Syd.

Do it now.

"Liam O'Dane," I said. "Will you marry me?"

I'd never seen such sweet tenderness before,

tempered with a flare of doubt.

"You're sure," he said. "That I'm good enough?"

Oh.

My.

Swearword.

I kissed him, lingering, letting him feel all of my egos embracing him and wanting him to say yes.

When I pulled away again, his eyes shone with tears, lips curling into a smile.

"Sydlynn Hayle," he said. "You only had to ask."

I hugged him as he carried me into his room, only the soft growling from Galleytrot's wide chest making me pause.

Until Liam closed the door firmly in the hound's face.

And then it was just the two of us.

I could live with that.

chapter thirty six

Endings can be bitter or sweet. I chose sweet.

Though the stronghold remained in the hands of the Brotherhood, that was all they managed to hold. I had no idea what kind of friends Piers hung out with, but the term "hacker" seemed to fit.

How did I know? Coterie Industries took a nose dive only weeks after conclave ended and, from what I could tell, was about to collapse altogether under allegations of fraud and deception.

The other Councils kept Mom—and through her, me—in gleeful information, mostly about the uncovering of Brotherhood members scattered through all territories. I had no doubt, with the loss of Mom not so long ago, Belaisle planned to infiltrate another Council to balance his hold on Applegate.

Now he wouldn't get the chance.

Most of the fleeing Brotherhood members did manage to escape, though, from the sick look on Mom's face the time or two I was present when she received mental updates, I didn't want to know what the witches did to the sorcerers they managed to capture.

Eva Southway blossomed into quite the leader, coming to visit on a regular basis with her own updates. I worried she might turn arrogant now she had the power and backing to act, but, to my relief, she just settled into her newly elevated position with dedication and focus.

At least I didn't have to worry about the Steam Union getting delusions of world domination with her at the helm. Though, from what we knew, there really were other branches of the Union out there as well, branches Eva had not as yet any success contacting.

I just hoped they weren't being mobbed.

She liked me better now I was engaged, not so cold. And I was relieved she would never be my mother-in-law.

Sonja O'Dane had been bad enough.

Since there had already been a few instances of mistaken identity, though all had been resolved without the accused party actually dying, I knew we still had a lot to worry about and had concerns our new allies might turn on us if such incidents escalated.

Not my problem.

Nor was the new housing that had to be arranged for our Enforcers. Mom and the Council created a nice little barracks for them at Harvard, an offshoot of Coven Hall, but I knew Pender had to be torturing himself over the fact he was the Leader who lost possession of the stronghold.

In fact, I was there when he tried to step down, begging Mom to let him go. And I wished she would. But she refused to hear a word of it and ordered him to hunt the Brotherhood.

He did. I just hoped she hadn't created a monster needing revenge.

I attended the interment of the ashes of the fallen Enforcers. Belaisle's attempt at an insult appeared on Mom's desk one afternoon, a plain, cardboard box full of ashes and shattered skeletal fragments. We all knew who they belonged to. And though their bones were broken, we would never forget the fallen Enforcers—the ones left behind—who tried to hold the line and keep the Brotherhood from seizing their home.

Heroes came in all shapes and sizes. Like the wild magicks. They vanished again once conclave was over, whisking off to where ever it was they chose, with my thanks.

And my hope I'd see them again.

I wished Gram's interest had lasted past conclave. But her sense of duty faded as quickly as it came. Especially when I, Liam holding my hand, announced our news to the family.

Her scowl of disappointment hung between us like a curse long after she spun and walked off, slamming the door behind her.

Poor Liam. I felt terrible for him, though the rest of the family embraced him, just happy I made a choice, I think.

If only Galleytrot wasn't being such a jerk about it. Wasn't this what he wanted?

Stupid dog.

Surprise, surprise, Ameline vanished again, though now I knew she was able to hide in plain sight. I'd be watching for her, feeling for Gram. I warned Meira about Ameline's request, but my sister only laughed. Made a "let her try" face.

Didn't stop me from having a private conversation first with Dad, then with Ahbi.

No way was I letting Ameline do to Meems what she'd done to Gram.

Even while I simmered over what to do about the dark maji, I knew something had to be done if we wanted this to be over anytime soon.

I hated conundrums. They made my head hurty.

At least Femke Svensson was awesome. Every time I met her, I liked her more, from her easy laugh to her wide-open welcome, to her progressive thinking. Margaret Applegate may have done a lot of harm to her covens when under the influence of the Brotherhood, but her last act as leader was a solid.

Femke was more than happy to listen as I appealed to her about Sebastian. While she didn't immediately tell me to run off and kick Pannera Sthol's undead ass, she promised to look into it. And, if no resolution was forthcoming in the next few weeks, promised she would give me permission to act.

I'd take it.

Helped a lot Femke invited Sunny in on the conversation.

Funny, but the fear I had our little alliances would fall apart shortly after our united front came together seemed to be founded in empty air. Everyone was getting along like best buds at a strawberry social in their honor.

Amazing no one turned on each other yet.

There was still time.

Trill and the brothers Zornov were safely parked in my back yard for the time being. Nice to be able to sit with them, talk without trouble hanging imminently over our heads. Apollo's cheek didn't bother me as much as I thought it would, Owen's sweetness reminding me of Liam.

Trill and I had a long talk about her contact with the Brotherhood. Turned out one of Apollo's old friends was one of them. And not so happy with the way things were going. Enough he was willing to talk a little.

I really had to meet him. Thank him, after pinning

him to the ground and going through his mind with a jackhammer to make sure he wasn't a bad guy in sheep's clothing.

She trusted him. So.

Okay then.

And wouldn't you know, Apollo had his own sources in the underground community, promising to beat Piers to the punch with a death-blow for the Brotherhood.

I let them play, knowing everything they did made Liander's Belaisle's life here on this plane more uncomfortable.

Yup, a damned shame, that.

It was nice to have a full house, especially with the wedding coming. Just so nice to have all my family and friends around me.

I had momentary panic attacks when I thought about Mia. They popped up at the oddest times, like when I was brushing my teeth or lacing up my sneakers. Anything could set me off, chest heaving, heart pounding.

Because I knew, when Mom caught her, the former Goth leader of the Dumont family would be dead. Andre was still demanding it on a regular basis, enough Mom was ready to string him up if he didn't shut the hell up.

And that made me sick to my stomach with worry, no matter what Mia had done.

Damned sense of loyalty. When I had a kid, Sassafras was keeping his fuzzy, meddling paws the hell off.

Thinking about Mia inevitably led me to ponder Alison's involvement. Why she'd sided with Belaisle in the first place, especially when he was just draining the power she'd managed to steal... she had to know what he was doing.

Then again, maybe not. Alison was unstable in life and death hadn't been kind.

I tried not to fret over the fact Belaisle had control of the battle site, knowing Ameline was right about that at least. When the time came—if the time came—we'd find a way to reach him and have it out at last.

Who was I kidding, if?

Delusions didn't become me these days.

And as for Iepa, I was still ripping mad at the maji for her little announcement about all sorcerers having a claim on the empty plane. She might have been trying to back me in her own twisted way, but I was seriously going to plant my boot in her butt the next time she had the nerve to show up and crap on my parade.

If I had any doubt, any thought about going through with my wedding to Liam, it crumbled to dust the day after conclave ended, the morning I emerged from the Sidhe cavern and felt a rubber-band snap of agony as the family magic severed on Quaid's end and slammed into me, returning home.

I knew then he'd made his choice, the faint touch of Enforcer magic telling me he'd taken his vows to the order.

At least I could hope Payten hit him hard for cheating on her. Would serve him right to end up alone, the jerkasaurus.

Sigh.

No. No way. I would not ruin the rest of my life over him.

I had a wedding to plan. And a future to focus on.

He and Payten could have each other.

Time to shake off the old and embrace the love I felt. To wed and commit to Liam for as long as he lived.

Yes, I had to go there, didn't I?

Like what you read? Find out more at
pattilarsen.com

Here's a look at the first chapter of
Book Nineteen of the Hayle Coven Novels

COVEN LEADER

chapter one

So weird, this image of me reflected back from the mirror. I'd wanted cream or even a color, but Mom and Shenka—and all the other women in my life who thought they had a say—insisted on white.

I wasn't an angel. But as I stood there, looking at myself in my wedding dress, I smiled.

And felt like one.

Slow breathing did wonders for the wild pounding of my heart as Mom lifted the lace veil and pinned it to the back of my piled curls. Tears glistened in her eyes while, with trembling hands, she let the fall of soft fabric go, the sigh of it falling to the floor behind me like the exhale of all the sadness I'd ever felt.

Gone with the excitement of what I was about to do. I fidgeted a little with the skirt of my gown, loving the halter style, the way the dress clung to me in shining folds of satin. While I knew Mom would have preferred to dress me in a princess concoction of froth and poof, I'd won this argument.

Mostly because I didn't give her a choice and just went out to the local bridal boutique and bought it without telling a soul.

"Perfect choice," Mom said with a sweet smile as she smoothed a dangling curl back from my bare shoulder. "You are so beautiful."

I turned in a rush and hugged her, not caring if my dress was crumpled, if my hair and veil suffered. "Mom," I whispered, doing my very best not to cry. "Thank you."

She waved one hand in front of her face when she let me go, cheeks pink, laughing through sparkling tears.

"Don't you dare," she said. "You'll ruin your makeup."

Tastefully applied, thanks to Shenka, who stood back with a beaming smile, her knee-length dress the perfect shade of family magic blue.

"Miriam's right," my second said with a hitch in her voice. "You're gorgeous, Syd."

I felt it. Turned to look at myself again, catching the glitter of my engagement ring in my reflection. Liam presented me with the large diamond the very night I proposed, a ring, it turned out, he had in his possession for almost a year.

Imagine that.

I smiled down on it, focusing on right now. Refusing to allow the craziness of my life to intrude for this one lovely, perfect evening. The sun had already set and I knew the rest of the wedding guests and party would be arriving any minute, now the vampires were able to join us.

Shenka touched up Mom's eyes as I sat carefully on the edge of the bed and watched, smiling as they spoke in low, soft voices, giggling together over something I missed. Because my mind, traitor that it was, already drifted elsewhere.

I still found it hard to believe it had only been two weeks since conclave. Even more that Mom allowed thirteen days to go by before she married me off. I was sure, that first morning Liam and I made our announcement, she'd have us out in the back yard, calling for an officiator, the second she saw the sparkly on my finger.

But she showed amazing restraint and, considering the Council was now happy I was getting married, it might have been the fact the pressure was off her shoulders granting me even such a short bit of breathing room.

I shouldn't have been surprised the wedding came together so quickly. Shenka being the mistress of organized, after all, must have had a plan already in place, mobilizing the coven into immediate action. And because our family had such diverse interests—from photographers to bakers to florists and part-time musicians—the entire process was covered and arranged before I could say otherwise.

Just as well, considering how bad I was at keeping track of details. Or running my own life, let alone a wedding. I'd been part of Sunny and Uncle Frank's, but my involvement stopped at trying on dresses and shoes and arranging Sunny's bachelorette party. Which I'd forgotten all about. Leaving it to Mom and her old second, now my rep on the Council, Erica Plower to save my forgetful butt.

At least nothing blew up in the past two weeks, alliances formed during conclave still holding together. The new European Council Leader, Femke Svensson, suggested Steam Union members be assigned to the various Councils and, in doing so, ensured the safety of most sorcerers as well as serving as protection against the Brotherhood.

I was still waiting on word from her about my vampire friend, Sebastian DeWinter. She promised to look into the Pannera Sthol issue, now aware the undead queen was under the thrall of the taint introduced by the dark sorcerers. She was also informed the handsome blood clan leader was trapped and most likely being tortured by my former Hayle coven member turned undead spy for the Brotherhood, Celeste Oberman.

What I wouldn't do to get my hands around her neck and squeeze. She'd been a thorn in my side for years now and yet always remained outside my grip. But I had a feeling, once Femke gave me permission to act, Celeste's days of irking me would end in a short walk to a tall stake and a very, very hot fire.

Couldn't wait. I was bringing marshmallows.

The fact the Brotherhood went back to ground did nothing to make me feel better. Now that my friends and allies were making the sorcerer's lives here on this plane almost impossible—instant death if caught could be an excellent deterrent to making their presence known—I knew the threat Liander Belaisle and his sect presented was far from over.

With his possession of the stronghold and the empty plane Mom's Enforcers once called home, Belaisle was in full control of the site where our last battle was meant to be fought. Ameline Benoit, my nemesis, had been right when she said it didn't matter who held possession. When the day came, we'd be there to meet Belaisle no matter what. But it still bugged me knowing I'd be walking into a situation he controlled rather than the other way around.

Sigh. I had to force my hands into stillness, the constant twisting of my new ring a habit I'd picked up to add to the others I fell into when my churning mind took over. At this rate, I'd either rub my finger raw or thin the platinum band to nothing before I even made it down the aisle.

Couldn't help it. Thinking about the last battle made me worry over Ameline and her power shortfall. Which pushed my mind toward my sister. Ameline already demanded I turn over Meira's demon magic to her so she could complete her journey to maji. The resounding "NO" I'd delivered didn't seem to have phased Ameline's plans. Which meant my almost constant stress about Meira surfaced about as often as any of my other nibbling anxieties.

A lot, in other words.

Meems insisted she was fine, that all was well. Our daily talks reassured me that was true. And knowing my demon grandmother, former Ruler Ahbi Sanghamitra, was embedded in the Node power source keeping Demonicon stable, her spirit part of the veil Ameline was forced to cross if she wanted to go after Meira, made me feel a little better.

But Ahbi wouldn't be much help if Ameline came after my sister while she was here on my plane.

I must have been frowning, because the giggling pair went silent. The sudden quiet snapped me out of my thoughts, raised my eyes to see them watching me with irritation.

"You," Shenka shook an eyebrow pencil at me, "are going to be happy tonight or I'm going to kick your butt."

Mom nodded once, definitive. "Me first," she said.

I cleared away my thoughts with a mental sweep of a broom and smiled at both of them. "Sorry," I said. "Just keep me distracted and I'll be fine."

Mom rose and came to me, taking my hands, pulling me to my feet just demon power surged downstairs.

"That would be your sister," Mom said. "And your father." Her voice wavered just a little, her smile a bit too bright. "Are you ready?"

A flutter of butterflies woke in my stomach, rising to beat themselves against my ribcage in response.

Was I?

Mom turned before I could answer, fished out a bottle of perfume from the back of my drawer. I laughed, remembering she'd left it for me. Lilac, her signature. I shook my head when she offered it up.

"I think I need to find my own," I said. "He'll just have to smell me as I am for now."

Shenka hugged me, pressing her cheek to mine. "Liam will be in such a daze when he sees you, his brain won't be functioning anyway."

I laughed nervously, dancing insects increasing their pace. "I'm going to throw up."

Shenka pulled back and grinned. "This from a woman who's faced death, destruction, mayhem and almost certain collapse of a plane or two."

That was different. In fact, I'd rather face a horde of Brotherhood than the aisle waiting for me in the back yard.

Running sounded good about now. Gulp.

Shenka winked. "I have a bucket out there," she said with glee. "Just in case."

Oh. My. Swearword.

Another rush of power broke through the family wards, spirit magic tied to the undead. I turned to the door as it creaked open after a quick knock, and opened my arms to my sister as Meira came in. She wore her human persona tonight, my height, no giant platform boots in sight, her strapless dress a match for Shenka's, only hers in the deepest amber.

"Gorgeous," she said. "Liam's going to drop."

Another nervous giggle escaped me paired with the sudden need to sprint through the door as Charlotte entered, her wolf crawling over her eyes. I squeezed her, too, pretty sure I'd be all hugged out by the time tonight was over.

She wore an iridescent fabric, shimmering with a soft gold sheath of gauze over top. Mom's brilliant idea made me smile as she dressed each of my bridesmaids in their magic colors. Sunny's stunning face shone with joy as she embraced me, silver gown tightly fitted to her perfect body.

Finally, Trill entered, shy and, from the way she walked in her heels, more than a little uncomfortable. But her deep crimson dress was the perfect color for her.

The girls all gathered to admire each other's outfits, the first time they'd all been together in them since Shenka started putting this dog and Persian show together. I stepped aside, let them ooh and ahh over each other as the door creaked one last time and Dad poked his head in, blue eyes and tanned skin of his human mask firmly in place.

"It's almost time," he said, deep voice rumbling in the sudden silence. "But I'd like a moment alone with the bride first, please."

My bridesmaids and maid of honor—Meira, naturally—all left in a flutter of brilliant dresses and laughter. Mom was last to go, pausing beside Dad, one hand reaching out. But, just before she could touch him, she let her hand fall as she ducked her head and disappeared out into the hall.

I couldn't help the soft sigh of sadness that escaped me. Dad sighed, too, broad shoulders sagging in his black tux. "I'm sorry, cupcake," he said. "I didn't want to ruin your night."

I went to him, hugged him, felt the warmth and strength I remembered from my childhood, laughed at the nickname I used to hate and now adored.

"Dad," I said, "I'm so glad you're here."

He leaned back after a moment, his eyes damp, handsome face smiling as a flicker of amber danced through his gaze. "All your mother and I ever wanted was for you to be happy," he said. "Are you, Syd?"

I stopped, drew a breath. Thought about running one last time.

Asked my heart.

Already knew the answer as my itchy feet calmed, my pounding heart falling into a softer rhythm.

"Yes, Dad," I said, amazed to believe it. "I am. As happy as I think I'll ever be."

He bent and kissed my forehead. "Then I'm happy for you," he said. "Are you ready?"

Mom's question again.

I nodded, paused. "I just need a second?"

Dad left me with a soft squeeze of my hand. "I'll be right downstairs," he said.

Left me alone.

I turned one last time to look in the mirror, at the woman I'd become, the bride I was. Hugged myself as the diamond ring flashed and a trail of tears escaped to track down my right cheek.

We love you, my vampire sent, her magic flowing around me.

We will always be here for you, my demon's graveled growl went on as amber fire lit my insides.

No matter where life takes you, Shaylee sent, Sidhe green flaring within, *we are one, forever*.

The family magic swirled in joy while my maji power stirred. Even the black flower of my sorcery answered, blossoming a moment before falling still.

Thank you, I sent to all of them, pulling myself together. *I love you, too. And would be nothing without you.*

But it wasn't their love I longed for, wept for. My hand trembled as I lifted it to look at the diamond on my finger, fighting the face trying to rise in my mind. The feel of magic I'd loved and lost. The taste of chocolate and the heat of power.

I loved Liam. We would be happy together as long as he lived.

And I refused to think of anyone else.

A tissue cleared up the moisture, a soft dab with a cotton stick erasing the moment of weakness.

All right, Sydlynn Thaddea Hayle.

Time to get married.

I left my reflection behind with my longing and sadness and closed the door firmly behind me.

about the author

Everything you need to know about me is in this one statement: I've wanted to be a writer since I was a little girl, and now I'm doing it. How cool is that, being able to follow your dream and make it reality? I've tried everything from university to college, graduating the second with a journalism diploma (I sucked at telling real stories), am part of an all-girl improv troupe (if you've never tried it, I highly recommend making things up as you go along as often as possible). I've even been in a Celtic girl band (some of our stuff is on YouTube!) and was an independent film maker. My life has been one creative thing after another—all leading me here, to writing books for a living.

Now with multiple series in happy publication, I live on beautiful and magical Prince Edward Island (I know you've heard of Anne of Green Gables) with my very patient husband and multitude of pets.

I love-love-love hearing from you! You can reach me (and I promise I'll message back) at patti@pattilarsen.com. And if you're eager for your next dose of Patti Larsen books (usually about one release a month) come join my mailing list! All the best up and coming, giveaways, contests and, of course, my observations on the world (aren't you just dying to know what I think about everything?) all in one place: http://smarturl.it/PattiLarsenEmail.

Last—but not least!—I hope you enjoyed what you read! Your happiness is my happiness. And I'd love to hear just what you thought. A review where you found this book would mean the world to me—reviews feed writers more than you will ever know. So, loved it (or not so much), **your honest review would make my day**. Thank you!